The Middle of Things

By J. S. Fletcher

Originally published in 1922

The Middle of Things

© 2010 Resurrected Press
www.ResurrectedPress.com

Published by Intrepid Ink, LLC

Intrepid Ink, LLC provides full publishing services to authors of fiction and non-fiction books, eBooks and websites. From editing to formatting, to publishing, to marketing, Intrepid Ink gets your creative works into the hands of the people who want to read them.
Find out more at www.IntrepidInk.com.

ISBN 13: 978-1-935774-13-6

Printed in the United States of America

FOREWORD

In The Middle of Things J. S. Fletcher weaves a complicated tale of murder, hidden identities, and buried secrets all set in the London neighborhood of Bayswater. London isn't so much a city as a collection of neighborhoods, some poor, some posh. Bayswater lies on the latter end of the spectrum, a fashionable area of elegant private residences just to the north of Kensington Gardens and Hyde Park and just south of Paddington Station. It is perhaps not as close to the seats of power as such other fashionable neighborhoods such as Belgravia or Mayfair, but that is part of its charm.

Bayswater is a quiet neighborhood whose residents are successful lawyers or medical men, people of independent means, or wealthy colonials returned to their homeland. It is hardly the place to expect a brutal murder and apparent robbery, yet that is exactly what Richard Viner finds himself caught up in when he discovers the body of a neighbor on his nightly stroll after having spent an evening reading a detective story to his aunt.

He protests to his aunt that the events in detective stories never occur in real life. She counters with several mysteries from her own experience. He is still doubtful, but finds she is right when he finds himself in... *The Middle of Things.*

About the Author

Joseph Smith Fletcher (1863-1935) was a journalist and the author of over 200 books. Born in Halifax, West Yorkshire, he studied law before turning to journalism. His earlier works were either histories or historical fiction, and he was made a fellow of the Royal Historical Society. He didn't start writing mysteries until 1914, though before he died he had written over 100 in the genre.

Greg Fowlkes
Editor-In-Chief
Resurrected Press
www.ResurrectedPress.com

TABLE OF CONTENTS

1
FACED WITH REALITY

On that particular November evening, Viner, a young gentleman of means and leisure, who lived in a comfortable old house in Markendale Square, Bayswater, in company with his maiden aunt Miss Bethia Penkridge, had spent his after-dinner hours in a fashion which had become a habit. Miss Penkridge, a model housekeeper and an essentially worthy woman, whose whole day was given to supervising somebody or something, had an insatiable appetite for fiction, and loved nothing so much as that her nephew should read a novel to her after the two glasses of port which she allowed herself every night had been thoughtfully consumed and he and she had adjourned from the dining-room to the hearthrug in the library. Her tastes, however, in Viner's opinion were somewhat, if not decidedly, limited. Brought up in her youth on Miss Braddon, Wilkie Collins and Mrs. Henry Wood, Miss Penkridge had become a confirmed slave to the sensational. She had no taste for the psychological, and nothing but scorn for the erotic. What she loved was a story which began with crime and ended with a detection—a story which kept you wondering who did it, how it was done, and when the doing was going to be laid bare to the light of day. Nothing pleased her better than to go to bed with a brain titivated with the mysteries of the last three chapters; nothing gave her such infinite delight as to find, when the final pages were turned, that all her own theories were wrong, and that the real criminal was somebody quite other than the person she had fancied. For a novelist who was so little master of his trade as to let you see when and how things were going,

Miss Penkridge had little but good-natured pity; for one who led you by all sorts of devious tracks to a startling and surprising sensation she cherished a whole-souled love; but for the creator of a plot who could keep his secret alive and burning to his last few sentences she felt the deepest thing that she could give to any human being–respect. Such a master was entered permanently on her mental library list.

At precisely ten o'clock that evening Viner read the last page of a novel which had proved to be exactly suited to his aunt's tastes. A dead silence fell on the room, broken only by the crackling of the logs in the grate. Miss Penkridge dropped her knitting on her silk-gowned knees and stared at the leaping flames; her nephew, with an odd glance at her, rose from his easy-chair, picked up a pipe and began to fill it from a tobacco-jar on the mantelpiece. The clock had ticked several times before Miss Penkridge spoke.

"Well!" she said, with the accompanying sigh which denotes complete content. "So he did it! Now, I should never have thought it! The last person of the whole lot! Clever–very clever! Richard, you'll get all the books that that man has written!"

Viner lighted his pipe, thrust his hands in the pockets of his trousers and leaned back against the mantelpiece.

"My dear aunt!" he said half-teasingly, half-seriously. "You're worse than a drug-taker. Whatever makes a highly-respectable, shrewd old lady like you cherish such an insensate fancy for this sort of stuff?"

"Stuff?" demanded Miss Penkridge, who had resumed her knitting. "Pooh! It's not stuff–it's life! Real life–in the form of fiction!"

Viner shook his head, pityingly. He never read fiction for his own amusement; his tastes in reading lay elsewhere, in solid directions. Moreover, in those directions he was a good deal of a student, and he knew more of his own library than of the world outside it. So he shook his head again.

"Life!" he said. "You don't mean to say that you think those things"–he pointed a half-scornful finger to a pile of novels which had come in from Mudie's that day–"really represent life?"

"What else?" demanded Miss Penkridge.

"Oh–I don't know," replied Viner vaguely. "Fancy, I suppose, and imagination, and all that sort of thing–invention, you know, and so on. But–life! Do you really think such things happen in real life, as those we've been reading about?"

"I don't think anything about it," retorted Miss Penkridge sturdily. "I'm sure of it. I never had a novel yet, nor heard one read to me, that was half as strong as it might have been!"

"Queer thing, one never hears or sees of these things, then!" exclaimed Viner. "I never have!–and I've been on this planet thirty years."

"That sort of thing hasn't come your way, Richard," remarked Miss Penkridge sententiously. "And you don't read the popular Sunday newspapers. I do! They're full of crime of all sorts. So's the world. And as to mysteries–well, I've known of two or three in my time that were much more extraordinary than any I've ever read of in novels. I should think so!"

Viner dropped into his easy-chair and stretched his legs.

"Such as–what?" he asked.

"Well," answered Miss Penkridge, regarding her knitting with appraising eyes, "there was a case that excited great interest when your poor mother and I were mere girls. It was in our town–young Quainton, the banker. He was about your age, married to a very pretty girl, and they'd a fine baby. He was immensely rich, a strong healthy young fellow, fond of life, popular, without a care in the world, so far as anyone knew. One morning, after breakfasting with his wife, he walked away from his house, on the outskirts of the town–only a very small town, mind you–to go to the bank, as usual. He never reached the bank–in fact, he was never seen again, never heard of again. He'd only half a mile to walk, along a fairly frequented road, but–complete, absolute, final disappearance! And–never cleared up!"

"Odd!" agreed Viner. "Very odd, indeed. Well–anymore?"

"Plenty!" said Miss Penkridge, with a click of her needles. "There was the case of poor young Lady Marshflower–as sweet a young thing as man could wish to see! Your mother and I saw her married–she was a Ravenstone, and only nineteen. She married Sir Thomas Marshflower, a man of forty. They'd only just come home from the honeymoon when it–happened. One morning Sir Thomas rode into the market-town to preside at the petty sessions–he hadn't been long gone when a fine, distinguished-looking man called, and asked to see Lady Marshflower. He was shown into the morning-room–she went to him. Five minutes later a shot was heard. The servants rushed in–to find their young mistress shot through the heart, dead. But the murderer? Disappeared as completely as last year's snow! That was never solved, never!"

"Do you mean to tell me the man was never caught?" exclaimed Viner.

"I tell you that not only was the man never caught, but that although Sir Thomas spent a fortune and nearly lost his senses in trying to find out who he was, what he wanted and what he had to do with Lady Marshflower, he never discovered one single fact!" affirmed Miss Penkridge. "There!"

"That's queerer than the other," observed Viner. "A veritable mystery!"

"Veritable mysteries!" said Miss Penkridge, with a sniff. "The world's full of 'em! How many murders go undetected–how many burglaries are never traced–how many forgeries are done and never found out? Piles of 'em–as the police could tell you. And talking about forgeries, what about old Barrett, who was *the* great man at Pumpney, when your mother and I were girls there? That was a fine case of crime going on for years and years and years, undetected–aye, and not even suspected!"

"What was it?" asked Viner, who had begun by being amused and was now becoming interested. "Who was Barrett?"

"If you'd known Pumpney when we lived there," replied Miss Penkridge, "you wouldn't have had to ask twice who Mr. Samuel Barrett was. He was everybody. He was everything–except honest. But nobody knew that–until it was too late. He was a solicitor by profession, but that was a mere nothing–in comparison. He was chief spirit in the place. I don't know how many times he wasn't mayor of Pumpney. He held all sorts of offices. He was a big man at the parish church–vicar's warden, and all that. And he was trustee for half the moneyed people in the town–everybody wanted Samuel Barrett, for trustee or executor; he was such a solid, respectable, square-toed man, the personification of integrity. And he died, suddenly, and then it was found that he'd led a double life, and had an establishment here in London, and was a gambler and a speculator, and Heaven knows what, and all the money that had been intrusted to him was nowhere, and he'd systematically forged, and cooked accounts, and embezzled corporation money–and he'd no doubt have gone on doing it for many a year longer if he hadn't had a stroke of apoplexy. And that wasn't in a novel!" concluded Miss Penkridge triumphantly. "Novels–Improbability–pooh! Judged by what some people can tell of life, the novel that's improbable hasn't yet been written!"

"Well!" remarked Viner after a pause, "I dare say you're right, Aunt Bethia. Only, you see, I haven't come across the things in life that you read about in novels."

"You may yet," replied Miss Penkridge. "But when anybody says to me of a novel that it's impossible and far-fetched and so on, I'm always inclined to remind him of the old adage. For you can take it from me, Richard, that truth is stranger than fiction, and that life's full of queer things. Only, as you say, we don't all come across the strange things."

The silvery chime of the clock on the mantelpiece caused Miss Penkridge, at this point, to bring her work and her words to a summary conclusion. Hurrying her knitting into the hand-bag which she carried at her belt, she rose, kissed her nephew and departed bedward; while Viner, after refilling his pipe, proceeded to carry out another nightly proceeding which had become a habit. Every night, throughout the year, he always went for a walk before going to bed. And now, getting into an overcoat and pulling a soft cap over his head, he let himself out of the house, and crossing the square, turned down a side-street and marched slowly in the direction of the Bayswater Road.

November though it was the night was fine and clear, and there was a half-moon in the heavens; also there was rather more than a suspicion of frost in the air, and the stars, accordingly, wore a more brilliant appearance. To one who loved night strolling, as Viner did, this was indeed an ideal night for the time of year; and on this occasion, therefore, he went further than usual going along Bayswater Road as far as Notting Hill Gate, and thence returning through the various streets and terraces which lay between Pembridge Gardens and Markendale Square. And while he strolled along, smoking his pipe, watching the twinkling lights of passing vehicles and enjoying the touch of frost, he was thinking, in a half-cynical, half-amused way, of his Aunt Bethia's taste for the sensational fiction and of her evidently sincere conviction that there were much stranger things in real life than could be found between the covers of any novel.

"Those were certainly two very odd instances which she gave me," he mused, "those of the prosperous banker and the pretty bride. In the first, how on earth did the man contrive to get away unobserved from a town in which, presumably, every soul knew him? Why did he go? Did he go? Is his body lying at the bottom of some hole by some roadside? Was he murdered in broad daylight on a public road? Did he lose his reason or his memory, and wander away and away? I think, as my aunt sagely remarked, that nobody is ever going to find anything about that affair! Then my Lady Marshflower–there's a fine mystery! Who was the man? What did she know about him? Where had they met? Had they ever met? Why did he shoot her? How on earth did he contrive to disappear without leaving some trace? How–"

At this point Viner's musings and questionings were suddenly and rudely interrupted. Unconsciously he had walked back close to his own Square, but on the opposite side to that by which he had left it, approaching it by one of the numerous long terraces which run out of the main road in the Westbourne Grove district–when his musings were rudely interrupted. Between this terrace and Markendale Square was a narrow passage, little frequented save by residents, or by such folk familiar enough with the neighbourhood to know that it afforded a shortcut. Viner was about to turn into this passage, a dark affair set between high walls, when a young man darted hurriedly out of it, half collided with him, uttered a hasty word of apology, ran across the road and disappeared round the nearest corner. But just there stood a street-lamp, and in its glare Viner caught sight of the hurrying young man's face. And when the retreating footsteps had grown faint, Viner still stood staring in the direction in which they had gone.

"That's strange!" he muttered. "I've seen that chap somewhere–I know him. Now, who is he? And what made him in such a deuce of a hurry?"

It was very quiet at that point. There seemed to be nobody about. Behind him, far down the long, wide terrace, he heard slow, measured steps–that, of course, was a policeman on his beat. But beyond the subdued murmur of the traffic in the Bayswater Road in one direction and in Bishop's Road, Viner heard nothing but those measured steps. And after listening to them for a minute, he turned into the passage out of which the young man had just rushed so unceremoniously.

There was just one lamp in that passage–an old-fashioned affair, fixed against the wall, halfway down. It threw but little light on its surroundings. Those surroundings were ordinary enough. The passage itself was about thirty yards in length. It was inclosed on each-side by old brick walls, so old that the brick had grown black with age and smoke. These walls were some fifteen feet in height; here and there they were pierced by doors–the doors of the yards at the rear of the big houses on either side. The doors were set flush with the walls–Viner, who often walked through that passage at night, and who had something of a whimsical fancy, had thought more than once that after nightfall the doors looked as if they had never been opened, never shut. There was an air of queer, cloistral or prisonlike security in their very look. They were all shut now, as he paced down the passage, as lonely a place at that hour as you could find in all London. It was queer, he reflected, that he scarcely ever remembered meeting anybody in that passage.

And then he suddenly paused, pulling himself up with a strange consciousness that at last he was to meet something. Beneath the feeble light of the one lamp Viner saw a man. Not a man walking, or standing still, or leaning against the wall, but lying full length across the flagged pavement, motionless–so motionless that at the end of the first moment of surprise, Viner felt sure that he was in the presence of death. And then he stole nearer, listening, and looked down, and drawing his match-box from his pocket added the flash of a match to the poor rays from above. Then he saw white linen, and a bloodstain slowly spreading over its glossy surface.

2
NUMBER SEVEN IN THE SQUARE

Before the sputter of the match had died out, Viner had recognized the man who lay dead at his feet. He was a man about whom he had recently felt some curiosity, a man who, a few weeks before, had come to live in a house close to his own, in company with an elderly lady and a pretty girl; Viner and Miss Penkridge had often seen all three in and about Markendale Square, and had wondered who they were. The man looked as if he had seen things in life—a big, burly, bearded man of apparently sixty years of age, hard, bronzed; something about him suggested sun and wind as they are met with in the far-off places. Usually he was seen in loose, comfortable, semi-nautical suits of blue serge; there was a roll in his walk that suggested the sea. But here, as he lay before Viner, he was in evening dress, with a light overcoat thrown over it; the overcoat was unbuttoned and the shirt-front exposed. And on it that sickening crimson stain widened and widened as Viner watched.

Here, without doubt, was murder, and Viner's thoughts immediately turned to two things—one the hurrying young man whose face he thought he had remembered in some vague fashion; the other the fact that a policeman was slowly pacing up the terrace close by. He turned and ran swiftly up the still deserted passage. And there was the policeman, twenty yards away, coming along with the leisureliness of one who knows that he has a certain area to patrol. He pulled himself to an attitude of watchful attention as Viner ran up to him; then suddenly recognizing Viner as a well-known inhabitant of the Square, touched the rim of his helmet.

"I say!" said Viner in the hushed voice of one who imparts strange and confidential tidings. "There's a man lying dead in the passage round here. And without doubt murdered! There's blood all over his shirt-front."

The policeman stood stock still for the fraction of a second. Then he pulled out his whistle and blew loudly and insistently. Before the shrill call had died away, he was striding towards the passage, with Viner at his side.

"Did you find him, Mr. Viner?" he asked.

"I found him," asserted Viner. "Just now—halfway down the passage!"

"Sure he's dead, sir?"

"Dead—yes! And murdered, too! And—"

He was about to mention the hurrying young man, but they had just then arrived at the mouth of the passage, and the policeman once more drew out his whistle and blew more insistently than before.

"There's my sergeant and inspector not far off," he remarked. "Some of 'em'll be on the spot in a minute or two. Now then, sir."

He marched down the passage to the dead man, glanced at the lamp, and turning on his own lantern, directed its light on the body.

"God bless me!" he muttered. "Mr. Ashton!"

"You know him?" said Viner.

"Gent that came to live at number seven in your square a while back, Mr. Viner," answered the policeman. "Australian or New Zealander, I fancy. He's gone right enough, sir! And—knifed! You didn't see anybody about, sir?"

"Yes," replied Viner, "that's just it. As I turned into the passage, I met a young fellow running out of it in a great hurry—he ran into me, and then, shot off across the road, Westbourne Grove way. Then I came along and found—this!"

The policeman bent lower and suddenly put a knowing finger on certain of the dead man's pockets.

"Robbed!" he said. "No watch there, anyway, and nothing where you'd expect to find his purse. Robbery and murder–murder for the sake of robbery–that's what it is, Mr. Viner! Westbourne Grove way, you say this fellow went? And five minutes' start!"

"Is it any good getting a doctor?" asked Viner.

"A thousand doctors'll do him no good," replied the policeman grimly. "But–there's Dr. Cortelyon somewhere about here–number seven in the terrace. One of these back doors is his. We might call him."

He turned the light of his lantern on the line of doors in the right-hand wall, and finding the number he wanted, pulled the bell. As its tinkle sounded somewhere up the yard behind, he thrust his whistle into Viner's hand.

"Mr. Viner," he said, "go up to the end of the passage and blow on that as loud as you can, three times. I'll stand by here till you come back. If you don't hear or see any of our people coming from either direction, blow again."

Viner heard steps coming down the yard behind the door as he walked away. And he heard more steps, hurrying steps, as he reached the end of the passage. He turned it to find an inspector and a sergeant approaching from one part of the terrace, a constable from another.

"You're wanted down here," said Viner as they all converged on him. "There's been murder! One of your men's there–he gave me this whistle to summon further help. This way!"

The police followed him in silence down the passage. Another figure had come on the scene. Bending over the body and closely scrutinizing it in the light of the policeman's lantern was a man whom Viner knew well enough by sight–a tall, handsome man, whose olive-tinted complexion, large lustrous eyes and Vandyke beard gave him the appearance of a foreigner. Yet though he had often seen him, Viner did not know his name; the police-inspector, however, evidently knew it well enough.

"What is it, Dr. Cortelyon?" he asked as he pushed himself to the front. "Is the man dead?"

Dr. Cortelyon drew himself up from his stooping position to his full height–a striking figure in his dress jacket and immaculate linen. He glanced round at the expectant faces.

"The man's been murdered!" he said in calm, professional accents. "He's been stabbed clean through the heart. Dead? Yes, for several minutes."

"Who found him here?" demanded the inspector.

"I found him," answered Viner. He gave a hurried account of the whole circumstances as he knew them, the police watching him keenly. "I should know the man again if I saw him," he concluded. "I saw his face clearly enough as he passed me."

The inspector bent down and hastily felt the dead man's pockets.

"Nothing at all here," he said as he straightened himself. "No watch or chain or purse or anything. Looks like robbery as well as murder. Does anybody know him?"

"I know who this gentleman is, sir," answered the policeman to whom Viner had first gone. "He's a Mr. Ashton, who came to live not so long since at number seven in Markendale Square, close by Mr. Viner there. I've heard that he came from the Colonies."

"Do you know him," asked the inspector, turning to Viner.

"Only by sight," answered Viner. "I've seen him often, but I didn't know his name. I believe he has a wife and daughter–"

"No sir," interrupted the policeman. "He was a single gentleman. The young lady at number seven is his ward, and the older lady looked after her–sort of a companion."

The Inspector looked round. Other policemen, attracted by the whistle, were coming into the passage at each end, and he turned to his sergeant.

"Put a man at the top and another at the bottom of this passage," he said. "Keep everybody out. Send for the divisional surgeon. Dr. Cortelyon, will you see him when he comes along? I want him to see the body before its removal. Now, then, about these ladies–they'll have to be told." He turned to Viner. "I understand you live close by them?" he asked. "Perhaps you'll go there with me?"

Viner nodded; and the inspector, after giving a few more words of instruction to the sergeant, motioned him to follow; together they went down the passage into Markendale Square.

"Been resident here long, Mr. Viner?" asked the Inspector as they emerged. "I noticed that some of my men knew you. I've only recently come into this part myself."

"Fifteen years," answered Viner.

"Do you know anything of this dead man?"

"Nothing–not so much as your constable knows."

"Policemen pick things up. These ladies, now? It's a most unpleasant thing to have to go and break news like this. You know nothing about them, sir?"

"Not even as much as your man knew. I've seen them often–with him, the dead man. There's an elderly lady and a younger one, a mere girl. I took them for his wife and daughter. But you heard what your man said."

"Well, whatever they are, they've got to be told. I'd be obliged if you'd come with me. And then–that fellow you saw running away! You'll have to give us as near a description of him as you can. What number did my man say it was–seven?"

Viner suddenly laid a hand on his companion's sleeve. A smart car, of the sort let out on hire from the more pretentious automobile establishments, had just come round the corner and was being pulled up at the door of a house in whose porticoed front hung a brilliant lamp.

"That's number seven," said Viner. "And–those are the two ladies."

The Inspector stopped and watched. The door of the house opened, letting a further flood of light on the broad step beneath the portico and on the pavement beyond; the door of the car opened too, and a girl stepped out, and for a second or two stood in the full glare of the lamps. She was a slender, lissome young creature, gowned in white, and muffled to the throat in an opera cloak out of which a fresh, girlish face, bright in colour, sparkling of eye, crowned by a mass of hair of the tint of dead gold, showed clearly ere she rapidly crossed to the open door. After her came an elderly, well-preserved woman in an elaborate evening toilette, the personification of the precise and conventional chaperon. The door closed; the car drove away; the Inspector turned to Viner with a shake of his head.

"Just home from the theatre!" he said. "And—to hear this! Well, it's got to be done, Mr. Viner, anyhow."

Viner, who had often observed the girl whom they had just seen with an interest for which he had never troubled to account, found himself wishing that Miss Penkridge was there in his place. He did not know what part he was to play, what he was to do or say; worse than that, he did not know if the girl in whose presence he would certainly find himself within a minute or two was very fond of the man whom he had just found done to death. In that case—but here his musings were cut short by the fact that the Inspector had touched the bell in the portico of number seven, and that the door had opened, to reveal a smart and wondering parlour-maid, who glanced with surprise at the inspector's uniform.

"Hush! This is Mr. Ashton's?" said the Inspector. "Yes—well, now, what is the name of the lady—the elderly lady—I saw come in just now? Keep quiet, there's a good girl,—the fact is, Mr. Ashton's had an accident, and I want to see that lady."

"Mrs. Killenhall," answered the parlour-maid.

"And the young lady—her name?" asked the Inspector.

"Miss Wickham."

The Inspector walked inside the house.

"Just ask Mrs. Killenhall and Miss Wickham if they'll be good enough to see Inspector Drillford for a few minutes," he said. Then, as the girl closed the door and turned away up the inner hall, he whispered to Viner. "Better see both and be done with it. It's no use keeping bad news too long; they may as well know—both."

The parlour-maid reappeared at the door of a room along the hall; and the two men, advancing in answer to her summons, entered what was evidently the dining-room of the house. The two ladies had thrown off their wraps; the younger one sat near a big, cheery fire, holding her slender fingers to the blaze; the elder stood facing the door in evident expectancy. The room itself was luxuriously furnished in a somewhat old-fashioned, heavy style; everything about it betokened wealth and comfort. And that its owner was expected home every minute was made evident to the two men by the fact that a spirit-case was set on the centre table, with glasses and mineral waters and cigars; Viner remembered, as his eyes encountered these things, that a half-burned cigar lay close to the dead man's hand in that dark passage so close by.

"Mrs. Killenhall? Miss Wickham?" began Drillford, looking sharply from one to the other. "Sorry to break in on you like this, ladies, but the fact is, there has been an accident to Mr. Ashton, and I'm obliged to come and tell you about it."

Viner, who had remained a little in the background, was watching the faces of the two to whom this initial breaking of news was made. And he saw at once that there was going to be no scene. The girl by the fire looked for an instant at the inspector with an expression of surprise, but it was not the surprise of great personal concern. As for the elder woman, after one quick glance from Drillford to Viner, whom she evidently recognized, she showed absolute self-possession.

"A bad accident?" she asked.

Drillford again looked from the elder to the younger lady.

"You'll excuse me if I ask what relation you ladies are to Mr. Ashton?" he said with a significant glance at Mrs. Killenhall.

"None!" replied Mrs. Killenhall. "Miss Wickham is Mr. Ashton's ward. I am Miss Wickham's chaperon–and companion."

"Well, ma'am," said Drillford, "then I may tell you that my news is–just about as serious as it possibly could be, you understand."

In the silence that followed, the girl turned toward the visitors, and Viner saw her colour change a little. And it was she who first spoke.

"Don't be afraid to tell us," she said. "Is Mr. Ashton dead?"

Drillford inclined his head, and spoke as he was bidden.

"I'm sorry to say he is," he replied. "And still more to be obliged to tell you that he came to his death by violence. The truth is–"

He paused, looking from one to the other, as if to gauge the effect of his words. And again it was the girl who spoke.

"What is the truth?" she asked.

"Murder!" said Drillford. "Just that!"

Mrs. Killenhall, who had remained standing until then, suddenly sat down, with a murmur of horror. But the girl was watching the inspector steadily.

"When was this? And how, and where?" she inquired.

"A little time ago, near here," answered Drillford. "This gentleman, Mr. Viner, a neighbour of yours, found him–dead. There's no doubt, from what we can see, that he was murdered for the sake of robbery. And I want some information about him, about his habits and–"

Miss Wickham got up from her chair and looked meaningly at Mrs. Killenhall.

"The fact is," she said, turning to Drillford; "strange as it may seem, neither Mrs. Killenhall nor myself know very much about Mr. Ashton."

3
WHO WAS MR. ASHTON?

For the first time since they had entered the room, Drillford turned and glanced at Viner; his look indicated the idea which Miss Wickham's last words had set up in his mind. Here was a mystery! The police instinct was aroused by it.

"You don't know very much about Mr. Ashton?" he said, turning back to the two ladies. "Yet–you're under his roof? This is his house, isn't it?"

"Just so," assented Miss Wickham. "But when I say we don't know much, I mean what I say. Mrs. Killenhall has only known Mr. Ashton a few weeks, and until two months ago I had not seen Mr. Ashton for twelve years. Therefore, neither of us can know much about him."

"Would you mind telling me what you do know?" asked Drillford. "We've got to know something–who he is, and so on."

"All that I know is this," replied Miss Wickham. "My father died in Australia, when I was about six years old. My mother was already dead, and my father left me in charge of Mr. Ashton. He sent me, very soon after my father's death, to school in England, and there I remained for twelve years. About two months ago Mr. Ashton came to England, took this house, fetched me from school and got Mrs. Killenhall to look after me. Here we've all been ever since–and beyond that I know scarcely anything."

Drillford looked at the elder lady.

"I know, practically, no more than Miss Wickham has told you," said Mrs. Killenhall. "Mr. Ashton and I got in touch with each other through his advertisement in the *Morning Post*. We exchanged references, and I came here."

"Ah!" said Drillford. "And—what might his references be, now?"

"To his bankers, the London and Orient, in Threadneedle Street," answered Mrs. Killenhall promptly. "And to his solicitors, Crawle, Pawle and Rattenbury, of Bedford Bow."

"Very satisfactory they were, no doubt, ma'am?" suggested Drillford.

Mrs. Killenhall let her eye run round the appointments of the room.

"Eminently so," she said dryly. "Mr. Ashton was a very wealthy man."

Drillford pulled out a pocketbook and entered the names which Mrs. Killenhall had just mentioned.

"The solicitors will be able to tell something," he murmured as he put the book back. "We'll communicate with them first thing in the morning. But just two questions before I go. Can you tell me anything about Mr. Ashton's usual habits? Had he any business? What did he do with his time?"

"He was out a great deal," said Mrs. Killenhall. "He used to go down to the City. He was often out of an evening. Once, since I came here, he was away for a week in the country—he didn't say where. He was an active man—always in and out. But he never said much as to where he went."

"The other question," said Drillford, "is this: Did he carry much on him in the way of valuables or money? I mean—as a rule?"

"He wore a very fine gold watch and chain," answered Mrs. Killenhall; "and as for money—well, he always seemed to have a lot in his purse. And he wore two diamond rings—very fine stones."

"Just so!" murmured Drillford. "Set upon for the sake of those things, no doubt. Well, ladies, I shall telephone to Crawle's first thing in the morning, and they'll send somebody along at once, of course. I'm sorry to have brought you such bad news, but—"

He turned toward the door; Miss Wickham stopped him.

"Will Mr. Ashton's body be brought here–tonight?" she asked.

"No," replied Drillford. "It will be taken to the mortuary. If you'll leave everything to me, I'll see that you are spared as much as possible. Of course, there'll have to be an inquest–but you'll hear all about that tomorrow. Leave things to us and to Mr. Ashton's solicitors."

He moved towards the door, and Viner, until then a silent spectator, looked at Miss Wickham, something impelling him to address her instead of Mrs. Killenhall.

"I live close by you," he said. "If there is anything that I can do, or that my aunt Miss Penkridge, who lives with me, can do? Perhaps you will let me call in the morning."

The girl looked at him steadily and frankly.

"Thank you, Mr. Viner," she said. "It would be very kind if you would. We've no men folk–yes, please do."

"After breakfast, then," answered Viner, and went away to join the Inspector, who had walked into the hall.

"What do you think of this matter?" he asked, when they had got outside the house.

"Oh, a very clear and ordinary case enough, Mr. Viner," replied Drillford. "No mystery about it at all. Here's this Mr. Ashton been living here some weeks– some fellow, the man, of course, whom you saw running away, has noticed that he was a very rich man and wore expensive jewellery, has watched him, probably knew that he used that passage as a short cut, and has laid in wait for him and murdered him for what he'd got on him. It wouldn't take two minutes to do the whole thing. Rings, now! They spoke of diamond rings, in there. Well, I didn't see any diamond rings on his hands when I looked at his body, and I particularly noticed his hands, to see if there were signs of any struggle. No sir–it's just a plain case of what used to be called highway robbery and murder. But come round with me to the police-station, Mr. Viner–they'll have taken him to the mortuary by now, and I should like to hear what our divisional surgeon has to say, and what our people actually found on the body."

As Viner and the Inspector walked into the police-station, Dr. Cortelyon came out. Drillford stopped him.

"Found out anything more, Doctor?" he asked.

"Nothing beyond what I said at first," replied Cortelyon. "The man has been stabbed through the heart, from behind, in one particularly well-delivered blow. I should say the murderer had waited for him in that passage, probably knowing his habits. That passage, now–you know it really will have to be seen to! That wretched old lamp in the middle gives no light at all. The wonder is that something of this sort hasn't occurred before."

Drillford muttered something about local authorities and property-owners and went forward into an office, motioning Viner to follow. The divisional surgeon was there in conversation with the sergeant whom Drillford had left in charge of the body. "That is something on which I'd stake my professional reputation," he said. "I'm sure of it."

"What's that, Doctor?" asked Drillford. "Something to do with this affair?"

"I was saying that whoever stabbed this unfortunate man had some knowledge of anatomy," remarked the doctor. "He was killed by one swift blow from a particularly keen-edged, thin-bladed weapon which was driven through his back at the exact spot. You ought to make a minute search behind the walls on either side of that passage–the probability is that the murderer threw his weapon away."

"We'll do all that, Doctor," said Drillford. "As to your suggestion–don't you forget that there are a good many criminals here in London who are regular experts in the use of the knife–I've seen plenty of instances of that myself. Now," he went on, turning to the sergeant, "about that search? What did you find on him?"

The sergeant lifted the lid of a desk and pointed to a sheet of foolscap paper whereon lay certain small articles at which Viner gazed with a sense of strange fascination. A penknife, a small gold matchbox, a gold-mounted pencil-case, some silver coins, a handkerchief, and conspicuous among the rest, a farthing.

"That's the lot," said the sergeant, "except another handkerchief, and a pair of gloves in the overcoat, where I've left them. Nothing else—no watch, chain, purse or pocketbook. And no rings—but it's very plain from his fingers that he wore two rings one on each hand, third finger in each case."

"There you are!" said Drillford with a glance at Viner. "Murdered and robbed—clear case! Now, Mr. Viner, give us as accurate a description as possible of the fellow who ran out of that passage."

Viner did his best. His recollections were of a young man of about his own age, about his own height and build, somewhat above the medium; it was his impression, he said, that the man was dressed, if not shabbily, at least poorly; he had an impression, too, that the clean-shaven face which he had seen for a brief moment was thin and worn.

"Got any recollection of his exact look?" inquired the Inspector. "That's a lot to go by."

"I'm trying to think," said Viner. "Yes—I should say he looked to be pretty hard-up. There was a sort of desperate gleam in his eye. And—"

"Take your time," remarked Drillford. "Anything you can suggest, you know—"

"Well," replied Viner. "I'd an idea at the moment, and I've had it since, that I'd seen this man before. Something in his face was familiar. The only thing I can think of is this: I potter round old bookshops and curiosity-shops a good deal–I may have seen this young fellow on some occasion of that sort."

"Anyway," suggested Drillford, glancing over the particulars which he had written down, "you'd know him again if you saw him?"

"Oh, certainly!" asserted Viner. "I should know him anywhere."

"Then that's all we need trouble you with now, sir," said Drillford. "The next business will be–tomorrow."

Viner walked slowly out of the police-station and still more slowly homeward. When he reached the first lamp, he drew out his watch. Half-past twelve! Just two hours ago he had been in his own comfortable library, smiling at Miss Penkridge's ideas about the very matters into one of which he was now plunged. He would not have been surprised if he had suddenly awoke, to find that all this was a bad dream, induced by the evening's conversation. But just then he came to the passage in which the murder had been committed. A policeman was on guard at the terrace end–and Viner, rather than hear any more of the matter, hastened past him and made a circuitous way to Markendale Square.

He let himself into his house as quietly as possible, and contrary to taste and custom, went into the dining-room, switched on the electric light and helped himself to a stiff glass of brandy and soda at the sideboard. When the mixture was duly prepared, he forgot to drink it. He stood by the sideboard, the glass in his hand, his eyes staring at vacancy. Nor did he move when a very light foot stole down the stairs, and Miss Penkridge, in wraps and curl-papers, looked round the side of the door.

"Heavens above, Richard!" she exclaimed, "What is the matter! I wondered if you were burglars! Half-past twelve!"

Viner suddenly became aware of the glass which he was unconsciously holding. He lifted it to his lips, wondering whatever it was that made his mouth feel so dry. And when he had taken a big gulp, and then spoke, his voice–to himself–sounded just as queer as his tongue had been feeling.

"You were right!" he said suddenly. "There are queerer, stranger affairs in life than one fancies! And I– I've been pitchforked–thrown–clean into the middle of things! I!"

Miss Penkridge came closer to him, staring. She looked from him to the glass, from the glass to him.

"No–I haven't been drinking," said Viner with a harsh laugh. "I'm drinking now, and I'm going to have another, too. Listen!"

He pushed her gently into a chair, and seating himself on the edge of the table, told her the adventure. And Miss Penkridge, who was an admirable listener to fictitious tales of horror, proved herself no less admirable in listening to one of plain fact, and made no comment until her nephew had finished.

"That poor man!" she said at last. "Such a fine, strong, healthy-looking man, too! I used to wonder about him, when I saw him in the square, I used to think of him as somebody who'd seen things!"

Viner made a sudden grimace.

"Don't!" he said. "Ugh! I've seen things tonight that I never wished to see! And I wish–"

"What?" demanded Miss Penkridge after a pause, during which Viner had sat staring at the floor.

"I wish to God I'd never seen that poor devil who was running away!" exclaimed Viner with sudden passion. "They'll catch him, and I shall have to give evidence against him, and my evidence'll hang him, and–"

"There's a lot to do, and a lot'll happen before that comes off, Richard," interrupted Miss Penkridge. "The man may be innocent."

"He'd have a nice job to prove it!" said Viner with a forced laugh. "No, if the police get him–besides, he was running straight from the place! Isn't it a queer thing?" he went on, laughing again. "I don't mind remembering the–the dead man, but I hate the recollection of that chap hurrying away! I wonder what it feels like when you've just murdered another fellow, to slink off like–"

"You've no business to be wondering any such thing!" said Miss Penkridge sharply. "Here–get yourself another brandy and soda, and let us talk business. These two women–did they feel it much?"

"They puzzled me," replied Viner. He took his aunt's advice about the extra glass, and obeyed her, too, when she silently pointed to a box of cigars which lay on the sideboard. "All right," he said after a minute or two. "I'm not going to have nerves. What was I saying? They puzzled me? Yes, puzzled. Especially the girl; she seemed so collected about everything. And yet, according to her own story, she's only just out of the schoolroom. You'll go round there with me?"

"If we can be of any service to them? Certainly," assented Miss Penkridge.

"The girl said they'd no men folk," remarked Viner.

"In that case I shall certainly go," said Miss Penkridge. "Now, Richard, smoke your cigar, and think no more about all this till tomorrow."

Viner flung himself into an easy-chair.

"All right!" he said. "Don't bother! It's been a bit of a facer, but–"

He was astonished when he woke the next morning, much later than was his wont, to find that he had not dreamed about the events of the midnight. And he was his usual practical and cool-headed self when, at eleven o'clock, he stood waiting in the hall for Miss Penkridge to go round with him to number seven. But the visit was not to be paid just then–as they were about to leave the house, a police-officer came hurrying up and accosted Viner. Inspector Drillford's compliments, and would Mr. Viner come round? And then the messenger gave a knowing grin.

"We've got the man, sir!" he whispered. "That's why you're wanted."

4
THE RING AND THE KNIFE

Viner was hoping that the police had got hold of the wrong man as he reluctantly walked into Drillford's office, but one glance at the inspector's confident face, alert and smiling, showed him that Drillford himself had no doubts on that point.

"Well, Mr. Viner," he said with a triumphant laugh, "we haven't been so long about it, you see! Much quicker work than I'd anticipated, too."

"Are you sure you've got the right man?" asked Viner. "I mean–have you got the man I saw running away from the passage?"

"You shall settle that yourself," answered Drillford. "Come this way."

He led Viner down a corridor, through one or two locked doors, and motioning him to tread softly, drew back a sliding panel in the door of a cell and silently pointed. Viner, with a worse sickness than before, stole up and looked through the barred opening. One glance at the man sitting inside the cell, white-faced, staring at the drab, bare wall, was enough; he turned to Drillford and nodded. Drillford nodded too, and led him back to the office.

"That's the man I saw," said Viner.

"Of course!" assented Drillford. "I'd no doubt of it. Well, it's been a far simpler thing than I'd dared to hope. I'll tell you how we got him. This morning, about ten o'clock, this chap, who won't give his name, went into the pawnbroker's shop in Edgware Road, and asked for a loan on a diamond ring which he produced. Now, Pelver, who happened to attend to him himself, is a good deal of an expert in diamonds–he's a jeweller as well as a pawnbroker, and he saw at once that the diamond in this ring was well worth all of a thousand pounds—a gem of the first water! He was therefore considerably astonished when his customer asked for a loan of ten pounds on it—still more so when the fellow suggested that Pelver should buy it outright for twenty-five. Pelver asked him some questions as to his property in the ring—he made some excuses about its having been in his family for some time, and that he would be glad to realize on it. Under pretence of examining it, Pelver took the ring to another part of his shop and quietly sent for a policeman. And the end was, this officer brought the man here, and Pelver with him, and the ring. Here it is!"

He opened a safe and produced a diamond ring at which Viner stared with feelings for which he could scarcely account.

"How do you know that's one of Mr. Ashton's rings?" he asked.

"Oh, I soon solved that!" laughed Drillford. "I hurried round to Markendale Square with it at once. Both the ladies recognized it—Mr. Ashton had often shown it to them, and told them its value, and there's a private mark of his inside it. And so we arrested him, and there he is! Clear case!"

"What did he say?" asked Viner.

"He's a curious customer," replied Drillford. "I should say that whatever he is now, he has been a gentleman. He was extremely nervous and so on while we were questioning him about the ring, but when it came to the crucial point, and I charged him and warned him, he turned strangely cool. I'll tell you what he said, in his exact words. 'I'm absolutely innocent of that!' he said. 'But I can see that I've placed myself in a very strange position.' And after that he would say no more—he hasn't even asked to see a solicitor."

"What will be done next?" asked Viner.

"He'll be brought before the magistrate in an hour or two," said Drillford. "Formal proceedings—for a remand, you know. I shall want you there, Mr. Viner; it won't take long. I wish the fellow would tell us who he is."

"And I wish I could remember where and when I have seen him before!" exclaimed Viner.

"Ah, that's still your impression?" remarked Drillford. "You're still convinced of it?"

"More than ever–since seeing him just now," affirmed Viner. "I know his face, but that's all I can say. I suppose," he continued, looking diffidently at the inspector, as if he half-expected to be laughed at for the suggestion he was about to make, "I suppose you don't believe that this unfortunate fellow may have some explanation of his possession of Mr. Ashton's ring?"

Drillford, who had been replacing the ring in a safe, locked the door upon it with a snap, and turned on his questioner with a look which became more and more businesslike and official with each succeeding word.

"Now, Mr. Viner," he said, "you look at it from our point of view. An elderly gentleman is murdered and robbed. A certain man is seen–by you, as it happens–running away as fast as he can from the scene of the murder. Next morning that very man is found trying to get rid of a ring which, without doubt, was taken from the murdered man's finger. What do you think? Or–another question–what could we, police officials, do?"

"Nothing but what you're doing, I suppose," said Viner. "Still–there may be a good deal that's–what shall I say?–behind all this."

"It's for him to speak," observed Drillford, nodding in the direction of the cells. "He's got a bell within reach of his fingers; he's only got to ring it and to ask for me or any solicitor he likes to name. But–we shall see!"

Nothing had been seen or heard, in the way hinted at by Drillford, when, an hour later, Viner, waiting in the neighbouring police-court, was aware that the humdrum, sordid routine was about to be interrupted by something unusual. The news of an arrest in connection with the

Lonsdale Passage murder had somehow leaked out, and the court was packed to the doors —Viner himself had gradually been forced into a corner near the witness-box in which he was to make an unwilling appearance. And from that corner he looked with renewed interest at the man who was presently placed in the dock, and for the hundredth time asked himself what it was in his face that woke some chord of memory in him.

There was nothing of the criminal in the accused man's appearance. Apparently about thirty years of age, spare of figure, clean-shaven, of a decidedly intellectual type of countenance, he looked like an actor. His much-worn suit of tweed was well cut and had evidently been carefully kept, in spite of its undoubtedly threadbare condition. It, and the worn and haggard look of the man's face, denoted poverty, if not recent actual privation, and the thought was present in more than one mind there in possession of certain facts: if this man had really owned the ring which he had offered to the pawnbroker, why had he delayed so long in placing himself in funds through its means? For if his face expressed anything, it was hunger.

Viner, who was now witnessing police-court proceedings for the first time in his life, felt an almost morbid curiosity in hearing the tale unfolded against the prisoner. For some reason, best known to themselves, the police brought forward more evidence than was usual on first proceedings before a magistrate. Viner himself proved the finding of the body; the divisional surgeon spoke as to the cause of death; the dead man's solicitor testified to his identity and swore positively as to the ring; the pawnbroker gave evidence as to the prisoner's attempt to pawn or sell the ring that morning. Finally, the police proved that on searching the prisoner after his arrest, a knife was found in his hip-pocket which, in the opinion of the divisional surgeon, would have caused the wound found in the dead man's body. From a superficial aspect, no case could have seemed clearer.

But in Viner's reckoning of things there was mystery. Two episodes occurred during the comparatively brief proceedings which made him certain that all was not being brought out. The first was when he himself went into the witness-box to prove his discovery of the body and to swear that the prisoner was the man he had seen running away from the passage. The accused glanced at him with evident curiosity as he came forward; on hearing Viner's name, he looked at him in a strange manner, changed colour and turned his head away. But when a certain question was put to Viner, he looked round again, evidently anxious to hear the answer.

"I believe you thought, on first seeing him, that the prisoner's face was familiar to you, Mr. Viner?"

"Yes–I certainly think that I have seen him before, somewhere."

"You can't recollect more? You don't know when or where you saw him?"

"I don't. But that I have seen him, perhaps met him, somewhere, I am certain."

This induced the magistrate to urge the accused man–who had steadfastly refused to give name or address–to reveal his identity. But the prisoner only shook his head.

"I would rather not give my name at present," he answered. "I am absolutely innocent of this charge of murder, but I quite realize that the police are fully justified in bringing it against me. I had nothing whatever to do with Mr. Ashton's death–nothing! Perhaps the police will find out the truth; and meanwhile I had rather not give my name."

"You will be well advised to reconsider that," said the magistrate. "If you are innocent, as you say, it will be far better for you to say who you are, and to see a solicitor. As things are, you are in a very dangerous position."

But the prisoner shook his head.

"Not yet, at any rate," he answered. "I want to hear more."

When the proceedings were over and the accused, formally remanded for a week, had been removed to the cells previous to being taken away, Viner went round to Drillford's office.

"Look here!" he said abruptly, finding the Inspector alone, "I dare say you think I'm very foolish, but I don't believe that chap murdered Ashton. I don't believe it for one second!"

Drillford who was filling up some papers, smiled.

"No?" he said. "Now, why, Mr. Viner?"

"You can call it intuition if you like," answered Viner. "But I don't! And I shall be surprised if I'm not right. There are certain things that I should think would strike you."

"What, for instance?" asked Drillford.

"Do you think it likely that a man who must have known that a regular hue and cry would be raised about that murder, would be such a fool as to go and offer one of the murdered man's rings within a mile of the spot where the murder took place?" asked Viner.

Drillford turned and looked steadily at his questioner.

"Well, but that's precisely what he did, Mr. Viner!" he exclaimed. "There's no doubt whatever that the ring in question was Ashton's; there's also no doubt that this man did offer it to Pelver this morning. Either the fellow is a fool or singularly ignorant, to do such a mad thing! But–he did it! And I know why."

"Why, then?" demanded Viner.

"Because he was just starving," answered Drillford. "When he was brought in here, straight from Pelver's, he hadn't a halfpenny on him, and in the very thick of my questionings–and just think how important they were!– he stopped me. 'May I say a word that's just now much more important to me than all this?' he said. 'I'm starving! I haven't touched food or drink for nearly three days. Give me something, if it's only a crust of bread!' That's fact, Mr. Viner."

"What did you do?" inquired Viner.

"Got the poor chap some breakfast, at once," answered Drillford, "and let him alone till he'd finished. Have you ever seen a starved dog eat? No–well, I have, and he ate like that–he was ravenous! And when a man's at that stage, do you think he's going to stop at anything? Not he! This fellow, you may be sure, after killing and robbing Ashton, had but one thought–how soon he could convert some of the property into cash, so that he could eat. If Pelver had made him that advance, or bought the ring, he'd have made a bee-line for the nearest coffee-shop. I tell you he was mad for food!"

"Another thing," said Viner. "Where is the rest of Mr. Ashton's property–his watch, chain, the other ring, his purse, and–wasn't there a pocketbook? How is it this man wasn't found in possession of them?"

"Easy enough for him to hide all those things, Mr. Viner," said Drillford, with an indulgent smile. "What easier? You don't know as much of these things as I do–he could quite easily plant all those articles safely during the night. He just stuck to the article which he could most easily convert into money."

"Well, I don't believe he's guilty," repeated Viner. "And I want to do something for him. You may think me quixotic, but I'd like to help him. Is there anything to prevent you from going to him, telling him that I'm convinced of his innocence and that I should like to get him help–legal help?"

"There's nothing to prevent it, to be sure," answered Drillford. "But Mr. Viner, you can't get over the fact that this fellow had Ashton's diamond ring in his possession!"

"How do I–how do you–know how he came into possession of it?" demanded Viner.

"And then–that knife!" exclaimed Drillford. "Look here! I've got it. What sort of thing is that for an innocent, harmless man to carry about him? It's an American bowie-knife!"

He opened a drawer and exhibited a weapon which, lying on a pile of paper, looked singularly suggestive and fearsome.

"I don't care!" said Viner with a certain amount of stubbornness. "I'm convinced that the man didn't kill Ashton. And I want to help him. I'm a man of considerable means; and in this case–well, that's how I feel about it."

Drillford made no answer. But presently he left the room, after pointing Viner to a chair. Viner waited–five, ten minutes. Then the door opened again, and Drillford came back. Behind him walked the accused man, with a couple of policemen in attendance upon him.

"There, Mr. Viner!" said Drillford. "You can speak to him yourself!"

Viner rose from his chair. The prisoner stepped forward, regarding him earnestly.

"Viner!" he said, in a low, concentrated tone, "don't you know me? I'm Langton Hyde! You and I were at Rugby together. And–we meet again, here!"

5
LOOK FOR THAT MAN!

At these words Viner drew back with an exclamation of astonishment, but in the next instant he stepped forward again, holding out his hand.

"Hyde!" he said. "Then–that's what I remembered! Of course I know you! But good heavens, man, what does all this mean? What's brought you to this–to be here, in this place?"

The prisoner looked round at his captors, and back at Viner, and smiled as a man smiles who is beginning to realize hopelessness to the full.

"I don't know if I'm allowed to speak," he said.

Drillford, who had been watching this episode with keen attention, motioned to the two policemen.

"Wait outside," he said abruptly. "Now, then," he continued when he, Viner and Hyde were alone, "this man can say anything he likes to you, Mr. Viner, so long as you've asked to see him. This is all irregular, but I've no wish to stop him from telling you whatever he pleases. But remember," he went on, glancing at the prisoner, "you're saying it before me–and in my opinion, you'd a deal better have said something when you were in court just now."

"I didn't know what to say," replied Hyde doubtfully. "I'm pretty much on the rocks, as you can guess; but–I have relatives! And if it's possible, I don't want them to know about this."

Drillford looked at Viner and shook his head, as if to signify his contempt of Hyde's attitude.

"Considering the position you're in," he said, turning again to Hyde, "you must see that it's impossible that your relations should be kept from knowing. You'll have to give particulars about yourself, sooner or later. And charges of murder, like this, can't be kept out of the newspapers."

"Tell me, Hyde!" exclaimed Viner. "Look here, now, to begin with–you didn't kill this man?"

Hyde shook his head in a puzzled fashion–something was evidently causing him surprise.

"I didn't know the man was killed, or dead, until they brought me here, from that pawnbroker's this morning!" he said. Then he laughed almost contemptuously, and with some slight show of spirit. "Do you think I'd have been such a fool as to try to pawn or sell a ring that belonged to a man who'd just been murdered?" he demanded. "I'm not quite such an ass as that!"

Viner looked round at Drillford.

"There!" he said quietly. "What did I tell you? Isn't that what I said? You're on the wrong track, Inspector!"

But Drillford, sternly official in manner, shook his head.

"How did he come by the ring, then?" he asked, pointing at his prisoner. "Let him say!"

"Hyde!" said Viner. "Tell! I've been certain for an hour that you didn't kill this man, and I want to help you. But– tell us the truth! What do you know about it? How did you get that ring?"

"I shall make use of anything he tells," remarked Drillford warningly.

"He's going to tell–everything," said Viner. "Come now, Hyde, the truth!"

Hyde suddenly dropped into a chair by which he was standing, and pressed his hand over his face with a gesture which seemed to indicate a certain amount of bewilderment.

"Let me sit down," he said. "I'm weak, tired, too. Until this morning I hadn't had a mouthful of food for a long time, and I'd–well, I'd been walking about, night as well as day. I was walking about all yesterday, and a lot of last night. I'm pretty nearly done, if you want to know!"

"Take your time," said Drillford. "Here, wait a bit," he went on after a sudden glance at his prisoner. "Keep quiet a minute." He turned to a cupboard in the corner of the room and presently came back with something in a glass. "Drink that," he said not unkindly. "Drop of weak brandy and water," he muttered to Viner. "Do him no harm—I see how it is with him—he's been starving."

Hyde caught the last word and laughed feebly as he handed the glass back.

"Starving!" he said. "Yes—that's it! I hope neither of you'll know what it means! Three days without—"

"Now, Hyde!" interrupted Viner. "Never mind that—you won't starve again. Come—tell us all about this—tell everything."

Hyde bent forward in his chair, but after a look at the two men, his eyes sought the floor and moved from one plank to another as if he found it difficult to find a fixed point.

"I don't know where to begin, Viner," he said at last. "You see, you've never met me since we left school. I went in for medicine—I was at Bart's for a time, but—well, I was no good, somehow. And then I went in for the stage—I've had some fairly decent engagements, both here and in the States, now and then. But you know what a precarious business that is. And some time ago I struck a real bad patch, and I've been out of a job for months. And lately it's gone from bad to worse—you know, or rather I suppose you don't know, because you've never been in that fix—pawning everything, and so on, until—well, I haven't had a penny in my pockets for days now!"

"Your relations?" questioned Viner.

"Didn't want them to know," answered Hyde. "The fact is, I haven't been on good terms with them for a long time, and I've got some pride left or I had, until yesterday. But here's the truth: I had to clear out of my lodgings—which was nothing but an attic, three days since, and I've been wandering about, literally hungry and homeless, since that. If it hadn't been for that, I should never have been in this hole! And that's due to circumstances that beat me, for I tell you again, I don't know anything about this man's murder–at least, not about it actually."

"What do you know?" asked Viner. "Tell us plainly."

"I'm going to," responded Hyde. "I was hanging about the Park and around Kensington Gardens most of yesterday. Then, at night, I got wandering about this part–didn't seem to matter much where I went. You don't know, either of you, what it means to wander round, starving. You get into a sort of comatose state–you just go on and on. Well, last night I was walking, in that way, in and out about these Bayswater squares. I got into Markendale Square. As I was going along the top side of it, I noticed a passage and turned into it–as I've said, when a man's in the state I was in, it doesn't matter where he slouches–anywhere! I turned into that passage, I tell you, just aimlessly, as a man came walking out. Viner, look for that man! Find him! He's the fellow these police want! If there's been murder–"

"Keep calm, Hyde!" said Viner. "Go on, quietly."

"This man passed me and went on into the square," continued Hyde. "I went up the passage. It was very dark, except in the middle, where there's an old-fashioned lamp. And then I saw another man, who was lying across the flags. I don't know that I'd any impression about him– I was too sick and weary. I believe I thought he was drunk, or ill or something. But you see, at the same instant that I saw him, I saw something else which drove him clean out of my mind. In fact, as soon as I'd seen it, I never thought about him anymore, nor looked at him again."

"What was it?" demanded Viner, certain of what the answer would be.

"A diamond ring," replied Hyde. "It was lying on the flags close by the man. The light from the lamp fell full on it. And I snatched it up, thrust it into my pocket and ran up the passage. I ran into somebody at the far end–it turns out to have been you. Well, you saw me hurry off–I got as far away as I could, lest you or somebody else should follow. I wandered round Westbourne Grove, and then up into the Harrow Road, and in a sort of back street there I sneaked into a shanty in a yard, and stopped in it the rest of the night. And this morning I tried to pawn the ring."

"Having no idea of its value," suggested Viner, with a glance at Drillford, who was listening to everything with an immovable countenance.

"I thought it might be worth thirty or forty pounds," answered Hyde. "Of course, I'd no idea that it was worth what's been said. You see, I'm fairly presentable, and I thought I could tell a satisfactory story if I was asked anything at the pawnshop. I didn't anticipate any difficulty about pawning the ring–I don't think there'd have been any if it hadn't been for its value. A thousand pounds! Of course, I'd no idea of that!"

"And that's the whole truth?" asked Viner.

"It's the whole truth as far as I'm concerned," answered Hyde. "I certainly picked up that ring in that passage, close by this man who was lying there. But I didn't know he was dead; I didn't know he'd been murdered. All I know is that I was absolutely famishing, desperate, in no condition to think clearly about anything. I guess I should do the same thing again, under the circumstances. I only wish–"

He paused and began muttering to himself, and the two listeners glanced at each other. "You only wish what, Hyde?" asked Viner.

"I wish it had been a half-crown instead of that ring!" said Hyde with a queer flashing glance at his audience. "I could have got a bed for fourpence, and have lived for three days on the rest. And now–"

Viner made no remark; and Drillford, who was leaning against his desk, watching his prisoner closely, tapped Hyde on the shoulder.

"Can you describe the man who came out of the passage as you entered it?" he asked. "Be accurate, now!"

Hyde's face brightened a little, and his eyes became more intelligent.

"Yes!" he answered. "You know—or you don't know—how your mental faculties get sharpened by hunger. I was dull enough, in one way, but alert enough in another. I can describe the man—as much as I saw of him. A tall man—neither broad nor slender—half-and-half. Dressed in black from top to toe. A silk hat—patent leather boots—and muffled to the eyes in a white silk handkerchief."

"Could you see his face?" asked Drillford. "Was he clean-shaved, or bearded, or what?"

"I tell you he was muffled to the very eyes," answered Hyde. "One of those big silk handkerchiefs, you know—he had it drawn up over his chin and nose—right up."

"Then you'd have difficulty in knowing him again," observed Drillford. "There are a few thousand men in the West End of London who'd answer the description you've given."

"All right!" muttered Hyde doggedly. "But—I know what I saw. And if you want to help me, Viner, find that man—because he must have come straight away from the body!"

Drillford turned to Viner, glancing at the same time at the clock.

"Do you want to ask him any more questions?" he inquired. "No? Well, there's just one I want to ask. What were you doing with that knife in your possession?" he went on, turning to Hyde. "Be careful, now; you heard what the doctor said about it, in court?"

"I've nothing to conceal," replied Hyde. "You heard me say just now that I'd had engagements in the States. I bought that knife when I was out West—more as a curiosity than anything–and I've carried it in my pocket ever since."

Drillford looked again at Viner.

"He'll have to go, now," he said. "If you're going to employ legal help for him, the solicitor will know where and when he can see him." He paused on his way to the door and looked a little doubtfully at his prisoner. "I'll give you a bit of advice," he said, "not as an official, but as an individual. If you want to clear yourself, you'd better give all the information you can."

"I'll send my own solicitor to you, Hyde, at once," said Viner. "Be absolutely frank with him about everything."

When Viner was once more alone with Drillford, the two men looked at each other.

"My own impression," said Viner, after a significant silence, "is that we have just heard the plain truth! I'm going to work on it, anyway."

"In that case, Mr. Viner, there's no need for me to say anything," remarked Drillford. "It may be the plain truth. But as I am what I am, all I know is the first-hand evidence against this young fellow. So he really was a schoolmate of yours?"

"Certainly!" said Viner. "His people live, or did live, in the north. I shall have to get into communication with them. But now–what about the information he gave you? This man he saw?"

Drillford shook his head.

"Mr. Viner," he answered, "you don't understand police methods. We've got very strong evidence against Hyde. We know nothing about a tall man in a white muffler. If you want to clear Hyde, you'd better do what he suggested–find that man! I wish you may–if he ever existed!"

"You don't believe Hyde?" asked Viner.

"I'm not required to believe anything, sir, unless I've good proof of it," said Drillford with a significant smile. "If there is any mystery in this murder, well–let's hope something will clear it up."

Viner went away troubled and thoughtful. He remembered Hyde well enough now, though so many years had elapsed since their last meeting. And he was genuinely convinced of his innocence: there had been a ring of truth in all that he had said. Who, then, was the guilty man? And had robbery been the real motive of the murder? Might it not have been that Ashton had been murdered for some quite different motive, and that the murderer had hastily removed the watch, chain, purse, and rings from the body with the idea of diverting suspicion, and in his haste had dropped one of the rings?

"If only one knew more about Ashton and his affairs!" mused Viner. "Even his own people don't seem to know much."

This reminded him of his promise to call on Miss Wickham. He glanced at his watch: it was not yet one o'clock: the proceedings before the magistrate and the subsequent talk with Hyde had occupied comparatively little time. So Viner walked rapidly to number seven in the square, intent on doing something toward clearing Hyde of the charge brought against him. The parlour-maid whom he had seen the night before admitted him at once; it seemed to Viner that he was expected. She led him straight to a room in which Mrs. Killenhall and Miss Wickham were in conversation with an elderly man, who looked at Viner with considerable curiosity when his name was mentioned, and who was presently introduced to him as Mr. Ashton's solicitor, Mr. Pawle, of Crawle, Pawle and Rattenbury.

6
SPECULATIONS

Mr. Pawle, an alert-looking, sharp-eyed little man, whom Viner at once recognized as having been present in the magistrate's court when Hyde was brought up, smiled as he shook hands with the new visitor.

"You don't know me, Mr. Viner," he said. "But I knew your father very well–he and I did a lot of business together in our time. You haven't followed his profession, I gather?"

"I'm afraid I haven't any profession, Mr. Pawle," answered Viner. "I'm a student–and a bit, a very little bit, of a writer."

"Aye, well, your father was a bit in that way too," remarked Mr. Pawle. "I remember that he was a great collector of books–you have his library, no doubt?"

"Yes, and I'm always adding to it," said Viner. "I shall be glad to show you my additions, any time."

Mr. Pawle turned to the two ladies, waving his hand at Viner.

"Knew his father most intimately," he said, as if he were guaranteeing the younger man's status. "Fine fellow, was Stephen Viner. Well," he continued, dropping into a chair, and pointing Viner to another, "this is a sad business that we've got concerned in, young man! Now, what do you think of the proceedings we've just heard? Your opinion, Mr. Viner, is probably better worth having than anybody's, for you saw this fellow running away from the scene, and you found my unfortunate client lying dead. What, frankly, *is* your opinion?"

"I had better tell you something that's just happened," replied Viner. He went on to repeat the statements which Hyde had just made to Drillford and himself. "My opinion," he concluded, "is that Hyde is speaking the plain truth–that all he really did was, as he affirms, to pick up that ring and run away. I don't believe he murdered Mr. Ashton, and I'm going to do my best to clear him."

He looked round from one listener to another, seeking opinion from each. Mr. Pawle maintained a professional imperturbability; Mrs. Killenhall looked mildly excited on hearing this new theory. But from Miss Wickham, Viner got a flash of intelligent comprehension.

"The real thing is this," she said, "none of us know anything about Mr. Ashton, really. He may have had enemies."

Pawle rubbed his chin; the action suggested perplexity.

"Miss Wickham is quite right," he said. "Mr. Ashton is more or less a man of mystery. He had been here in England two months. His ward knows next to nothing about him, except that she was left in his guardianship many a year ago, that he sent her to England, to school, and that he recently joined her here. Mrs. Killenhall knows no more than that he engaged her as chaperon to his ward, and that they exchanged references. His references were to his bankers and to me. But neither his bankers nor I know anything of him, except that he was a very well-to-do man. I can tell precisely what his bankers know. It is merely this: he transferred his banking-account from an Australian bank to them on coming to London. I saw them this morning on first getting the news. They have about two hundred thousand pounds lying to his credit. That's absolutely all they know about him–all!"

"The Australian bankers would know more," suggested Viner.

"Precisely!" agreed Mr. Pawle. "We can get news from them, in time. But now, what do I know? No more than this–Mr. Ashton called on me about six or seven weeks ago, told me that he was an Australian who had come to settle in London, that he was pretty well off, and that he wanted to make a will. We drafted a will on his instructions, and he duly executed it. Here it is! Miss Wickham has just seen it. Mr. Ashton has left every penny he had to Miss Wickham. He told me she was the only child of an old friend of his, who had given her into his care on his death out in Australia, some years ago, and that as he, Ashton, had no near relations, he had always intended to leave her all he had. And so he has, without condition, or reservation, or anything–all is yours, Miss Wickham, and I'm your executor. But now," continued Mr. Pawle, "how far does this take us toward solving the mystery of my client's death? So far as I can see, next to nowhere! And I am certain of this, Mr. Viner: if we are going to solve it, and if this old school friend of yours is being unjustly accused, and is to be cleared, we must find out more about Ashton's doings since he came to London. The secret lies–there!"

"I quite agree," answered Viner. "But–who knows anything?"

Mr. Pawle looked at the two ladies.

"That's a stiff question!" he said. "The bankers tell me that Ashton only called on them two or three times; he called on me not oftener; neither they nor I ever had much conversation with him. These two ladies should know more about him than anybody–but they seem to know little."

Viner, who was sitting opposite to her, looked at Miss Wickham.

"You must know something about his daily life?" he said. "What did he do with himself?"

"We told you and the police-inspector pretty nearly all we know, last night," replied Miss Wickham. "As a rule, he used to go out of a morning–I think, from his conversation, he used to go down to the City. I don't think it was on business: I think, he liked to look about him. Sometimes he came home to lunch; sometimes he didn't.

Very often in the afternoon he took us for motor-rides into the country–sometimes he took us to the theatres. He used to go out a good deal, alone at night–we don't know where."

"Did he ever mention any club?" asked Mr. Pawle.

"No, never!" replied Miss Wickham. "He was reticent about himself–always very kind and thoughtful and considerate for Mrs. Killenhall and myself, but he was a reserved man."

"Did he ever have anyone to see him?" inquired the solicitor. "Any men to dine, or anything of that sort?"

"No–not once. No one has ever even called on him," said Miss Wickham. "We have had two or three dinner-parties, but the people who came were friends of mine–two or three girls whom I knew at school, who are now married and live in London."

"A lonely sort of man!" commented Mr. Pawle. "Yet–he must have known people. Where did he go when he went into the City? Where did he go at night? There must be somebody somewhere who can tell more about him. I think it will be well if I ask for information through the newspapers."

"There is one matter we haven't mentioned," said Mrs. Killenhall. "Just after we got settled down here, Mr. Ashton went away for some days–three or four days. That, of course, may be quite insignificant."

"Do you know where he went?" asked Mr. Pawle.

"No, we don't know," answered Mrs. Killenhall. "He went away one Monday morning, saying that now everything was in order we could spare him for a few days. He returned on the following Thursday or Friday,–I forget which,–but he didn't tell us where he had been."

"You don't think any of the servants would know?" asked Mr. Pawle.

"Oh, dear me, no!" replied Mrs. Killenhall. "He was the sort of man who rarely speaks to his servants–except when he wanted something."

Mr. Pawle looked at his watch and rose.

"Well!" he said. "We shall have to find out more about my late client's habits and whom he knew in London. There may have been a motive for this murder of which we know nothing. Are you coming, Mr. Viner? I should like a word with you!"

Viner, too, had risen; he looked at Miss Wickham.

"I hope my aunt called on you this morning?" he asked. "I was coming with her, but I had to go round to the police-station."

"She did call, and she was very kind indeed, thank you," said Miss Wickham. "I hope she'll come again."

"We shall both be glad to do anything," said Viner. "Please don't hesitate about sending round for me if there's anything at all I can do." He followed Mr. Pawle into the square, and turned him towards his own house. "Come and lunch with me," he said. "We can talk over this at our leisure."

"Thank you–I will," answered Mr. Pawle. "Very pleased. Between you and me, Mr. Viner, this is a very queer business. I'm quite prepared to believe the story that young fellow Hyde tells. I wish he'd told it straight out in court. But you must see that he's in a very dangerous position–very dangerous indeed! The police, of course, won't credit a word of his tale–not they! They've got a strong *prima facie* case against him, and they'll follow it up for all they're worth. The real thing to do, if you're to save him, is to find the real murderer. And to do that, you'll need all your wits! If one only had some theory!"

Viner introduced Mr. Pawle to Miss Penkridge with the remark that she was something of an authority in mysteries, and as soon as they had sat down to lunch, told her of Langton Hyde and his statement.

"Just so!" said Miss Penkridge dryly. "That's much more likely to be the real truth than that this lad killed Ashton. There's a great deal more in this murder than is on the surface, and I dare say Mr. Pawle agrees with me."

"I dare say I do," assented Mr. Pawle. "The difficulty is—how to penetrate into the thick cloak of mystery."

"When I was round there, at Number Seven, this morning," observed Miss Penkridge, "those two talked very freely to me about Mr. Ashton. Now, there's one thing struck me at once—there must be men in London who knew him. He couldn't go out and about, as he evidently did, without meeting men. Even if it wasn't in business, he'd meet men somewhere. And if I were you, I should invite men who knew him to come forward and tell what they know."

"It shall be done—very good advice, ma'am," said Mr. Pawle.

"And there's another thing," said Miss Penkridge. "I should find out what can be told about Mr. Ashton where he came from. I believe you can get telegraphic information from Australia within a few hours. Why not go to the expense—when there's so much at stake? Depend upon it, the real secret of this murder lies back in the past—perhaps the far past."

"That too shall be done," agreed Mr. Pawle. "I shouldn't be surprised if you're right."

"In my opinion," remarked Miss Penkridge, dryly, "the robbing of this dead man was all a blind. Robbery wasn't the motive. Murder was the thing in view! And why? It may have been revenge. It may be that Ashton had to be got out of the way. And I shouldn't wonder a bit if that isn't at the bottom of it, which is at the top and bottom of pretty nearly everything!"

"And that, ma'am?" asked Mr. Pawle, who evidently admired Miss Penkridge's shrewd observations, "that is what, now?"

"Money!" said Miss Penkridge. "Money!"

The old solicitor went away, promising to get to work on the lines suggested by Miss Penkridge, and next day he telephoned to Viner asking him to go down to his offices in Bedford Row. Viner hurried off, and on arriving found Mr. Pawle with a cablegram before him.

"I sent a pretty long message to Melbourne, to Ashton's old bankers, as soon as I left you yesterday," he said. "I gave them the news of his murder, and asked for certain information. Here's their answer. I rang you up as soon as I got it."

Viner read the cablegram carefully:

Deeply regret news. Ashton well known here thirty years dealer in real estate. Respected, wealthy. Quiet man, bachelor. Have made inquiries in quarters likely to know. Cannot trace anything about friend named Wickham. Ashton was away from Melbourne, up country, four years, some years ago. May have known Wickham then. Ashton left here end July, by *Maraquibo*, for London. Was accompanied by two friends Fosdick and Stephens. Please inform if can do more.

"What do you think of that?" asked Mr. Pawle. "Not much in it, is there?"

"There's the mention of two men who might know something of Ashton's habits," said Viner. "If Fosdick and Stephens are still in England and were Ashton's friends, one would naturally conclude that he'd seen them sometimes. Yet we haven't heard of their ever going to his house."

"We can be quite certain that they never did–from what the two ladies say," remarked Mr. Pawle. "Perhaps they don't live in London. I'll advertise for both. But now, here's another matter. I asked these people if they could tell me anything about Wickham, the father of this girl to whom Ashton's left his very considerable fortune. Well, you see, they can't. Now, it's a very curious thing, but Miss Wickham has no papers, has, in fact, nothing whatever to prove her identity. Nor have I. Ashton left nothing of that sort. I know no more, and she knows no more, than what he told both of us–that her father died when she was a mere child, her mother already being dead, that the father left her in Ashton's guardianship, and that Ashton, after sending her here to school, eventually came and took her to live with him. There isn't a single document really to show who she is, who her father was, or anything about her family."

"Is that very important?" asked Viner.

"It's decidedly odd!" said Mr. Pawle. "This affair seems to be getting more mysterious than ever."

"What's to be done next?" inquired Viner.

"Well, the newspapers are always very good about that," answered the solicitor. "I'm getting them to insert paragraphs asking the two men, Fosdick and Stephens, to come forward and tell us if they've seen anything of Ashton since he came to England; I'm also asking if anybody can tell us where Ashton was when he went away from home on that visit that Mrs. Killenhall spoke of. If–"

Just then a clerk came into Mr. Pawle's room, and bending down to him, whispered a few words which evidently occasioned him great surprise.

"At once!" he said. "Bring them straight in, Parkinson. God bless me!" he exclaimed, turning to Viner. "Here are the two men in question–Fosdick and Stephens! Saw our name in the paper as Ashton's solicitors and want to see me urgently."

7
WHAT WAS THE SECRET?

The two men who were presently ushered in were typical Colonials–big, hefty fellows as yet in early middle age, alert, evidently prosperous, if their attire and appointments were anything to go by, and each was obviously deeply interested in the occasion of his visit to Mr. Pawle. Two pairs of quick eyes took in the old solicitor and his companion, and the elder of the men came forward in a businesslike manner.

"Mr. Pawle, I understand?" he said. "I'm Mr. Fosdick, of Melbourne, Victoria; this is my friend Mr. Stephens, same place."

"Take a seat, Mr. Fosdick–have this chair, Mr. Stephens," responded Mr. Pawle. "You wish to see me–on business?"

"That's so," answered Fosdick as the two men seated themselves by the solicitor's desk. "We saw your name in the newspapers this morning in connection with the murder of John Ashton. Now, we knew John Ashton–he was a Melbourne man, too–and we can tell something about him. So we came to you instead of the police. Because, Mr. Pawle, what we can tell is maybe more a matter for a lawyer than for a policeman. It's mysterious."

"Gentlemen," said Mr. Pawle, "I'll be frank with you. I recognized your names as soon as my clerk announced them. Here's a cablegram which I have just received from Melbourne–you'll see your names mentioned in it."

The two callers bent over the cablegram, and Fosdick looked up and nodded.

"Yes, that's right," he said. "We came over with John Ashton in the *Maraquibo*. We knew him pretty well before that–most folk in Melbourne did. But of course, we were thrown into his company on board ship rather more than we'd ever been before. And we very much regret to hear of what's happened to him."

"You say there is something you can tell?" observed Mr. Pawle. "If it's anything that will help to solve the mystery of this murder,–for there is a mystery,–I shall be very glad to hear it."

Fosdick and Stephens glanced at each other and then at Viner, who sat a little in Mr. Pawle's rear.

"Partner of yours?" asked Fosdick.

"Not at all! This gentleman," replied Mr. Pawle, "is Mr. Viner. It was he who found Ashton's dead body. They were neighbours."

"Well, you found the body of a very worthy man, sir," remarked Fosdick gravely. "And we'd like to do something toward finding the man who killed him. For we don't think it was this young fellow who's charged with it, nor that robbery was the motive. We think John Ashton was– removed. Put out of the way!"

"Why, now?" asked Mr. Pawle.

"I'll tell you," replied Fosdick. "My friend Stephens, here, is a man of few words; he credits me with more talkativeness than he'll lay claim to. So I'm to tell the tale. There mayn't be much in it, and there may be a lot. We think there's a big lot! But this is what it comes to: Ashton was a close man, a reserved man. However, one night, when the three of us were having a quiet cigar in a corner of the smoking saloon in the *Maraquibo*, he opened out to us a bit. We'd been talking about getting over to England–we'd all three emigrated, you'll understand, when we were very young–and the talk ran on what we'd do. Fosdick and Stephens, d'ye see, were only on a visit,– which is just coming to an end, Mr. Pawle; we sail home in a day or two,–but Ashton was turning home for good. And he said to us, in a sort of burst of confidence, that he'd have plenty to do when he landed. He said that he was   in   possession–sole   possession–of   a   most extraordinary secret, the revelation of which would affect one of the first families in England, and he was going to bring it out as soon as he'd got settled down in London. Well–you may be surprised, but–that's all."

"All you can tell?" exclaimed Mr. Pawle.

"All! But we can see plenty in it," said Fosdick. "Our notion is that Ashton was murdered by somebody who didn't want that secret to come out. Now, you see if events don't prove we're right."

"Gentlemen," said Mr. Pawle, "allow me to ask you a few questions."

"Many as you please, sir," assented Fosdick. "We'll answer anything."

"He didn't tell you what the secret was?" asked Mr. Pawle.

"No. He said we'd know more about it in time," replied Fosdick. "It would possibly lead to legal proceedings, he said–in that case, it would be one of the most celebrated cases ever known."

"And romantic," added Stephens, speaking for the first time. "Romantic! That was the term he used."

"And romantic–quite so," assented Fosdick. "Celebrated and romantic–those were the words. But in any case, he said, whether it got to law matters or not, it couldn't fail to be in the papers, and we should read all about it in due time."

"And you know no more than that?" inquired Mr. Pawle.

"Nothing!" said Fosdick with decision.

Mr. Pawle looked at Viner as if to seek some inspiration. And Viner took up the work of examination.

"Do you know anything of Mr. Ashton's movements since he came to London?" he asked.

"Next to nothing," replied Fosdick. "Ashton left the *Maraquibo* at Naples, and came overland–he wanted to put in a day or two in Rome and a day or two in Paris. We came round by sea to Tilbury. Then Stephens and I separated–he went to see his people in Scotland, and I went to mine in Lancashire. We met–Stephens and I–in London here last week. And we saw Ashton for just a few minutes, down in the City."

"Ah!" exclaimed Mr. Pawle. "You have seen him, then! Did anything happen?"

"You mean relating to what he'd told *us*?" said Fosdick. "Well, no more than I asked him sort of jokingly, how the secret was. And he said it was just about to come out, and we must watch the papers."

"There was a remark he made," observed Stephens. "He said it would be of just as much interest, perhaps of far more, to our Colonial papers as to the English."

"Yes–he said that," agreed Fosdick. "He knew, you see, that we were just about setting off home."

"He didn't ask you to his house?" inquired Mr. Pawle.

"That was mentioned, but we couldn't fix dates," replied Fosdick. "However, we told him we were both coming over again on business, next year, and we'd come and see him then."

Mr. Pawle spread out his hands with a gesture of helplessness.

"We're as wise as ever," he exclaimed.

"No," said Fosdick emphatically, "wiser! The man had a secret, affecting powerful interests. Many a man's been put away for having a secret."

Mr. Pawle put his finger-tips together and looked thoughtfully at his elder visitor.

"Well, there's a good deal in that," he said at last. "Now, while you're here, perhaps you can tell me something else about Ashton. How long have you known him?"

"Ever since we were lads," answered Fosdick readily. "He was a grown man, then, though. Stephens and I are about forty–Ashton was sixty."

"You've always known of him as a townsman of Melbourne?"

"That's so. We were taken out there when we were about ten or twelve—Ashton lived near where we settled down. He was a speculator in property—made his money in buying and selling lots."

"Was he well known?"

"Everybody knew Ashton."

"Did you ever know of his having a friend named Wickham?" inquired Mr. Pawle with a side-glance at Viner. "Think carefully, now!"

But Fosdick shook his head, and Stephens shook his.

"Never heard the name," said Fosdick.

"Did you ever hear Ashton mention the name!" asked Mr. Pawle.

"Never!"

"Never heard him mention it on board ship—when he was coming home?"

"No—never!"

"Well," said Mr. Pawle, "I happen to know that Ashton, some years ago, had a very particular friend named Wickham, out in Australia."

A sudden light came into Fosdick's keen grey-blue eyes.

"Ah," he said. "I can tell how that may be. A good many years ago, when we were just familiar enough with Melbourne to know certain people in it, I remember that Ashton was away up country for some time—as that cablegram says. Most likely he knew this Wickham then. Is that the Wickham mentioned there?"

"It is," assented Mr. Pawle, "and I want to know who he was."

"Glad to set any inquiries going for you when we get back," said Fosdick. "We sail in two days."

"Gentlemen," answered Mr. Pawle gravely, "it takes, I believe, five or six weeks to reach Australia. By the time you get there, this unfortunate fellow Hyde, who's charged with the murder of Ashton, on evidence that is quite sufficient to satisfy an average British jury, will

probably have been tried, convicted and hanged. No! I'm
afraid we must act at once if we're to help him, as Mr.
Viner here is very anxious to do. And there's something
you can do. The coroner's inquest is to be held tomorrow.
Go there and volunteer the evidence you've just told us! It
mayn't do a scrap of good–but it will introduce an element
of doubt into the case against Hyde, and that will benefit
him."

"Tomorrow?" said Fosdick. "We'll do it. Give us the
time and place. We'll be there, Mr. Pawle. I see your
point, sir–to introduce the idea that there's more to this
than the police think."

When the two callers had gone, Mr. Pawle turned to
Viner.

"Now, my friend," he said, "You've already sent your
own solicitor to Hyde, haven't you? Who is he, by the by?"

"Felpham, of Chancery Lane," replied Viner.

"Excellent man! Now," said Mr. Pawle, "you go to
Felpham and tell him what these two Australians have
just told us, and say that in my opinion it will be well
worth while, in his client's interest, to develop their
evidence for all it's worth. That theory of Fosdick's may
have a great deal in it. And another thing–Felpham must
insist on Hyde being present at the inquest tomorrow and
giving evidence. That, I say, must be done! Hyde must
make his story public as soon as possible. He must be
brought to the inquest. He'll be warned by the coroner, of
course, that he's not bound to give any evidence at all, but
he must go into the box and tell, on oath, all that he told
you and Drillford. Now be off to Felpham and insist on all
this being done."

Viner went away to Chancery Lane more puzzled
than ever. What was this secret affecting one of the first
families in England, of which Ashton had told his two
Melbourne friends? How was it, if legal proceedings were
likely to arise out of it, that Ashton had not told Pawle
about it? Was it possible that he had gone to some other
solicitor? If so, why didn't he come forward? And what,

too, was this mystery about Miss Wickham and her father? Why, as Pawle had remarked, were there no papers or documents, concerning her to be found anywhere? Had she anything to do with the secret? It seemed to him that the confusion was becoming more confounded. But the first thing to do was to save Hyde. And he was relieved to see that Felpham jumped at Pawle's suggestion.

"Good!" said Felpham. "Of course, I'll have Hyde brought up at the inquest, and he shall tell his story. And we'll save these Australian chaps until Hyde's been in the box. I do wish Hyde himself could tell us more about that man whom he saw leaving the passage. Of course, that man is the actual murderer."

"You think that?" asked Viner.

"Don't doubt it for one moment–and a cool, calculating hand, too!" declared Felpham. "A man who knew what he was doing. How long do you suppose it would take to strike the life out of a man and to snatch a few valuables from his clothing? Pooh! To a hand such as this evidently was, a minute. Then, he walks calmly away. And–who is he? But–we're not doing badly."

That, too, was Viner's impression when he walked out of the coroner's court next day. After having endured its close and sordid atmosphere for four long hours, he felt, more from intuition than from anything tangible, that things had gone well for Hyde. One fact was plain– nothing more could be brought out against Hyde, either there, when the inquest was resumed a week later, or before the magistrate, or before a judge and jury. Every scrap of evidence against him was produced before the coroner: it was obvious that the police could rake up no more, unless indeed they could prove him to have hidden Ashton's remaining valuables somewhere which was ostensibly an impossibility. And the evidence of Hyde himself had impressed the court. Two days' rest and refreshment, even in a prison and on prison fare, had

pulled him together, and he had given his evidence
clearly and confidently. Viner had seen that people were
impressed by it: they had been impressed, too, by the
evidence volunteered by the two Australians. And when
the coroner announced that he should adjourn the inquiry
for a week, the folk who had crowded the court went away
asking each other not if Hyde was guilty, but what was
this secret of which Ashton had boasted the possession?

Drillford caught Viner up as he walked down the
street and smiled grimly at him.

"Well, you're doing your best for him, and no mistake,
Mr. Viner," he said. "He's a lucky chap to have found such
a friend!"

"He's as innocent as I am," answered Viner. "Look
here; if you police want to do justice, why don't you try to
track the man whom Hyde has told of?"

"What clue have we?" exclaimed Drillford almost
contemptuously. "A tall man in black clothes, muffled to
his eyes! But I'll tell you what, Mr. Viner," he added with
a grin: "as you're so confident, why don't you find him?"

"Perhaps I shall," said Viner, quietly.

He meant what he said, and he was thinking deeply
what might be done towards accomplishing his desires,
when, later in the afternoon, Mr. Pawle rang him up on
the telephone.

"Run down!" said Mr. Pawle cheerily. "There's a new
development!"

8
NEWS FROM ARCADIA

When Viner, half an hour later, walked into the waiting-room at Crawle, Pawle and Rattenbury's, he was aware of a modestly attired young woman, evidently, from her dress and appearance, a country girl, who sat shyly turning over the pages of an illustrated paper. And as soon as he got into Pawle's private room, the old solicitor jerked his thumb at the door by which Viner had entered, and smiled significantly.

"See that girl outside?" he asked. "She's the reason of my ringing you up."

"Yes?" said Viner. "But what—why? More mystery?"

"Don't know," said Mr. Pawle. "I've kept her story till you came. She turned up here about three-quarters of an hour ago, and said that her grandmother, who keeps an inn at Marketstoke, in Buckinghamshire, had seen the paragraph in the papers this morning in which I asked if anybody could give any information about Mr. John Ashton's movements, and had immediately sent her off to me with the message that a gentleman of that name stayed at their house for a few days some weeks since, and that if I would send somebody over there, she, the grandmother, could give some particulars about him. So that solves the question we were talking of at Markendale Square, as to where Ashton went during the absence Mrs. Killenhall told us of."

"If this is the same Ashton," suggested Viner.

"We'll soon decide that," answered Mr. Pawle as he touched the bell on his desk. "I purposely awaited your coming before hearing what this young woman had to tell. Now, my dear," he continued as a clerk brought the girl into the room, "take a chair and tell me what your message is, more particularly. You're from Marketstoke eh? Just so–and your grandmother, who sent you here, keeps an inn there?"

"Yes, sir, the Ellingham Arms," replied the girl as she sat down and glanced a little nervously at her two interviewers.

"To be sure. And your grandmother's name is–what?"

"Hannah Summers, sir."

"Mrs. Hannah Summers. Grandfather living?"

"No, sir."

"Very well–Mrs. Hannah Summers, landlady at the Ellingham Arms, Marketstoke, in Buckinghamshire. Now then–but what's your name, my dear?"

"Lucy Summers, sir."

"Very pretty name, I'm sure! Well, and what's the message your grandmother sent me? I want this gentleman to hear it."

"Grandmother wished me to say, sir, that we read the piece in the paper this morning asking if anybody could give you any news about a Mr. John Ashton, and that as we had a gentleman of that name staying with us for three or four days some weeks since, she sent me to tell you, and to say that if you would send somebody down to see her, she could give some information about him."

"Very clearly put, my dear–much obliged to you," said Mr. Pawle. "Now, I suppose you were at the Ellingham Arms when this Mr. Ashton came there?"

"Oh, yes, sir; I live there!"

"To be sure! Now, what sort of man was he–in appearance?"

"A tall, big gentleman, sir, with a beard, going a little grey. He was wearing a blue serge suit."

Mr. Pawle nodded at Viner.

"Seems like our man," he remarked. "Now," he went on, turning again to Lucy Summers, "you say he stayed there three or four days. What did he do with himself while he was there?"

"He spent a good deal of time about the church, sir," answered the girl, "and he was at Ellingham Park a good deal–"

"Whose place is that?" interrupted Mr. Pawle.

"Lord Ellingham's, sir."

"Do you mean that Mr. Ashton called on Lord Ellingham, or what?"

"No, sir, because Lord Ellingham wasn't there–he scarcely ever is there," replied Lucy Summers. "I mean that Mr. Ashton went into the park a good deal and looked over the house–a good many people come to see Ellingham Park, sir."

"Well, and what else?" asked Mr. Pawle. "Did he go to see people in the town at all?"

"I don't know, sir–but he was out most of the day. And at night he talked a great deal with my grandmother, in her sitting-room, I think," added the girl with a glance which took in both listeners. "I think that's what she wants to tell about. She would have come here herself, but she's over seventy and doesn't like travelling."

Mr. Pawle turned to Viner.

"Now we know where we are," he said. "There's no doubt that this is our Ashton, and that Mrs. Summers has something she can tell about him. Viner, I suggest that you and I go down to Marketstoke this afternoon. You've accommodations for a couple of gentlemen, I suppose, my dear?" he added, turning to the girl. "Couple of nice bedrooms and a bit of dinner, eh?"

"Oh, yes sir!" replied Lucy Summers. "We constantly have gentlemen there, sir."

"Very well," said Mr. Pawle. "Now, then, you run away home to Marketstoke, my dear, and tell your grandmother that I'm very much obliged to her, and that I am coming down this evening, with this gentleman, Mr. Viner, and that we shall be obliged if she'll have a nice, plain, well-cooked dinner ready for us at half-past seven. We shall come in my motorcar–you can put that up for the night, and my driver too? Very well–that's settled. Now, come along, and one of my clerks shall get you a cab to your station. Great Central, isn't it? All right–mind you get yourself a cup of tea before going home."

"Viner," Pawle continued when he had taken the girl into the outer office, "we can easily run down to Marketstoke in under two hours. I'll call for you at your house at half-past five. That'll give us time to wash away the dirt before our dinner. And then–we'll hear what this old lady has to tell."

Viner, who was musing somewhat vaguely over these curious developments, looked at Mr. Pawle as if in speculation about his evident optimism.

"You think we shall hear something worth hearing?" he asked.

"I should say we probably shall," replied Mr. Pawle. "Put things together. Ashton goes away–as soon as he's got settled down in Markendale Square–on a somewhat mysterious journey. Now we hear that he had a secret. Perhaps something relating to that secret is mixed up with his visit to Marketstoke. Depend upon it, an old woman of over seventy–especially a landlady of a country-town inn, whose wits are presumably pretty sharp–wouldn't send for me unless she'd something to tell. Before midnight, my dear sir, we may have learnt a good deal."

Viner picked up his hat.

"I'll be ready for you at half-past five," he said. Then, halfway to the door, he turned with a question: "By the by," he added, "You wouldn't like me to tell the two ladies that we've found out where Ashton went when he was away?"

"I think not until we've found out why he went away," answered the old lawyer with a significant smile. "We may draw the covert blank, you know, after all. When we've some definite news–"

Viner nodded, went out, into the afternoon calm of Bedford Row. As he walked up it, staring mechanically at the old-fashioned red brick fronts, he wondered how many curious secrets had been talked over and perhaps unravelled in the numerous legal sanctuaries approached through those open doorways. Were there often as strange ones as that upon which he had so unexpectedly stumbled? And when they first came into the arena of thought and speculation did they arouse as much perplexity and mental exercise as was now being set up in him? Did every secret, too, possibly endanger a man's life as his old schoolfellow's was being endangered? He had no particular affection or friendship for Langton Hyde, of whom, indeed, he had known very little at school, but he had an absolute conviction that he was innocent of murder, and that conviction had already aroused in him a passionate determination to outwit the police. He had been quick to see through Drillford's plans. There was a case, a strong *prima facie* case against Hyde, and the police would work it up for all they were worth. Failing proofs in other directions, failing the discovery of the real murderer, how was that case going to be upset? And was it likely that he and Pawle were going to find any really important evidence in an obscure Buckinghamshire market-town?

He jumped into a cab at the top of Bedford Row and hastened back to Markendale Square to pack a bag and prepare for his journey. Miss Penkridge called to him from the drawing-room as he was running upstairs; he turned into the room to find her in company with two ladies–dismal, pathetic figures in very plain and obviously countrified garments, both in tears and evident great distress, who, as Viner walked in, rose from their chairs and gazed at him sadly and wistfully. They reminded him at once of the type of spinster found in quiet, unpretentious cottages in out-of-the-way villages– the neither young nor old women, who live on circumscribed means and are painfully shy of the rude world outside. And before either he or Miss Penkridge could speak, the elder of the two broke into an eager exclamation.

"Oh, Mr. Viner, we are Langton's sisters! And we are so grateful to you–and oh, do you think you can save him?"

Viner was quick to seize the situation. He said a soothing word or two, begged his visitors to sit down again, and whispered to Miss Penkridge to ring for tea.

"You have come to town today?" he asked.

"We left home very, very early this morning," replied the elder sister. "We learned this dreadful news last night in the evening paper. We came away at four o'clock this morning–we live in Durham, Mr. Viner,–and we have been to Mr. Felpham's office this afternoon. He told us how kind you had been in engaging his services for our unfortunate brother, and we came to thank you. But oh, do you think there is any chance for him?"

"Every chance!" declared Viner, pretending more conviction than he felt. "Don't let yourselves be cast down. We'll move heaven and earth to prove that he's wrongly accused. I gather–if you don't mind my asking– that your brother has been out of touch with you for some time?"

The two sisters exchanged mournful glances.

"We had not heard anything of Langton for some years," replied the elder. "He is much–much younger than ourselves, and perhaps we are too staid and old-fashioned for him. But if we had known that he was in want! Oh, dear me, we are not at all well-to-do, Mr. Viner, but we would have sacrificed anything. Mr. Felpham says that we shall be allowed to visit him–he is going to arrange for us to do so. And of course we must remain in London until this terrible business is over–we came prepared for that."

"Prepared for that!" repeated the other sister, who seemed to be a fainter replica of the elder. "Yes, prepared, of course, Mr. Viner."

"Now that we have found Langton, though in such painful circumstances," said the first speaker, "we must stand by him. We must find some quiet lodging, and settle down to help. We cannot let all the burden fall on you, Mr. Viner."

Viner glanced at Miss Penkridge. They were quick to understand each other, these two, and he knew at once that Miss Penkridge saw what was in his mind.

"You must stay with us," he said, turning to the two mournful figures. "We have any amount of room in this house, and we shall be only too glad–"

"Oh, but that is too–" began both ladies.

"I insist," said Viner, with a smile.

"We both insist!" echoed Miss Penkridge. "We are both given to having our own way, too; so say no more about it. We are all in the same boat just now, and its name is *Mystery*, and we must pull together until we're in harbour."

"Listen!" said Viner. "I have to go away tonight, on a matter closely connected with this affair. Let me leave you in my aunt's charge, and tomorrow I may be able to give you some cheering news. You'll be much more comfortable here than in any lodgings or hotel and–and I should like to do something for Hyde; we're old schoolfellows, you know."

Then he escaped from the room and made ready for his journey; and at half-past five came Mr. Pawle in his private car and carried him off into the dark. An hour and a half later the car rolled smoothly into the main street of a quiet, wholly Arcadian little town, and pulled up before an old-fashioned many-gabled house over the door of which was set up one of those ancient signs which, in such places, display the coat of arms of the lord of the manor. Viner had just time to glance around him, and in a clear, starlit evening, to see the high tower of a church, the timbered fronts of old houses, and many a tall, venerable tree, before following Mr. Pawle into a stone hall filled with dark oak cabinets and bright with old brass and pewter, on the open hearth of which burnt a fine and cheery fire of logs.

"Excellent!" muttered the old lawyer as he began to take off his multitudinous wraps. "A real bit of the real old England! Viner, if the dinner is as good as this promises, I shall be glad we've come, whatever the occasion."

"Here's the landlady, I suppose," said Viner as a door opened.

A tall, silver-haired old woman, surprisingly active and vivacious in spite of her evident age, came forward with a polite, old-fashioned bow. She wore a silk gown and a silk apron and a smart cap, and her still bright eyes took in the two visitors at a glance.

"Your servant, gentlemen," she said. "Your rooms are ready, and dinner will be ready, too, when you are. This way, if you please."

"A very fine old house this, ma'am," observed Mr. Pawle as they followed her up a curious staircase, all nooks and corners. "And you have, no doubt, been long in it?"

"Born in it, sir," said the landlady, with a laugh. "Our family—on one side—has been here two hundred years. This is your room, sir—this is your friend's." She paused, and with a significant look, pointed to another door. "That," she said, "is the room which Mr. Ashton had when he was here."

"Ah! We are very anxious to know what you can tell us about him, ma'am," said Mr. Pawle.

Mrs. Summers paused, and again glanced significantly at her visitors.

"I wish I knew the meaning of what I shall tell you," she answered.

9
LOOKING BACKWARD

On the principle that business should never be discussed when one is dining, Mr. Pawle made no reference during dinner to the matter which had brought Viner and himself to the Ellingham Arms. He devoted all his attention and energies to the pleasures of the table; he praised the grilled soles and roast mutton and grew enthusiastic over some old Burgundy which Mrs. Summers strongly recommended. But when dinner was over and he had drunk a glass or two of old port, his eyes began to turn toward the door of the quaint little parlour in which he and Viner had been installed, and to which the landlady had promised to come.

"I confess I'm unusually curious about what we're going to hear, Viner," he said, as he drew out a well-filled cigar-case. "There's an atmosphere of mystery about our presence and our surroundings that's like an aperitif to an already hungry man. Ashton, poor fellow, comes over to this quiet, out-of-the-way place; why, we don't know; what he does here we don't know, yet–but all the circumstances, up to now, seem to point to secrecy, if not to absolute romance and adventure."

"Is it going, after all, to clear up the mystery of his death?" asked Viner. "That's what concerns me–I'm afraid I'm a bit indifferent to the rest of it. What particular romance, do you think, could be attached to the mere fact that Ashton paid a three days' visit to Marketstoke?"

Mr. Pawle drew out a well-filled cigar-case.

"In my profession," he answered, "we hear a great deal more of romance than most folk could imagine. Now, here's a man who returns to this country from a long residence in Australia. The first thing he does, after

getting settled down in London, is to visit Marketstoke.
Why Marketstoke? Marketstoke is an obscure place–there
are at least five or six towns in this very county that are
better known. Again, I say–why Marketstoke? And why
this, the very first place in England? For what reason?
Now, as a lawyer, a reason does suggest itself to me; I've
been thinking about it ever since that rosy-cheeked lass
called at my office this afternoon. What does the man
who's been away from his native land for the best part of
his life do, as a rule, when at last he sets foot on it again–
eh?"

"I'm not greatly experienced," replied Viner, smiling
at the old solicitor's professional enthusiasm. "What does
he do–usually?"

"Makes his way as soon as possible to his native
place!" exclaimed Mr. Pawle, with an expressive flourish
of his cigar. "That, usually, is the first thing he thinks of.
You're not old enough to remember the circumstances, my
boy, but I have, of course, a very distinct recollection of
the Tichborne affair in the early seventies. Now, if you
ever read the evidence in that *cause celebre*, you'll
remember that the claimant, Orton, on arriving in
England, posing as the missing heir, Sir Roger Tichborne,
did a certain thing, the evidence of which, I can assure
you, was not lost on the jury before whom he eventually
came. Instead of going direct to Tichborne, where you'd
naturally have thought all his affection and interests
rested, where did he go? To Whitechapel! Why? Because
the Ortons were Whitechapel folk! The native place called
him, do you see? The first thought he had on setting foot
on English soil was–Whitechapel!"

"Are you suggesting that Ashton was probably a
native of Marketstoke?" asked Viner.

"I mean to find out–no matter what we hear from the
landlady–if that name is to be found in the parish
register here, anyway," answered Mr. Pawle. "You can be
sure of this–Ashton came to this obscure country town for

some special purpose. What was it? And–had it anything to do with, did it lead up to, his murder? That–"

A light tap at the door heralded the approach of Mrs. Summers.

"That," repeated Mr. Pawle, as he jumped up from his chair and politely threw the door open, "is what I mean to endeavour–endeavour, at any rate–to discover. Come in, ma'am," he continued, gallantly motioning the old landlady to the easiest chair in the room. "We are very eager, indeed, to hear what you can tell us. Our cigars, now–"

"Pray, don't mention them, sir," responded Mrs. Summers. "I hope you are quite comfortable, and that you are having everything you wish?"

"Nothing ma'am, could be more pleasant and gratifying, as far as material comfort goes," answered Mr. Pawle with conviction. "The dinner was excellent; your wine is sound; this old room is a veritable haven! I wish we were visiting you under less sad conditions. And now about your recollections of this poor gentleman, ma'am?"

The landlady laid a large book on the table, and opening it at a page where at she had placed a marker, pointed to a signature.

"That is the writing of the Mr. John Ashton who came here," she said. "He registered his name and address the day he came–there it is: 'John Ashton, 7 Markendale Square, London, W.' You gentlemen will recognise it, perhaps?"

Mr. Pawle put up his glasses, glanced once at the open book, and turned to Viner with a confirmatory nod.

"That's Ashton's writing, without a doubt," he said. "It's a signature not to be forgotten when you've once seen it. Well, that establishes the fact that he undoubtedly came here on that date. Now, ma'am, what can you tell about him?"

Mrs. Summers took the chair which Viner drew forward to the hearth and folded her hands over her silk apron.

"Well sir," she answered, "a good deal. Mr. Ashton came here one Monday afternoon, in a motorcar, with his luggage, and asked if I could give him rooms and accommodation for a few days. Of course I could–he had this room and the room I pointed out upstairs, and he stayed here until the Thursday, when he left soon after lunch–the same car came for him. And he hadn't been in the house an hour, gentlemen, before I wondered if he hadn't been here before."

"Interesting–very!" said Mr. Pawle. "Now, why, ma'am did you wonder that?"

"Well, sir," replied Mrs. Summers, "because, after he'd looked round the house, and seen his room upstairs, he went out to the front door, and then I followed him, to ask if he had any particular wishes about his dinner that evening. Our front door, as you will see in the morning, fronts the market square, and from it you can see about all there is to see of the town. He was standing at the door, under the porch, looking all round him, and I overheard him talking to himself as I went up behind him.

"'Aye!' he was saying, as he looked this way and that, 'there's the old church, and the old moot-hall, and the old market-place, and the old gabled and thatched houses, and even the old town pump–they haven't changed a bit, I reckon, in all these years!' Then he caught sight of me, and he smiled. 'Not many changes in this old place, landlady, in your time?' he said pleasantly. 'No, sir,' I answered. 'We don't change much in even a hundred years in Marketstoke.' 'No!' he said, and shook his head. 'No–the change is in men, in men!' And then he suddenly set straight off across the square to the churchyard. 'You've known Marketstoke before,' I said to myself."

"You didn't ask him that?" inquired Mr. Pawle, eagerly.

"I didn't, sir," replied Mrs. Summers. "I never asked him a question all the time he was here. I thought that if I was correct in what I fancied, I should hear him say something. But he never did say anything of that sort—all the same, I felt more and more certain that he did know the place. And during the time he was here, he went about in it in a fashion that convinced me that my ideas were right. He was in and around the church a great deal—the vicar and the parish clerk can tell you more about his visits there than I can—and he was at the old moot-hall several times, looking over certain old things they keep there, and he visited Ellingham Park twice, and was shown over the house. And before he'd been here two days I came to a certain conclusion about him, and I've had it ever since, though he never said one word, or did one thing that could positively confirm me in it."

"Yes!" exclaimed Mr. Pawle. "And that, ma'am, was—"

"That he was somebody who disappeared from Marketstoke thirty-five years ago," answered the landlady, "disappeared completely, and has never been heard of from that day to this!"

Mr. Pawle turned slowly and looked at Viner. He nodded his head several times, then turned to Mrs. Summers and regarded her fixedly.

"And that somebody?" he asked in hushed accents. "Who was he?"

The landlady smoothed her silk apron and shook her head.

"It's a long story, sir," she answered. "I think you must have heard something of it—though to be sure, it was not talked of much at the time, and didn't become public until legal proceedings became necessary, some years ago. You're aware, of course, that just outside the town here is Ellingham Park, the seat of the Earl of Ellingham. Well, what I have to tell you has to do with them, and I shall have to go back a good way. Thirty-five years ago the head of the family was the seventh Earl, who was then getting on in life. He was a very overbearing, harsh old gentleman, not at all liked–the people here in Marketstoke, nearly all of them his tenants, used to be perpetually at variance with him about something or other; he was the sort of man who wanted to have his own way about everything. And he had trouble at home, at any rate with his elder son,–he only had two sons and no daughter,–and about the time I'm talking of it came to a head. Nobody ever knew exactly what it was all about, but it was well known that Lord Marketstoke–that was the elder son's name–and his father, the Earl, were at cross purposes, if not actually at daggers drawn, about something or other. And when Lord Marketstoke was about twenty five or twenty-six there was a great quarrel between them; it broke out one night, after dinner; the servants heard angry words between them. That night, gentlemen, Lord Marketstoke left the house and set off to London, and from that day to this he has never been heard of or seen again–hereabouts, at any rate."

Mr. Pawle, who was listening with the deepest interest and attention, glanced at Viner as if to entreat the same care on his part.

"I do remember something of this, now I come to think of it," he said. "There were some legal proceedings in connection with this disappearance, I believe, some years ago."

"Yes, sir–they were in the newspapers," asserted the old landlady. "But of course, those of us about here knew of how things stood long before that. Lord Marketstoke went away, as I have said. It was known that he had money of his own, that had come to him from his mother, who had died years before all this. But it wasn't known where he went. Some said he'd gone to the Colonies; some said to America. And at one time there was a rumour that he'd taken another name and joined some foreign army, and been killed in its service. Anyway, nobody ever heard a word of him–Mr. Marcherson, who was steward at

Ellingham Park for over forty years (he died last year, a very old man) assured me that from the day on which Lord Marketstoke left his father's house not one word of him, not a breath, ever reached any of those he'd left behind him. There was absolute silence—he couldn't have disappeared more completely if they'd laid him in the family vault in Marketstoke church."

"And evident intention to disappear!" observed Mr. Pawle. "You'll mark that, Viner—it's important. Well, ma'am," he added, turning again to Mrs. Summers. "And—what happened next?"

"Well sir, there was nothing much happened," continued the landlady. "Matters went on in pretty much the usual way. The old Earl got older, of course, and his temper got worse. Mr. Marcherson assured me that he was never known to mention his missing son—to anybody. And in the end, perhaps about fifteen years after Lord Marketstoke had gone away, he died. And then there was no end of trouble and bother. The Earl had left no will; at any rate, no will could be found, and no lawyer could be heard of who had ever made one. And of course, nobody knew where the new Earl was, nor even if he was alive or dead. There were advertisements sent out all over the world—Mr. Marcherson told me that they were translated into I don't know how many foreign languages and published in every quarter of the globe—asking for news of him and stating that his father was dead. That was done for some time."

"With no result?" asked Mr. Pawle.

"No result whatever, sir—I understand that the family solicitors never had one single reply," answered Mrs. Summers. "I understand, too, that for some time before the old Earl's death they'd been trying to trace Lord Marketstoke from his last known movements. But that had failed too. He had chambers in London, and he kept a manservant there; the manservant could only say that on the night on which his young master left Ellingham Park he returned to his chambers, went to bed–and had gone when he, the manservant, rose in the morning. No, sir; all the efforts and advertisements were no good whatever, and after some time–some considerable time–the younger brother, the Honourable Charles Cave-Gray–"

"Cave-Gray? Is that the family name?" interrupted Mr. Pawle.

"That's the family name, sir–Cave-Gray," replied Mrs. Summers. "One of the oldest families in these parts, sir– the earldom dates from Queen Anne. Well, the Honourable Charles Cave-Gray, and his solicitors, of course, came to the conclusion that Lord Marketstoke was dead, and so–I don't understand the legal niceties, gentlemen, but they went to the courts to get something done which presumed his death and let Mr. Charles come into the title and estates. And in the end that had been done, and Mr. Charles became the eighth Earl of Ellingham."

"I remember it now," muttered Mr. Pawle. "Yes– curious case. But it was proved to the court, I recollect, that everything possible had been done to find the missing heir–and without result."

"Just so, sir, and so Mr. Charles succeeded," asserted Mrs. Summers. "He was a very nice, pleasant man, not a bit like his father–a very good and considerate landlord, and much respected. But he's gone now–died three years ago; and his son, a young man of twenty-two or three, succeeded him–that's the present Earl, gentlemen. And of him we see very little; he scarcely ever stayed at Ellingham Park, except for a bit of shooting, since he came to the title. And now," she concluded, with a shrewd glance at the old lawyer, "I wonder if you see, sir, what it was that came into my mind when this Mr. John Ashton came here a few weeks ago, especially after I heard him say what he did, and after I saw how he was spending his time here?"

"I've no inkling, ma'am; I've no inkling!" said Mr. Pawle. "You wondered–"

"I wondered," murmured Mrs. Summers, bending closer to her listeners, "if the man who called himself John Ashton wasn't in reality the long-lost Lord Marketstoke."

10
THE PARISH REGISTER

Mr. Pawle, after a glance at Viner which seemed to be full of many meanings, bent forward in his chair and laid a hand on the old landlady's arm.

"Now, have you said as much as that to anybody before?" he asked, eking her significantly. "Have you mentioned it to your neighbours, for instance, or to anyone in the town?"

"No, sir!" declared Mrs. Summers promptly. "Not to a soul! I'm given to keeping my ideas to myself, especially on matters of importance. There is no one here in Marketstoke that I would have mentioned such a thing to, now that the late steward, Mr. Marcherson, is dead. I shouldn't have mentioned it to you two gentlemen if it hadn't been for this dreadful news in the papers. No, I've kept my thoughts at home."

"Wise woman!" said Mr. Pawle. "But now let me ask you a few questions. Did you know this Lord Marketstoke before he disappeared?"

"I only saw him two or three times," replied the landlady. "It was seldom that he came to Ellingham Park, after his majority. Of course, I saw him a good deal when he was a mere boy. But after he was grown up, only, as I say, a very few times."

"But you remember him?" suggested Mr. Pawle.

"Oh, very well indeed!" said Mrs. Summers. "I saw him last a day or two before he went away for good."

"Well, now, did you think you recognized anything of him–making allowance for the difference in age–in this man who called himself John Ashton?" asked Mr. Pawle. "For that, of course, is important!"

"Mr. Ashton," answered Mrs. Summers, "was just such a man as Lord Marketstoke might have been expected to become. Height, build–all the Cave-Grays that I've known were big men–colour, were alike. Of course, Mr. Ashton had a beard, slightly grey, but he was a grey-haired man. All the family had crown hair; the present Lord Ellingham is crown-haired. And Mr. Ashton had grey eyes–every Cave-Gray that I remember was grey-eyed. I should say that Mr. Ashton was just what I should have expected Lord Marketstoke to be at sixty."

"I suppose Ashton never said or did anything here to reveal his secret, if he had one?" asked Mr. Pawle, after a moment's thoughtful pause.

"Oh, nothing!" replied Mrs. Summers. "He occupied himself, as I tell you, while he was here, and finally he went away in the car in which he had come, saying that he had greatly enjoyed his stay, and that we should see him again sometime. No–he never said anything about himself, that is. But he asked me several questions; I used to talk to him sometimes, of an evening, about the present Lord Ellingham."

"What sort of questions?" inquired Mr. Pawle.

"Oh–as to what sort of young man he was, and if he was a good landlord and so on," replied Mrs. Summers. "And I purposely told him about the disappearance of thirty-five years ago, just to see what he would say about it."

"Ah! And what did he say?" asked Mr. Pawle.

"Nothing–except that it was extraordinary how people could disappear in this world," said Mrs. Summers. "Whether he was interested or not, he didn't show it."

"Probably felt that he knew more about it than you did," chuckled the old solicitor. "Well, ma'am, we're much obliged to you. Now take my advice and keep to your very excellent plan of saying nothing. Tomorrow morning we will just have a look into certain things, and see if we can discover anything really pertinent, and you shall know what conclusion we come to.

Viner!" Pawle went on, when the old landlady had left them alone, "what do you think of this extraordinary story? Upon my word, I think it quite possible that the old lady's theory might be right, and that Ashton may really have been the missing Lord Marketstoke!"

"You think it probable that a man who was heir to an English earldom and to considerable estates could disappear like that, for so many years, and then reappear?" asked Viner.

"I won't discuss the probability," answered Mr. Pawle, "but that it's possible I should steadily affirm. I've known several very extraordinary cases of disappearance. In this particular instance–granting things to be as Mrs. Summers suggests–see how easy the whole thing is. This young man disappears. He goes to a far-off colony under an assumed name. Nobody knows him. It is ten thousand to one against his being recognized by visitors from home. All the advertising in the world will fail to reveal his identity. The only person who knows who he is is himself. And if he refuses to speak–there you are!"

"What surprises me," remarked Viner, "is that a man who evidently lived a new life for thirty-five years and prospered most successfully in it, should want to return to the old one."

"Ah, but you never know!" said the old lawyer. "Family feeling, old associations, loss of the old place–eh? As men get older, their thoughts turn fondly to the scenes and memories of their youth, Viner. If Ashton was really the Lord Marketstoke who disappeared, he may have come down here with no other thought than that of just revisiting his old home for sentimental reasons. He may not have had the slightest intention, for instance, of setting up a claim to the title and estates."

"I don't understand much about the legal aspect of this," said Viner, "but I've been wondering about it while you and the landlady talked. Supposing Ashton to be the

long-lost Lord Marketstoke—could he have established a
claim such as you speak of?"

"To be sure!" answered Mr. Pawle. "Had he been able
to prove that he was the real Simon pure, he would have
stepped into title and estates at once. Didn't the old lady
say that the seventh Earl died intestate? Very well—the
holders since his time, that is to say, Charles, who, his
brother's death being presumed, became eighth Earl, and
his son, the present holder, would have had to account for
everything since the day of the seventh Earl's death.
When the seventh Earl died, his elder son, Lord
Marketstoke, *ipso facto*, stepped into his shoes, and if he
were, or is, still alive, he's in them still. All he had to do,
at any moment, after his father's death, no matter who
had come into title and estates, was to step forward and
say: 'Here I am!—now I want my rights!'"

"A queer business altogether!" commented Viner. "But
whoever Ashton was, he's dead. And the thing that
concerns me is this: if he really was Earl of Ellingham, do
you think that fact's got anything to do with his murder?"

"That's just what we want to find out," answered Mr.
Pawle eagerly. "It's quite conceivable that he may have
been murdered by somebody who had a particular
interest in keeping him out of his rights. Such things
have been known. I want to go into all that. But now
here's another matter. If Ashton really was the missing
Lord Marketstoke, who is this girl whom he put forward
as his ward, to whom he's left his considerable fortune,
and about whom nobody knows anything? I've already
told you there isn't a single paper or document about her
that I can discover. Was he really her guardian?"

"Has this anything to do with it?" asked Viner. "Does
it come into things?"

Mr. Pawle did not answer for a moment; he appeared
to have struck a new vein of thought and to be exploring
it deeply.

"In certain events, it would come into it pretty
strongly!" he muttered at last. "I'll tell you why, later on.

Now I'm for bed–and first thing after breakfast, in the morning, Viner, we'll go to work."

Viner had little idea of what the old solicitor meant as regards going to work; it seemed to him that for all practical purposes they were already in a maze out of which there seemed no easy way. And he was not at all sure of what they were doing when, breakfast being over next morning, Mr. Pawle conducted him across the square to the old four-square churchyard, and for half an hour walked him up one path and down another and in and around the ancient yew-trees and gravestones.

"Do you know what I've been looking for, Viner?" asked Mr. Pawle at last as he turned towards the church porch. "I was looking for something, you know."

"Not the faintest notion!" answered Viner dismally. "I wondered!"

"I was looking," replied Mr. Pawle with a faint chuckle, "to see if I could find any tombstones or monuments in this churchyard bearing the name Ashton. There isn't one! I take it from that significant fact that Ashton didn't come down here to visit the graves of his kindred. But now come into the church–Mrs. Summers told me this morning that there's a chapel here in which the Cave-Gray family have been interred for two or three centuries. Let's have a look at it."

Viner, who had a dilettante love of ancient architecture, was immediately lost in admiration of the fine old structure into which he and his companion presently stepped. He stood staring at the high rood, the fine old rood screen, the beauty of the clustered columns– had he been alone, and on any other occasion, he would have spent the morning in wandering around nave and aisles and transepts. But Mr. Pawle, severely practical, at once made for the northeast chapel; and Viner, after another glance round, was forced to follow him.

"The Ellingham Chapel!" whispered the old solicitor as they passed a fine old stone screen which Viner mentally registered as fifteenth-century. "No end of Cave-Grays laid here. What a profusion of monuments!"

Viner began to examine those monuments as well as the gloom of the November morning and the dark-painted glass of the windows would permit. And before very long he turned to his companion, who was laboriously reading the inscription on a great box-tomb which stood against the north wall.

"I say!" he whispered. "Here's a curious fact which, in view of what we heard last night, may be of use to us."

"What's that?" demanded Mr. Pawle.

Viner took him by the elbow and led him over to the south wall, on which was arranged a number of ancient tablets, grouped around a great altar-tomb whereon were set up the painted effigies of a gentleman, his wife, and several sons and daughters, all in ruffs, kneeling one after the other, each growing less in size and stature, in the attitude of prayer. He pointed to the inscription on this, and from it to several of the smaller monuments.

"Look here!" he said. "There are Cave-Grays commemorated here from 1570 until 1820. No end of 'em—men and women. And now, see—there's a certain Christian name—a woman's name—which occurs over and over again. There it is—and there—and here—and here—and here again; it's evidently been a favourite family name among the Cave-Gray women for three hundred years at least. You see what it is? Avice!"

Mr. Pawle peered at the various places to which his companion's finger pointed.

"Yes," he answered, "I see it—several times, as you say. Avice! Yes?"

"Miss Wickham's Christian name is Avice," said Viner.

Mr. Pawle started.

"God bless me!" he exclaimed. "So it is! I'd forgotten that. Dear me! Now, that's very odd—too odd, perhaps, to be a coincidence. Very interesting, indeed! Favourite family name without a doubt."

Viner silently went round the chapel, inspecting every monument its four walls sheltered.

"It occurs just nineteen times," he announced at last. "Now, is it a coincidence that Miss Wickham's name should be Avice? Or is it that there's some connection between her and all these dead and gone Avices?"

"Very strange!" admitted Mr. Pawle. "Viner—we'll go next and have a look at the parish registers. But look here! Not a word to parson or clerk about our business! We merely wish to make search for a certain legal purpose, eh?"

Three hours later Viner, heartily weary of turning over old registers full of crabbed writing, was glad when Mr. Pawle closed the one on which he was engaged, intimated that he had seen all he wanted, paid the fees for his search, and whispered to his companion that they would go to lunch.

"Well?" asked Viner as they walked across the square to the Ellington Arms. "Have we done anything?"

"Probably!" answered Mr. Pawle. "For you never know how these little matters might help. We've established two facts, anyway. One—that there have never been any folk of the name of Ashton in this town since the registers came into being in 1567; the other, that the name Avice was a very favourite one indeed amongst the women of the Cave-Gray family. And there's just another little fact which I discovered, and said nothing about while the vicar and clerk were about—it may be nothing, and it may be something."

"What is it?" asked Viner.

"Well," answered Mr. Pawle pausing a few yards away from the porch of the hotel, and speaking in a confidential voice, "it's this: In turning up the records of the Cave-Gray family, as far as they are shown in their parish registers, I found that Stephen John Cave-Gray, sixth Earl of Ellingham, married one Georgina Wickham. Now, is that another coincidence? There you get the two names

in combination–Avice Wickham. That particular
Countess of Ellingham would, of course, be the
grandmother of the Lord Marketstoke who disappeared.
Did he think of her maiden name, Wickham, when he
wanted a new one for himself? Possibly! And when he
married, and had a daughter, did he think of the
Christian name so popular with his own womenfolk of
previous generations, and call his daughter Avice? And
are Marketstoke and Wickham and Ashton all one and
the same man?"

"Upon my word, it's a strange muddle!" exclaimed
Viner.

"Nothing as yet to what it will be," remarked Mr.
Pawle sententiously. "Come on–I'm famishing. Let's
lunch–and then we'll go back to town."

Another surprise awaited them when they walked
into Mr. Pawle's office in Bedford Row at four o'clock that
afternoon. A card lay on the old lawyer's blotting-pad,
and after glancing at it, he passed it to Viner.

"See that?" he said. "Now, who on earth is Mr.
Armitstead Ashton Armitstead, of Rouendale House,
Rawtenstall? Who left this?" he went on, as a clerk
entered the room with some letters.

"A gentleman who called at three o'clock, sir," replied
the clerk. "He said he's travelled specially from
Lancashire to see you about the Ashton affair. He's going
to call again, sir. In fact," concluded the clerk, glancing
into the anteroom, "I think he's here now."

"Bring him in," commanded Mr. Pawle. He made a
grimace at Viner as the clerk disappeared. "You see how
things develop," he murmured. "What are we going to
hear next?"

11
WHAT HAPPENED IN PARIS

The man who presently walked in, a tall, grey-bearded, evidently prosperous person, dressed in the height of fashion, glanced keenly from one to the other of the two men who awaited him.

"Mr. Pawle?" he inquired as he dropped into the chair which the old lawyer silently indicated at the side of his desk. "One of your partners, no doubt!" he added, looking again at Viner.

"No sir," replied Mr. Pawle. "This is Mr. Viner, who gave evidence in the case you want to see me about. You can speak freely before him. What is it you have to say, Mr. Armitstead?"

"Not, perhaps, very much, but it may be of use," answered the visitor. "The fact is that, like most folk, I read the accounts of this Ashton murder in the newspapers, and I gave particular attention to what was said by the man Hyde at the inquest the other day. It was what he said in regard to the man whom he alleges he saw leaving Lonsdale Passage that made me come specially to town to see you. I don't know," he went on, glancing at the card which still lay on Mr. Pawle's blotting-pad, "if you know my name at all? I'm a pretty well-known Lancashire manufacturer, and I was a member of Parliament for some years–for the Richdale Valley division. I didn't put up again at the last General Election."

Mr. Pawle bowed.

"Just so, Mr. Armitstead," he answered. "And there's something you know about this case?"

"I know this," replied Mr. Armitstead. "I met John Ashton in Paris some weeks ago. We were at the Hotel

Bristol together. In fact, we met and introduced ourselves to each other in an odd way. We arrived at the Hotel Bristol at the same time–he from Italy, I from London, and we registered at the same moment. Now, I have a habit of always signing my name in full, Armitstead Ashton Armitstead. I signed first; he followed. He looked at me and smiled. 'You've got one of my names, anyway, sir,' he remarked. 'And I see you hail from where I hailed from, many a long year ago.' 'Then you're a Lancashire man?' I said. 'I left Lancashire more years ago than I like to think of,' he answered, with a laugh. And then we got talking, and he told me that he had emigrated to Australia when he was young, and that he was going back to England for the first time. We had more talk during the two or three days that we were at the Bristol together, and we came to the conclusion that we were distantly related–a long way back. But he told me that, as far as he was aware, he had no close relations living, and when I suggested to him that he ought to go down to Lancashire and look up old scenes and old friends, he replied that he'd no intention of doing so–he must, he said, have been completely forgotten in his native place by this time."

"Did he tell you what his native place was, Mr. Armitstead?" asked Mr. Pawle, who had given Viner two or three expressive glances during the visitor's story.

"Yes," replied Mr. Armitstead. "He did–Blackburn. He left it as a very young man."

"Well," said Mr. Pawle, "there's a considerable amount of interest in what you tell us, for Mr. Viner and myself have been making certain inquiries during the last twenty-four hours, and we formed, or nearly formed, a theory which your information upsets. Ashtons of Blackburn? We must go into that. For we particularly want to know who Mr. John Ashton was–there's a great deal depending on it. Did he tell you more?"

"About himself, no," replied the visitor, "except that he'd been exceedingly fortunate in Australia, and had made a good deal of money and was going to settle down here in London. He took my address and said he'd write and ask me to dine with him as soon as he got a house to his liking, and he did write, only last week, inviting me to call next time I was in town. Then I saw the accounts of his murder in the papers–a very sad thing!"

"A very mysterious thing!" remarked Mr. Pawle. "I wish we could get some light on it!"

The visitor looked from one man to the other and lowered his voice a little.

"It's possible I can give you a little," he said. "That, indeed, is the real reason why I set off to see you this morning. You will remember that Hyde, the man who is charged with the murder, said before the Coroner that as he turned into Lonsdale Passage, he saw coming out of it a tall man in black clothes who was swathed to the very eyes in a big white muffler?"

"Yes!" said Mr. Pawle. "Well?"

"I saw such a man with Ashton in Paris," answered Mr. Armitstead. "Hyde's description exactly tallies with what I myself should have said."

Mr. Pawle looked at his visitor with still more interest and attention.

"Now, that really is of importance!" he exclaimed. "If Hyde saw such a man–as I believe he did–and you saw such a man, then that man must exist, and the facts that you saw him with Ashton, and that Hyde saw him in close proximity to the place where Ashton was murdered, are of the highest consequence. But–you can tell us more, Mr. Armitstead?"

"Unfortunately, very little," replied the visitor. "What I saw was on the night before I left Paris–after it I never saw Ashton again to speak to. It was late at night. Do you know the Rue Royale? There is at the end of it a well-known restaurant, close to the Place de la Concorde–I was sitting outside this about a quarter to eleven when I saw Ashton and the man I am speaking of pass along the pavement in the direction of the Madeleine. What made me particularly notice the man was the fact that although it was an unusually warm night, he was closely muffled in a big white silk handkerchief. It was swathed about his throat, his chin, his mouth; it reached, in fact, right up to his eyes. An odd thing, on such a warm night–Ashton, who was in evening dress, had his light overcoat thrown well back. He was talking very volubly as they passed me–the other man was listening with evident attention."

"Would you know the man if you saw him again?" asked Viner.

"I should most certainly know him if I saw him dressed and muffled in the same way," asserted Mr. Armitstead. "And I believe I could recognize him from his eyes–which, indeed, were all that I could really see of him. He was so muffled, I tell you, that it was impossible to see if he was a clean-shaven man or a bearded man. But I did see his eyes, for he turned them for an instant full on the light of the restaurant. They were unusually dark, full and brilliant–his glance would best be described as flashing. And I should say, from my impression at the time, and from what I remember of his dress, that he was a foreigner–probably an Italian."

"You didn't see this man at your hotel?" asked Mr. Pawle.

"No–I never saw him except on this one occasion," replied Mr. Armitstead. "And I did not see Ashton after that. I left Paris very early the next morning, for Rouen, where I had some business. You think this matter of the man in the muffler important?"

"Now that you've told us what you have, Mr. Armitstead, I think it's of the utmost importance and consequence–to Hyde," answered Mr. Pawle. "You must see his solicitor–he's Mr. Viner's solicitor too–and offer to give evidence when Hyde's brought up again; it will be of the greatest help. There's no doubt, to me, at any rate, that the man Hyde saw leaving the scene of the murder is the man you saw with Ashton in Paris. But now, who is he? Ashton, as we happen to know, left his ship at Naples, and travelled to England through Italy and France. Is this man some fellow that he picked up on the way? His general appearance, now–how did that strike you?"

"He was certainly a man of great distinction of manner," declared Mr. Armitstead. "He had the air and bearing of–well, of a personage. I should say he was somebody–you know what I mean–a man of superior position, and so on."

"Viner," exclaimed Mr. Pawle, "that man must be found! There must be people in London who saw him that night. People can't disappear like that. We'll set to work on that track–find him we must! Now, all the evidence goes to show that he and Ashton were in company that night–probably they'd been dining together, and he was accompanying Ashton to his house. How is it that no one at all has come forward to say that Ashton was seen with this man? It's really extraordinary!"

Mr. Armitstead shook his head.

"There's one thing you're forgetting, aren't you?" he said. "Ashton and this man mayn't have been in each other's company many minutes when the murder took place. Ashton may have been trapped. I don't know much about criminal affairs, but in reading the accounts of the proceedings before the magistrate and the coroner, an idea struck me which, so far as I could gather from the newspapers, doesn't seem to have struck anyone else."

"What's that?" demanded Mr. Pawle. "All ideas are welcome."

"Well, this," replied Mr. Armitstead: "In one of the London newspapers there was a plan, a rough sketchmap of the passage in which the murder took place. I gathered from it that on each side of that passage there are yards or gardens, at the backs of houses–the houses on one side belong to some terrace; on the other to the square–Markendale Square–in which Ashton lived. Now, may it not be that the murder itself was actually committed in one of those houses, and that the body was carried out through a yard or garden to where it was found?"

"Ashton was a big and heavy man," observed Viner. "No one man could have carried him."

"Just so!" agreed Mr. Armitstead. "But don't you think there's a probability that more than one man was engaged in this affair! The man in the muffler, hurrying away, may have only been one of several."

"Aye!" said Mr. Pawle, with a deep sigh. "There's something in all that. It may be as you say–a conspiracy. If we only knew the real object of the crime! But it appears to be becoming increasingly difficult to find it.... What is it?" he asked, as his clerk came into the room with a card. "I'm engaged."

The clerk came on, however, laid the card before his employer, and whispered a few words to him.

"A moment, then–I'll ring," said Mr. Pawle. He turned to his two companions as the clerk retired and closed the door, and smiled as he held up the card. "Here's another man who wants to tell me something about the Ashton case!" he exclaimed.

"It's been quite a stroke of luck having that paragraph in the newspapers, asking for information from anybody who could give it!"

"What's this?" asked Viner.

"Mr. Jan Van Hoeren, Diamond Merchant," read Mr. Pawle from the card, "583 Hatton Garden–"

"Ah!" Mr. Armitstead exclaimed. "Diamonds!"

"I shouldn't wonder if you're right," remarked Mr. Pawle. "Diamonds, I believe, are to Hatton Garden what cabbages and carrots are to Covent." He touched his bell, and the clerk appeared. "Bring Mr. Van Hoeren this way," he said.

There entered, hat in hand, bowing all round, a little fat, beady-eyed man, whose beard was blue-black and glossy, whose lips were red, whose nose was his most decided feature. His hat was new and shining, his black overcoat of superfine cloth was ornamented with a collar of undoubted sable; he carried a gold-mounted umbrella. But there was one thing on him that put all the rest of his finery in the shade. In the folds of his artistically-arranged black satin stock lay a pearl–such a pearl as few folk ever have the privilege of seeing. It was as big as a moderately sized hazel nut, and the three men who looked at it knew that it was something wonderful.

"Take a chair, Mr. Van Hoeren," said Mr. Pawle genially. "You want to tell me something about this Ashton case? Very much obliged to you, I'm sure. These gentlemen are both interested–considerably–in that case, and if you can give me any information that will throw any light on it–"

Mr. Van Hoeren deposited his plump figure in a convenient chair and looked round the circle of faces.

"One thing there is I don't see in them newspapers, Mr. Pawle," he said in strongly nasal accents. "Maybe nobody don't know nothings about it, what? So I come to tell you what I know, see? Something!"

"Very good of you, I'm sure," replied Mr. Pawle. "What may it be?"

Mr. Van Hoeren made a significant grimace; it seemed to imply that there was a great deal to be told.

"Some of us, my way, we know Mr. Ashton," he said. "In Hatton Garden, you understand. Dealers in diamonds, see? Me, and Haas, and Aarons, and one or two more. Business!"

"You've done business with Mr. Ashton?" asked the old lawyer. "Just so!"

"No–done nothing," replied Mr. Van Hoeren. "Not a shilling's worth. But we know him. He came down there. And we don't see nothing in them papers that we expected to see, and today two or three of us, we lunch together, and Haas, he says: 'Them lawyer men,' he says, 'they want information. You go and give it to 'em. So!"

"Well–what is it?" demanded Mr. Pawle.

Mr. Van Hoeren leaned forward and looked from one face to another.

"Ashton," he said, "was carrying a big diamond about— in his pocketbook!"

Mr. Armitstead let a slight exclamation escape his lips. Viner glanced at Mr. Pawle. And Mr. Pawle fastened his eyes on his latest caller.

"Mr. Ashton was carrying a big diamond about in his pocketbook?" he said. "Ah—have you seen it?"

"Several times I see it," replied Mr. Van Hoeren. "My trade, don't it? Others of us—we see it too."

"He wanted to sell it?" suggested Mr. Pawle.

"There ain't so many people could afford to buy it," said Mr. Van Hoeren.

"Why!" exclaimed Mr. Pawle. "Was it so valuable, then?"

The diamond merchant shrugged his shoulders and waved the gold-mounted umbrella which he was carefully nursing in his tightly-gloved hands.

"Oh, well!" he answered. "Fifty or sixty thousand pounds it was worth—yes!"

12
THE GREY MARE INN

The three men who heard this announcement were conscious that at this point the Ashton case entered upon an entirely new phase. Armitstead's mind was swept clean away from the episode in Paris, Viner's from the revelations at Marketstoke, Mr. Pawle suddenly realized that here, at last, was something material and tangible which opened out all sorts of possibilities. And he voiced the thoughts of his two companions as he turned in amazement on the fat little man who sat complacently nursing his umbrella.

"What!" he exclaimed. "You mean to tell me that Ashton was walking about London with a diamond worth fifty thousand pounds in his pocket? Incredible!"

"Don't see nothing so very incredible about it," retorted Mr. Van Hoeren. "I could show you men what carries diamonds worth twice that much in their pockets about the Garden."

"That's business," said Mr. Pawle. "I've heard of such things—but you all know each other over there, I'm told. Ashton wasn't a diamond merchant. God bless me—he was probably murdered for that stone!"

"That's just what I come to you about, eh?" suggested Mr. Van Hoeren. "You see 'tain't nothing if he show that diamond to me, and such as me; we don't think nothing of that—all in our way of business. But if he gets showing it to other people, in public places—what?"

"Just so!" asserted Mr. Pawle. "Sheer tempting of Providence! I'm amazed! But—how did you get to know Mr. Ashton and to hear of this diamond? Did he come to you?"

"Called on me at my office," answered Mr. Van Hoeren laconically. "Pulled out the diamond and asked me what I thought it was worth. Well, I introduce him to some of the other boys in the Garden, see? He show them the diamond too. We reckon it's worth what I say–fifty to sixty thousand. So!"

"Did he want to sell it?" demanded Mr. Pawle.

"Oh, well, yes–he wouldn't have minded," replied the diamond merchant. "Wasn't particular about it, you know–rich man."

"Did he tell you anything about it–how he got it, and so on?" asked Mr. Pawle. "Was there any history attached to it?"

"Oh, nothing much," answered Mr. Van Hoeren. "He told me he'd had it some years–got it in Australia, where he come from to London. Got it cheap, he did–lots of things like that in our business."

"And carried it in his pocket!" exclaimed Mr. Pawle. He stared hard at Mr. Van Hoeren, as if his mind was revolving some unpleasant idea. "I suppose all the people you introduced him to are–all right?" he asked.

"Oh, they're all right!" affirmed Mr. Van Hoeren, with a laugh. "Give my word for any of 'em, eh? But Ashton–if he pulls that diamond out to show to anybody–out of the trade, you understand–well, then, there's lots of fellows in this town would settle him to get hold of it–what?"

"I think you're right," said Mr. Pawle. He glanced at Viner. "This puts a new complexion on affairs," he remarked. "We shall have to let the police know of this. I'm much obliged to you, Mr. Van Hoeren. You won't mind giving evidence about this if it's necessary?"

"Don't mind nothing," said Mr. Van Hoeren. "Me and the other boys, we think you ought to know about that diamond, see?"

He went away, and Mr. Pawle turned to Viner and Armitstead.

"I shouldn't wonder if we're getting at something like a real clue," he said. "It seems evident that Ashton was not very particular about showing his diamond to people! If he'd show it–readily–to a lot of Hatton Garden diamond merchants, who, after all, were strangers to him, how do we know that he wouldn't show it to other men? The fact is, wealthy men like that are often very careless about their possessions. Possibly a diamond worth fifty or sixty thousand pounds wasn't of so much importance in Ashton's eyes as it would have been in–well, in mine. And how do we know that he didn't show the diamond to the man with the muffler, in Paris, and that the fellow followed him here and murdered him for it?"

"Possible!" said Armitstead.

"Doesn't it strike you as strange, though," suggested Viner, "that the first news of this diamond comes from Van Hoeren? One would have thought that Ashton would have mentioned it–and shown it–to Miss Wickham and Mrs. Killenhall. Yet apparently–he never did."

"Yes, that does seem odd," asserted Mr. Pawle. "But there seems to be no end of oddity in this case. And there's one thing that must be done at once: we must have a full and thorough search and examination of all Ashton's effects. His house must be thoroughly searched for papers and so on. Viner, I suppose you're going home? Do me the favour to call at Miss Wickham's, and tell her that I propose to come there at ten o'clock tomorrow morning, to go through Ashton's desk and his various belongings with her–surely there must be something discoverable that will throw more light on the matter. And in the meantime, Viner, don't say anything to her about our journey to Marketstoke–leave that for a while."

Viner went away from Crawle, Pawle, and Rattenbury's in company with Armitstead. Outside, the Lancashire business man gave him a shrewd glance.

"I very much doubt if that diamond has anything whatever to do with Ashton's murder," he said. "From what I saw of him, he seemed to me to be a very practical man, full of business aptitude and common sense, and I don't believe that he'd make a practice of walking about London with a diamond of that value in his pocket. It's all very well that he should have it in his pocket when he went down to Hatton Garden–he had a purpose. But that he should always carry it–no, I don't credit that, Mr. Viner."

"I can scarcely credit such a foolish thing myself," said Viner. "But–where is the diamond?"

"Perhaps you'll find it tomorrow," suggested Armitstead. "The man would be sure to have some place in his house where he kept his valuables. I shall be curious to hear."

"Are you staying in town?" inquired Viner.

"I shall be at the Hotel Cecil for a fortnight at least," answered Armitstead. "And if I can be of any use to you or Mr. Pawle, you've only to ring me up there. You've no doubt yourself, I think, that the unfortunate fellow Hyde is innocent?"

"None!" said Viner. "No doubt whatever! But–the police have a strong case against him. And unless we can find the actual murderer, I'm afraid Hyde's in a very dangerous position."

"Well," said Armitstead, "in these cases, you never know what a sudden and unexpected turn of events may do. That man with the muffler is the chap you want to get hold of–I'm sure of that!"

Viner went home and dined with his aunt and their two guests, Hyde's sisters, whom he endeavoured to cheer up by saying that things were developing as favourably as could be expected, and that he hoped to have good news for them ere long. They were simple souls, pathetically grateful for any scrap of sympathy and comfort, and he strove to appear more confident about the chances of clearing this unlucky brother than he really felt. It was his intention to go round to Number Seven during the evening, to deliver Mr. Pawle's message to Miss Wickham, but before he rose from his own table, a message arrived by Miss Wickham's parlour-maid–would Mr. Viner be kind enough to come to the house at once?

At this, Viner excused himself to his guests and hurried round to Number Seven, to find Miss Wickham and Mrs. Killenhall, now in mourning garments, in company with a little man whom Viner at once recognized as a well-known tradesman of Westbourne Grove–a florist and fruiterer named Barleyfield, who was patronized by all the well-to-do folk of the neighbourhood. He smiled and bowed as Viner entered the room, and turned to Miss Wickham as if suggesting that she should explain his presence.

"Oh, Mr. Viner!" said Miss Wickham, "I'm so sorry to send for you so hurriedly, but Mr. Barleyfield came to tell us that he could give some information about Mr. Ashton, and as Mr. Pawle isn't available, and I don't like to send for a police-inspector, I thought that you, perhaps–"

"To be sure!" said Viner. "What is it, Mr. Barleyfield?"

Mr. Barleyfield, who had obviously attired himself in his Sunday raiment for the purposes of his call, and had further shown respect for the occasion by wearing a black cravat, smiled as he looked from the two ladies to Viner.

"Well, Mr. Viner," he answered, "I'll tell you what it is–it may help a bit in clearing up things, for I understand there's a great deal of mystery about Mr. Ashton's death. Now, I'm told, sir, that nobody–especially these good ladies–knows nothing about what the deceased gentleman used to do with himself of an evening–as a rule. Just so. Well, you know, Mr. Viner, a tradesman like myself generally knows a good deal about the people of his neighbourhood. I knew Mr. Ashton very well indeed–he was a good customer of mine, and sometimes he'd stop and have a bit of chat with me. And I can tell you where he very often spent an hour or two of an evening."

"Yes–where?" asked Viner.

"At the Grey Mare Inn, sir," answered Barleyfield promptly. "I have often seen him there myself."

"The Grey Mare Inn!" exclaimed Viner, while Mrs. Killenhall and Miss Wickham looked at each other wonderingly. "Where is that? It sounds like the name of some village tavern."

"Ah, but you don't know this part of London as I do, sir!" said Barleyfield, with a knowing smile. "If you did, you'd know the Grey Mare well enough—it's an institution. It's a real old-fashioned place, between Westbourne Grove and Notting Hill—one of the very last of the old taverns, with a tea-garden behind it, and a bar-parlour of a very comfortable sort, where various old fogies of the neighbourhood gather of an evening and smoke churchwarden pipes and tell tales of the olden days—I rather gathered from what I saw that it was the old atmosphere that attracted Mr. Ashton—made him think of bygone England, you know, Mr. Viner."

"And you say he went there regularly?" asked Viner.

"I've seen him there a great deal, sir, for I usually turn in there for half an hour or so, myself, of an evening, when business is over and I've had my supper," answered Barleyfield. "I should say that he went there four or five nights a week."

"And no doubt conversed with the people he met there?" suggested Viner.

"He was a friendly, sociable man, sir," said Barleyfield. "Yes, he was fond of a talk. But there was one man there that he seemed to associate with—an elderly, superior gentleman whose name I don't know, though I'm familiar enough with his appearance. Him and Mr. Ashton I've often seen sitting in a particular corner, smoking their cigars, and talking together. And—if it's of any importance—I saw them talking like that, at the Grey Mare, the very evening that—that Mr. Ashton died, Mr. Viner."

"What time was that?" asked Viner.

"About the usual time, sir—nine-thirty or so," replied Barleyfield. "I generally look in about that time—nine-thirty to ten."

"Did you leave them talking there?" inquired Viner.

"They were there when I left, sir, at a quarter past ten," answered Barleyfield. "Talking in their usual corner."

"And you say you don't know who this man is?"

"I don't! I know him by sight—but he's a comparatively recent comer to the Grey Mare. I've noticed him for a year or so—not longer."

Viner glanced at the two ladies.

"I suppose you never heard Mr. Ashton mention the Grey Mare?" he asked.

"We never heard Mr. Ashton say anything about his movements," answered Miss Wickham. "We used to wonder, sometimes, if he'd joined a club or if he had friends that we knew nothing about."

"Well," said Viner, turning to the florist, "do you think you could take me to the Grey Mare, Mr. Barleyfield?"

"Nothing easier, sir—open to one and all!"

"Then, if you've the time to spare, we'll go now," said Viner. He lingered behind a moment to tell Miss Wickham of Mr. Pawle's appointment for the morning, and then went away with Barleyfield in the Notting Hill direction. "I suppose you've been at the Grey Mare since Mr. Ashton's death?" he asked as they walked along.

"Once or twice, sir," replied Barleyfield. "And you've no doubt heard the murder discussed?" suggested Viner.

"I've heard it discussed hard enough, sir, there and elsewhere," replied the florist. "But at the Gray Mare itself, I don't think anybody knew that this man who'd been murdered was the same as the grey-bearded gentleman who used to drop in there sometimes. They didn't when I was last in, anyway. Perhaps this gentleman I've mentioned to you might know—Mr. Ashton might have told his name to him. But you know how it is in these places, Mr. Viner—people drop in, even regularly, and fellow-customers may have a bit of talk with them without having the least idea who they are. Between you and me, sir, I came to the conclusion that Mr. Ashton was a man who liked to see a bit of what we'll call informal, old-fashioned tavern life, and he hit on this place by accident, in one of his walks round, and took to coming where he could be at his ease—amongst strangers."

"No doubt," agreed Viner.

He followed his guide through various squares and streets until they came to the object of their pilgrimage—a four-square, old-fashioned house set back a little from the road, with a swinging sign in front, and a garden at the side. Barleyfield led him through this garden to a side-door, whence they passed into a roomy, low-ceilinged parlour which reminded Viner of old coaching prints—he would scarcely have believed it possible that such a pre-Victorian room could be found in London. There were several men in it, and he nudged his companion's elbow.

"Let us sit down in a quiet corner and have something to drink," he said. "I just want to take a look at this place—and its frequenters."

Barleyfield led him to a nook near the chimney-corner and beckoned to an aproned boy who hung about with a tray under his arm. But before Viner could give an order, his companion touched his arm and motioned towards the door.

"Here's the gentleman Mr. Ashton used to talk to!" he whispered. "The tall man—just coming in."

13
THE JAPANESE CABINET

Remembering that Barleyfield had said that the man who now entered had been in Ashton's company in that very room on the evening of the murder, Viner looked at him with keen interest and speculation. He was a tall, well-built, clean-shaven man, of professional appearance and of a large, heavy, solemn face the evidently usual pallor of which was deepened by his black overcoat and cravat. An eminently respectable, slow-going, unimaginative man, in Viner's opinion, and of a type which one may see by the dozen in the precincts of the Temple; a man who would be content to do a day's work in a placid fashion, and who cherished no ambition to set the Thames on fire; certainly, so Viner thought, from appearances, not the man to commit a peculiarly daring murder. Nevertheless, knowing what he did, he watched him closely.

The newcomer, on entering, glanced at once at a quiet corner of the room, and seeing it unoccupied, turned to the bar, where the landlord, who was as old-fashioned as his surroundings, was glancing over the evening paper. He asked for whisky and soda, and when he took up the glass, drank slowly and thoughtfully. Suddenly he turned to the landlord.

"Have you seen that gentleman lately that I've sometimes talked to in the corner there?" he asked.

The landlord glanced across the room and shook his head.

"Can't say that I have, sir," he answered. "The tallish gentleman with a grey beard? No, he hasn't been in this last night or two."

The other man sat down his glass and drew something from his pocket.

"I promised to bring him a specimen of some cigars I bought lately," he said, laying an envelope on the counter. "I can't stop tonight. If he should come in, will you give him that–he'll know what it is."

"Good heavens!" muttered Viner, as he turned in surprise to Barleyfield. "These men evidently don't know that the man they're talking about is–"

"Murdered!" whispered Barleyfield, with a grim smile. "Nothing wonderful in that, Mr. Viner. They haven't connected Mr. Ashton with the man they're mentioning– that's all."

"And yet Ashton's portrait has been in the papers!" exclaimed Viner. "It amazes me!"

"Aye, just so, sir," said Barleyfield. "But–a hundred yards in London takes you into another world, Mr. Viner. For all practical purposes, Lonsdale Passage, though it's only a mile away, is as much separated from this spot as New York is from London. Well–that's the man I told you of, sir."

The man in question drank off the remaining contents of his glass, nodded to the landlord, and walked out. And Viner was suddenly minded to do something towards getting information.

"Look here!" he said. "I'm going to ask that landlord a question or two. Come with me."

He went up to the bar, Barleyfield following in close attendance, and gave the landlord a significant glance.

"Can I have a word with you, in private?" he asked.

The landlord looked his questioner over and promptly opened a flap in the counter.

"Step inside, sir," he said, indicating a door in the rear. "Private room there, sir."

Viner and Barleyfield walked into a little snugly furnished sitting-room; the landlord followed and closed the door.

"Do you happen to know the name of the gentleman who was speaking to you just now?" asked Viner, going straight to his point. "I've a very particular reason for wishing to know it."

"No more idea than I have of yours, sir," replied the landlord with a shrewd glance.

Viner pulled out a card and laid it on the table.

"That is my name," he said. "You and the gentleman who has just gone out were speaking just now of another gentleman whom he used to meet here—who used to sit with him in that far corner. Just so—you don't know the name of that gentleman, either?"

"No more than I know the others', sir," replied the landlord, shaking his head. "Lord bless you, folks may come in here for a year or two, and unless they happen to be neighbours of mine, I don't know who they are. Now, there's your friend there," he went on, indicating Barleyfield with a smile, "I know his face as that of a customer, but I don't know who he is! That gentleman who's just gone out, he's been in the habit of dropping in here for a twelvemonth, maybe, but I never remember hearing his name. As for the gentleman he referred to, why, I know him as one that's come in here pretty regular for the last few weeks, but I don't know his name, either."

"Have you heard of the murder in Lonsdale Passage?" asked Viner.

"Markendale Square way? Yes," answered the landlord, with awakening interest. "Why, is it anything to do—"

Viner saw an illustrated paper lying on a side-table and caught it up. There was a portrait of Ashton in it, and he held it up before the landlord.

"Don't you recognize that?" he asked.

The landlord started and stared.

"Bless my life and soul!" he exclaimed. "Why, surely that's very like the gentleman I just referred to—I should say it was the very man!"

"It is the very man!" said Viner with emphasis, "the man for whom your customer who's just gone out left the envelope. Now, this man who was murdered in Lonsdale Passage was here in your parlour for some time on the evening of the night on which he was murdered, and he was then in conversation with the man who has just gone out. Naturally, therefore, I should like to know that man's name."

"You're not a detective?" suggested the landlord.

"Not at all!" replied Viner. "I was a neighbour of Mr. Ashton's, and I am interested–deeply interested–in an attempt to clear up the mystery of his death. Things keep coming out. I didn't know until this evening that Ashton spent some time here, at your house, the night he was killed. But when I got to know, I came along to make one or two inquiries."

"Bless me!" said the landlord, who was still staring at the portrait. "Yes, that's the gentleman, sure enough! I've often wondered who he was–pleasant, sociable sort, he was, poor fellow. Now I come to think of it I remember him being in here that night–last time, of course, he was ever in. He was talking to that gentleman who's just gone; in fact, they left together."

"They left together, did they!" exclaimed Viner with a sharp glance at Barleyfield. "Ah! What time was that, now?"

"As near as I can recollect, about ten-fifteen to ten-thirty," answered the landlord. "They'd been talking together for a good hour in that corner where they usually sat. But dear me," he went on, looking from one to the other of his two visitors, "I'm quite sure that gentleman who's just left doesn't know of this murder! Why, you heard him ask for the other gentleman, and leave him some cigars that he'd promised!"

"Just so–which makes it all the stranger," said Viner. "Well, I'm much obliged to you, landlord–and for the time being, just keep the matter of this talk strictly to yourself. You understand?"

"As you wish, sir," assented the landlord. "I shan't say anything. You wouldn't like me to find out this gentleman's name? Somebody'll know him. My own idea is that he lives in this part–he began coming in here of an evening about a year since."

"No–do nothing at present," said Viner. "The inquiries are only beginning."

He impressed the same obligation of silence on Barleyfield as they went away, and the florist readily understood.

"No hard work for me to hold my tongue, Mr. Viner," he said. "We tradespeople are pretty well trained to that, sir! There's things and secrets I could tell! But upon my word, I don't ever remember quite such a case as this. And I expect it'll be like most cases of the sort!"

"What do you mean?" asked Viner.

"Oh, there'll be a sudden flash of light on it, sir, all of a sudden," replied Barleyfield. "And then–it'll be as clear as noonday."

"I don't know where it's coming from!" muttered Viner. "I don't even see a rift in the clouds yet."

He had been at work for an hour or two with Miss Wickham and Mr. Pawle next morning, searching for whatever might be discovered among Ashton's effects, before he saw any reason to alter this opinion. The bunch of keys discovered in the murdered man's pocket had been duly delivered to Miss Wickham by the police, and she handed them over to the old solicitor with full license to open whatever they secured. But both Mr. Pawle and Viner saw at once that Ashton had been one of those men who have no habit of locking up things. In all that roomy house he had but one room which he kept to himself–a small, twelve-foot-square apartment on the ground floor, in which, they said, he used to spend an hour or two of a morning. It contained little in the way of ornament or comfort–a solid writing-desk with a hard chair, an easy-chair by the fireplace, a sofa against the wall, a map of

London and a picture or two, a shelf of old books, a collection of walking-sticks, and umbrellas: these made up all there was to see.

And upon examination the desk yielded next to nothing. One drawer contained a cash-box, a checkbook, a pass-book. Some sixty or seventy pounds in notes, gold and silver lay in the cash-box; the stubs of the checks revealed nothing but the payment of tradesmen's bills; the pass-book showed that an enormous balance lay at the bank. In another drawer rested a collection of tradesmen's books–Mr. Ashton, said Mrs. Killenhall, used to pay his tradesmen every week; these books had been handed to him on the very evening of his death for settlement next morning.

"Evidently a most methodical man!" remarked Mr. Pawle. "Which makes it all the more remarkable that so few papers are discoverable. You'd have thought that in his longish life he'd have accumulated a good many documents that he wanted to keep."

But documents there were next to none. Several of the drawers of the desk were empty, save for stationery. One contained a bunch of letters, tied up with blue ribbon– these, on examination, proved to be letters written by Miss Wickham, at school in England, to her guardian in Australia. Miss Wickham, present while Mr. Pawle and Viner searched, showed some emotion at the sight of them.

"I used to write to him once a month," she said. "I had no idea that he had kept the letters, though!"

The two men went silently on with their search. But there was no further result. Ashton did not appear to have kept any letters or papers relative to his life or doings prior to his coming to England. Private documents of any sort he seemed to have none. And whatever business had taken him to Marketstoke, they could find no written reference to it; nor could they discover anything about the diamond of which Mr. Van Hoeren had spoken. They went upstairs to his bedroom and examined the drawers, cabinets and dressing-case—they found nothing.

"This is distinctly disappointing," remarked Mr. Pawle when he and Viner returned to the little room. "I never knew a man who left such small evidence behind him. It's quite evident to me that there's nothing whatever in this house that's going to be of any use to us. I wonder if he rented a box at any of the safe-deposit places? He must have had documents of some sort."

"In that case, we should surely have found a key, and perhaps a receipt for the rent of the box," suggested Viner. "I should have thought he'd have had a safe in his own house," he added, "but we don't hear of one."

Mr. Pawle looked round the room, as if suspicious that Ashton might have hidden papers in the stuffing of the sofa or the easy-chair.

"I wonder if there's anything in that," he said suddenly. "It looks like a receptacle of some sort."

Viner turned and saw the old lawyer pointing to a curious Japanese cabinet which stood in the middle of the marble mantelpiece—the only really notable ornament in the room. Mr. Pawle laid hold of it and uttered a surprised exclamation. "That's a tremendous weight for so small a thing!" he said. "Feel it!"

Viner took hold of the cabinet—an affair of some eighteen inches in height and twelve in depth—and came to the conclusion that it was heavily weighted with lead. He lifted it down to the desk, giving it a slight shake.

"I took it for a cigar cabinet," he remarked. "How does it open? Have you a key that will fit it?"

But upon examination there was no keyhole, and nothing to show how the door was opened.

"I see what this is," said Viner, after looking closely over the cabinet, back, front and sides. "It opens by a trick—a secret. Probably you press something somewhere and the door flies open. But—where?"

"Try," counselled Mr. Pawle. "There's something inside—I heard it when you shook the thing."

It took Viner ten minutes to find out the secret. He would not have found it at all but for accident. But pressing here and pulling there, he suddenly touched what appeared to be no more than a cleverly inserted rivet in the ebony surface; there was a sharp click, and the panelled front flew open.

"There is something!" exclaimed Mr. Pawle. "Papers!"

He drew out a bundle of papers, folded in a strong sheet of cartridge-paper and sealed back and front. The enveloping cover was old and faded; the ribbon which had been tied round the bundle was discoloured by age; the wax of the seals was cracked all over the surface.

"No inscription, no writing," said Mr. Pawle. "Now, I wonder what's in here?"

"Shall I fetch Miss Wickham?" suggested Viner. Mr. Pawle hesitated.

"No!" he said at last. "I think not. Let us first find out what this packet contains. I'll take the responsibility."

He cut the ribbons beneath the seals, and presently revealed a number of letters, old and yellow, in a woman's handwriting. And after a hasty glance at one or two of the uppermost, he turned to Viner with an exclamation that signified much.

"Viner!" he said, "here is indeed a find! These are letters written by the Countess of Ellingham to her son, Lord Marketstoke, when he was a schoolboy at Eton!"

14
THE ELLINGHAM MOTTO

Viner looked over Mr. Pawle's shoulder at the letters–there were numbers of them, all neatly folded and arranged; a faint scent of dried flowers rose from them as the old lawyer spread them out on the desk.

"Which Countess of Ellingham, and which Lord Marketstoke?" asked Viner. "There have been–must have been–several during the last century."

"The Lord Marketstoke I mean is the one who disappeared," answered Mr. Pawle. "We've no concern with any other. Look at these dates! We know that if he were living, he would now be a man of sixty-one or so; therefore, he'd be at school about forty-five years ago. Now, look here," he went on, rapidly turning the letters over. "Compare these dates–they run through two or three years; they were all of forty-three to forty-six years since. You see how they're signed–you see how they're addressed? There's no doubt about it, Viner–this is a collection of letters written by the seventh Countess of Ellingham to her elder son, Lord Marketstoke, when he was at Eton."

"How came they into Ashton's possession, I wonder!" asked Viner.

"It's all of a piece!" exclaimed Mr. Pawle. "All of a piece with Ashton's visit to Marketstoke–all of a piece with the facts that Avice was a favourite name with the Cave-Gray family, and that one of the holders of the title married a Wickham. Viner, there's no doubt whatever–in my mind–that either Ashton was Lord Marketstoke or that he knew the man who was!"

"You remember what Armitstead told us," remarked Viner. "That Ashton told him, in Paris, that he, Ashton, hailed from Lancashire?"

"Then–he knew the missing man, and got these papers from him!" declared the old lawyer. "But why? Ah!–now I have an idea! It may be that Marketstoke, dying out there in Australia, handed these things to Ashton and asked him to give them to some members of the Cave-Gray family–perhaps an aunt, or a cousin, or so on–and that Ashton went down to Marketstoke to find out what relations were still in existence. That may be it– that would solve the problem!"

"No!" said Viner with sudden emphasis. He made sure that the door of the little room was closed, and then went up to the old lawyer's elbow. "Is that really all you can think of?" he asked, with a keen glance. "As for me–why, I'm thinking of something that seems absolutely– obvious!"

"What, then?" demanded Mr. Pawle. "Tell me!"

Viner pointed towards the door.

"Haven't we heard already, that a man named Wickham handed over his daughter Avice to Ashton's care and guardianship?" he asked. "Doesn't that seem to be an established fact?"

"No doubt of it!" assented Mr. Pawle. "Well?"

"In my opinion," said Viner, quietly, "Wickham was the missing Lord of Marketstoke!"

Mr. Pawle, who was still turning over the letters, examining their dates, let them slip out of his hands and gasped.

"By George!" he exclaimed in a wondering voice. "It may be–possibly is! Then, in that case, that girl outside there–"

"Well?" asked Viner, after a pause.

Mr. Pawle made a puzzled gesture and shook his head, as if in amazement. "In that case, if Wickham was the missing Lord Marketstoke, and this girl is his daughter, she's–" He broke off, and became still more puzzled.

"Upon my honour," he exclaimed, "I don't know who she is!"

"What do you mean?" asked Viner. "She's his daughter, of course–Wickham's. Only, in that case–I mean, if he was really Lord Marketstoke–her proper name, I suppose, is Cave-Gray."

Mr. Pawle looked his young assistant over with an amused expression.

"You haven't the old practitioner's *flair*, Viner, my boy!" he said. "When one's got to my age, and seen a number of queer things and happenings, one's quick to see possible cases. Look here!–if Wickham was really Lord Marketstoke, and that girl across the hall is his daughter, she's probably–I say probably, for I don't know if the succession in this case goes with the female line– Countess of Ellingham, in her own right!"

Viner looked his surprise.

"Is that really so–would it be so?" he asked.

"It may be–I'm not sure," replied Mr. Pawle. "As I say, I don't know how the succession runs in this particular instance. There are, as you are aware, several peeresses in their own rights–twenty-four or five, at least. Some are very ancient peerages. I know that three–Furnivale and Fauconberg and Conyers–go right back to the thirteenth century; three others–Beaumont, Darcy da Knayth, and Zorch of Haryngworth–date from the fourteenth. I'm not sure of this Ellingham peerage–but I'll find out when I get back to my office. However, granting the premises, and if the peerage does continue in the female line, it will be as I say–this girl's the rightful holder of the title!"

Viner made no immediate answer and Mr. Pawle began to put up the letters in their original wrappings.

"Regular romance, isn't it–if it is so?" he exclaimed. "Extraordinary!"

"Shall you tell her?" asked Viner.

Mr. Pawle considered the direct question while he completed his task.

"No," he said at last, "not at present. She evidently knows nothing, and she'd better be left in complete ignorance for a while. You see, Viner, as I've pointed out to you several times, there isn't a paper or a document of any description extant which refers to her. Nothing in my hands, nothing in the banker's hands, nothing here! And yet, supposing her father, Wickham, to have been Lord Marketstoke, and to have entrusted his secret to Ashton at the same time that he gave him the guardianship of his daughter, he must have given Ashton papers to prove his and her identity–must! Where are they?"

"Do you know what I think?" said Viner. "I think–if I'm to put it in plain language–that Ashton carried those papers on him, and that he was murdered for the possession of them!"

Mr. Pawle nodded, and put the packet of letters in his pocket.

"I shouldn't be surprised," he answered. "It's a very probable theory, my boy. But it presupposes one thing, and makes one horribly suspicious of another."

"Yes?" inquired Viner.

"It presupposes that Ashton let somebody into the secret," replied Mr. Pawle, "and it makes one suspect that the person to whom he did reveal it had such personal interest in suppressing it that he went to the length of murdering Ashton before Ashton could tell it to anyone else. How does that strike you, Viner?"

"It's this–and not the diamond!" declared Viner doggedly. "I've a sort of absolute intuition that I'm right."

"I think so too," assented the old lawyer, dryly. "The fifty-thousand-pound diamond is a side-mine. Very well, now we know a lot, you and I. And, we're going to solve matters. And we're not going to say a word to this young lady, at present–that's settled. But I want to ask her some questions–come along."

He led the way across the hall to the dining-room where a reminder of Ashton's death met his and Viner's view as soon as they had crossed the threshold. The funeral was to take place next day, and Mrs. Killenhall and Miss Wickham were contemplating a massive wreath of flowers which had evidently just arrived from the florist's and been deposited on the centre-table.

"All we can do for him, you know!" murmured Mrs. Killenhall, with a glance at the two men. "He–he had so few friends here, poor man!"

"That remark, ma'am," observed Mr. Pawle, "is apropos of a subject that I want to ask Miss Wickham two or three questions about. Friends, now? Miss Wickham, you always understood that Mr. Ashton and your father were very close friends, I believe?"

"I always understood so–yes, Mr. Pawle," replied Miss Wickham.

"Did he ever tell you much about your father?"

"No, very little indeed. He never told me more than that they knew each other very well, in Australia, that my father died out there, comparatively young, and that he left me in his, Mr. Ashton's care."

"Did he ever tell you whether your father left you any money?" demanded the old lawyer.

Miss Wickham looked surprised.

"Oh, yes!" she answered. "I thought you'd know that. My father left me a good deal of money. Didn't Mr. Ashton tell you?"

"Never a word!" said Mr. Pawle. "Now–where is it, then?"

"In my bank," replied Miss Wickham promptly. "The London and Universal. When Mr. Ashton fetched me away from school and brought me here, he told me that he had twelve thousand pounds of mine which my father had left me, and he handed it over to me then and there, and took me to the London and Universal Bank, where I opened an account with it."

"Spent any of it?" asked Mr. Pawle dryly.

"Only a few pounds," answered Miss Wickham.

The old solicitor glanced at Viner, who, while these private matters were being inquired into, was affecting to examine the pictures on the walls.

"Most extraordinary!" he muttered. "All this convinces me that Ashton must have had papers and documents! These must have been—however, we don't know where they are. But there would surely be, for instance, your father's will, Miss Wickham. I suppose you've never seen such a document? No, to be sure! You left all to Ashton. Well, now, do you remember your father?"

"Only just—and very faintly, Mr. Pawle," replied Miss Wickham. "You must remember I was little more than five years old."

"Can you remember what he was like?"

"I think he was a big, tall man—but it's a mere impression."

"Listen!" said Mr. Pawle. "Did you ever, at any time, hear Mr. Ashton make any reference—I'm talking now of the last few weeks—to the Ellingham family, or to the Earl of Ellingham?"

"Never!" replied Miss Wickham. "Never heard of them. He never—"

Mrs. Killenhall was showing signs of a wish to speak, and Mr. Pawle turned to her.

"Have you, ma'am?" he asked.

"Yes," said Mrs. Killenhall, "I have! It was one night when Miss Wickham was out—you were at Mrs. Murray-Sinclair's, my dear—and Mr. Ashton and I dined alone. He asked me if I remembered the famous Ellingham case, some years ago—something about the succession to the title—he said he'd read it in the Colonial papers. Of course, I remembered it very well."

"Well, ma'am," said Mr. Pawle, "and what then?"

"I think that was all," answered Mrs. Killenhall. "He merely remarked that it was an odd case, and said no more."

"What made him mention it?" asked Mr. Pawle.

"Oh, we'd been talking about romances of the peerage," replied Mrs. Killenhall. "I had told him of several."

"You're well up in the peerage, ma'am?" suggested the old lawyer.

"I know my Burke and my Debrett pretty thoroughly," said Mrs. Killenhall. "Very interesting, of course."

Mr. Pawle, who was sitting close to Miss Wickham, suddenly pointed to a gold locket which she wore.

"Where did you get that, my dear?" he asked. "Unusual device, isn't it?"

"Mr. Ashton gave it to me, a few weeks ago," answered Miss Wickham. "He said it had belonged to my father."

The old lawyer bent nearer, looked more closely at the locket, and got up.

"Elegant old thing!" he said. "Not made yesterday, that! Well, ladies, you will see me, for this very sad occasion"–he waved a hand at the wreath of flowers–"tomorrow. In the meantime, if there is anything you want done, our young friend here is close at hand. Just now, however, I want him."

"Viner," observed Pawle when they had left the house, "it's very odd how unobservant some people are! Now, there's that woman we've just left, Mrs. Killenhall, who says that she's well up in her Debrett, and her Burke,– and there, seen by her many a time, is that locket which Miss Wickham is wearing, and she's never noticed it! Never, I mean, noticed what's on it. Why, I saw it–and its significance–instantly, just now, which was the first time I'd seen it!"

"What is it that's on it?" asked Viner.

"After we came back from Marketstoke," replied Mr. Pawle, "I looked up the Cave-Gray family and their peerage. That locket bears their device and motto. The device is a closed fist, grasping a handful of blades of wheat; the motto is *Have and Hold*. Viner, as sure as fate, that girl's father was the missing Lord Marketstoke, and Ashton knew the secret! I'm convinced of it–I'm positive of it. And now see the extraordinary position in which we're all placed. Ashton's dead, and there isn't one scrap of paper to show what it was that he really knew. Nothing–not one written line!"

"Because, as I said before, he was murdered for his papers," affirmed Viner. "I'm sure of that as you are of the rest."

"I dare say you're right," agreed Mr. Pawle. "But, as *I've* said before, that presupposes that Ashton told somebody the secret. Now–who? Was it the man he was with in Paris? And if so, who is that man? But it's useless speculating. I've made up my mind to a certain course, Viner. Tomorrow, after the funeral, I'm going to call on the present Lord Ellingham–his town house is in Hertford Street, and I know he's in town–and ask him if he has heard anything of a mysterious nature relating to his long-missing uncle. We may hear something–you come with me."

Next day, toward the middle of the afternoon, Mr. Pawle and Viner got out of a taxicab in Park Lane and walked down Hertford Street, the old lawyer explaining the course he was about to take.

"This is a young man–not long come of age," he said. "He'll be quite well acquainted, however, with the family history, and if anything's happened lately, I dare say I can get him to talk. He–What is it?"

Viner had suddenly gripped his companion's arm and pulled him to a halt. He was looking ahead–at the house at which they were about to call. And there, just being shown out by a footman, was the man whom he had seen at the old-fashioned tavern in Notting Hill, and with him a tall, good-looking man whom he had never seen before.

15
THE PRESENT HOLDER

Mr. Pawle turned sharply on his companion as Viner pulled him up. He saw the direction of Viner's suddenly arrested gaze and looked from him to the two men who had now walked down the steps of the house and were advancing towards them.

"What is it?" he asked. "Those fellows are coming away from Lord Ellingham's house. You seem to know them?"

"One of them," murmured Viner. "The clean-shaven man. Look at him!"

The two men came on in close, evidently absorbed conversation, passed Mr. Pawle and Viner without as much as a glance at them, and went along in the direction of Park Lane.

"Well?" demanded Mr. Pawle.

"The clean-shaven man is the man I told you of–the man who was in conversation with Ashton at that tavern in Notting Hill the night Ashton was murdered," answered Viner. "The other man I don't know."

Mr. Pawle turned and looked after the retreating figures.

"You're sure of that?" he asked.

"Certain!" replied Viner. "I should know him anywhere."

Mr. Pawle came to another halt, glancing first at the two men, now well up the street, and then at the somewhat sombre front of Ellingham House.

"Now, this is an extraordinary thing, Viner!" he exclaimed. "There's the man who, you say, was with Ashton not very long before he came to his end, and we find him coming away–presumably–from Lord Ellingham, certainly from Lord Ellingham's house! What on earth does it mean? And I wonder who the man is?"

"What I'd like to know," said Viner, "is–who is the other man? But as you say, it is certainly a very curious thing that we should find the first man evidently in touch with Lord Ellingham–considering our recent discoveries. But–what are you going to do?"

"Going in here," affirmed Mr. Pawle, "to the fountain-head. We may get to know something. Have you a card?"

The footman who took the cards looked doubtfully at them and their presenters.

"His Lordship is just going out," he said, glancing over his shoulder. "I don't know–"

Mr. Pawle pointed to the name of his firm at the corner of his card.

"I think Lord Ellingham will see me," he said. "Tell his lordship I shall not detain him many minutes if he will be kind enough to give me an interview."

The man went away–to return in a few minutes and to lead the callers into a room at the rear of the hall, wherein, his back to the fire, his look and attitude one of puzzled surprise, stood a very young man, dressed in the height of fashion, who, as his servant had said, was obviously just ready to go out. Viner, remembering what had brought him and Mr. Pawle there, looked at Lord Ellingham closely–he seemed to be frank, ingenuous, and decidedly youthful. But there was something decidedly practical and business-like in his greeting of his visitors.

"I'm afraid I can't give you very long, Mr. Pawle," he said, glancing instinctively at the old lawyer. "I've a most important engagement in half an hour, and it won't be put off. But I can give you ten minutes."

"I am deeply obliged to your lordship," answered Mr. Pawle. "As your lordship will have seen from my card, I am one of the partners in Crawle, Pawle and Rattenbury– a firm not at all unknown, I think. Allow me to introduce my friend Mr. Viner, a gentleman who is deeply concerned and interested in the matter I want to mention to your lordship."

Lord Ellingham responded politely to Viner's bow and drew two chairs forward.

"Sit down, Mr. Pawle; sit down, Mr. Viner," he said. He dropped into a chair near a desk which stood in the centre of the room and looked interrogatively at his elder visitor. "Have you some business to discuss, Mr. Pawle?" he asked.

"Some business, my lord, which, I confess at once, is of extraordinary nature," answered the old lawyer. "I will go straight to it. Your lordship has doubtless read in the newspapers of the murder of a man named Ashton in Lonsdale Passage, in the Bayswater district?"

Lord Ellingham glanced at a pile of newspapers which lay on a side-table.

"Yes," he answered, "I have. I've been much interested in it—as a murder. A curious and mysterious case, don't you think?"

"We," replied Mr. Pawle, waving a hand toward Viner, "know it to be a much more mysterious case than anybody could gather from the newspaper accounts, for they know little who have written them, and we, who are behind the scenes, know a great deal. Now, your lordship will have seen that a young man, an actor named Langton Hyde, has been arrested and charged, and is on remand. This unfortunate fellow was an old schoolmate of Mr. Viner—they were at Rugby together; and Mr. Viner—and I may say I myself also—is convinced beyond doubt of his entire innocence, and we want to clear him; we are doing all we can to clear him. And it is because of this that we have ventured to call on your lordship."

"Oh!" exclaimed Lord Ellingham. "But—what can I do! How do I come in?"

"My lord," said Mr. Pawle in his most solemn manner, "I will go straight to this point also. We have reason to feel sure, from undoubted evidence, that Mr. John

Ashton, a very wealthy man, who had recently come from
Australia, where he had lived for a great many years, to
settle here in London, had in his possession when he was
murdered certain highly important papers relating to
your lordship's family, and that he was murdered for the
sake of them!"

The puzzled expression which Viner had noted in
Lord Ellingham's boyish face when they entered the room
grew more and more marked as Mr. Pawle proceeded,
and he turned on the old lawyer at the end with a stare of
amazement.

"You really think that!" he exclaimed.

"I shall be very much surprised if I'm not right!"
declared Mr. Pawle.

"But what papers?" asked Lord Ellingham. "And
what–how could this Mr. Ashton, who, you say, came
from Australia, be in possession of papers relating to my
family? I never heard of him."

"Your lordship," said Mr. Pawle, "is doubtless well
aware that some years ago there was a very strange–
shall we call it romance?–in your family. A very
remarkable episode, anyway, a most unusual–"

"You mean the strange disappearance of my uncle–
this Lord Marketstoke?" interrupted Lord Ellingham with
a smile. "Oh, of course, I know all about that."

"Very well, my lord," continued Mr. Pawle. "Then your
lordship is aware that Lord Marketstoke was believed to
have gone to the Colonies–Australia or New Zealand–and
was–lost there. His death was presumed. Now, Ashton
came from Australia, and as I say, we believe him to have
brought with him certain highly important papers
relative to Lord Marketstoke, whom we think to have
been well known to him at one time. Indeed, we felt sure
that Ashton knew Lord Marketstoke's secret. Now, my
lord, we are also confident that whoever killed John
Ashton did so in order to get hold of certain papers which,
I feel certain, Ashton made a habit of carrying on his

person–papers relating to his friend Lord Marketstoke's identity."

Lord Ellingham remained silent for a moment, looking from one visitor to another. It was very clear to Viner that some train of thought had been aroused in him and that he was closely pursuing it. He fixed his gaze at last on the old lawyer.

"Mr. Pawle," he said quietly, "have you any proof–undoubted proof–that Mr. Ashton did possess papers relating to my long-missing uncle?"

"Yes," answered Mr. Pawle, "I have!" He pulled out the bundle of letters which he and Viner had unearthed from the Japanese cabinet. "This! It is a packet of letters written by the seventh Countess of Ellingham to her elder son, the Lord Marketstoke we are talking of, when he was a boy at Eton. Your Lordship will probably recognize your grandmother's handwriting."

Lord Ellingham bent over the letter which Mr. Pawle spread before him.

"Yes," he said, "I know the writing quite well. And–these were in Mr. Ashton's possession?"

"We have just found them–Mr. Viner and I–in a cabinet in his house," replied Mr. Pawle. "They are the only papers we have so far been able to bring to light. But as I have said, we are convinced there were others–much more important ones!–in his possession, probably in his pocketbook."

Lord Ellingham handed the letters back.

"You think that this Mr. Ashton was in possession of a secret relating to the missing man–my uncle, Lord Marketstoke?" he asked.

"I am convinced of it!" declared Mr. Pawle.

Lord Ellingham glanced shrewdly at his visitors. "I should like to know what it was!" he said.

"Your lordship feels as I do," remarked Mr. Pawle. "But now I should like to ask a question which arises out of this visit. As we approached your lordship's door, just now, we saw, leaving it, two men. One of them, my friend Mr. Viner immediately recognized. He does not know who the man is–"

"Which of the two men do you mean!" interrupted Lord Ellingham. "I may as well say that they had just left me."

"The clean-shaven man," answered Viner.

"Whom Mr. Viner knows for a fact," continued Mr. Pawle, "to have been in Ashton's company only an hour or so before Ashton's murder!"

Lord Ellingham looked at Viner in obvious surprise.

"But you do not know who he is?" he exclaimed.

"No," replied Viner, "I don't. But there is no doubt of the truth of what Mr. Pawle has just said. This man was certainly with Mr. Ashton at a tavern in Notting Hill from about nine-thirty to ten-thirty on the evening of Ashton's death. In fact, they left the tavern together."

The young nobleman suddenly pulled open a drawer in his desk, produced a box of cigarettes and silently offered it to his visitors. He lighted a cigarette himself, and for a moment smoked in silence–it seemed to Viner that his youthful face had grown unusually grave and thoughtful.

"Mr. Pawle," he said at last, "I'm immensely surprised by what you've told me, and all the more so because this is the second surprise I've had this afternoon. I may as well tell you that the two gentlemen whom you saw going away just now brought me some very astonishing news– yours comes right on top of it! And, if you please, I'd rather not say any more about it, just now, but I'm going to make a proposal to you. Will you–and Mr. Viner, if he'll be so good–meet me tomorrow morning, say at noon, at my solicitors' offices?"

"With pleasure!" responded Mr. Pawle. "Your lordship's solicitors are–"

"Carless and Driver, Lincoln's Inn Fields," answered Lord Ellingham.

"Friends of ours," said Mr. Pawle. "We will meet your lordship there at twelve o 'clock to the minute."

"And–you'll bring that with you?" suggested Lord Ellingham, pointing to the packet of letters which Mr. Pawle held in his hand.

"Just so, my lord," assented Mr. Pawle. "And we'll be ready to tell all we know–for there are further details."

Outside the house the old lawyer gripped Viner's elbow.

"That boy knows something!" he said with a meaning smile. "He's astute enough for his age–smart youngster! But–what does he know? Those two men have told him something. Viner, we must find out who that clean-shaven man is. I have some idea that I have seen him before–I shouldn't be at all surprised if he's a solicitor, may have seen him in some court or other. But in that case I wonder he didn't recognize me."

"He didn't look at you," replied Viner. "He and the other man were too much absorbed in whatever it was they were talking about. I have been wondering since I first saw him at the tavern," he continued, "if I ought not to tell the police what I know about him–I mean, that he was certainly in Ashton's company on the evening of the murder. What do you think?"

"I think not, at present," replied Mr. Pawle. "It seems evident–unless, indeed, it was all a piece of bluff, and it may have been–that this man is, or was when you saw him, just as ignorant as the landlord of that place was that the man who used to drop in there and Ashton were one and the same person. No, let the police go on their own lines–we're on others. We shall hear of this man again, whoever he is. Now I must get back to my office– come there at half-past eleven tomorrow morning, Viner, and we'll go on to Carless and Driver's."

Viner went thoughtfully homeward, ruminating over the events of the day, and entered his house to find his two guests, the sisters of the unlucky Hyde, in floods of tears, and Miss Penkridge looking unusually grave. The elder Miss Hyde sprang up at sight of him and held a tear-soaked handkerchief towards him in pantomimic appeal.

"Oh, Mr. Viner," she exclaimed, "you are so kind, and so clever. I'm sure you'll see a way out of this! It looks, oh, so very black, and so very much against him; but oh, dear Mr. Viner, there must be some explanation!"

"But what is it?" asked Viner, looking from one to the other. "What has happened! Has anyone been here?"

Miss Penkridge silently handed to her nephew an early edition of one of the evening newspapers and pointed to a paragraph in large type. And Viner rapidly read it over, to the accompaniment of the younger Miss Hyde's sobs.

A sensational discovery in connection with the recent murder of Mr. Ashton in Lonsdale Passage, Bayswater, was made in the early hours of this morning. Charles Fisher, a greengrocer, carrying on business in the Harrow Road, found in his woodshed, concealed in a nook in the wall, a parcel containing Mr. Ashton's gold watch and chain and a diamond ring. He immediately communicated with the police, and these valuables are now in their possession. It will be remembered that Langton Hyde, the young actor who is charged with the crime, and who is now on remand, stated at the coroner's inquest that he passed the night on which the crime was committed in a shed in this neighbourhood.

Viner read this news twice over. Then a sudden idea occurred to him, and he turned to leave the room.

"I don't think you need be particularly alarmed about this," he said to the weeping sisters. "Cheer up, till I return–I am going round to the police."

16
THE OUTHOUSE

Near the police-station Viner fell in with his solicitor, Felpham, who turned a corner in a great hurry. Felpham's first glance showed his client that their purposes were in common.

"Seen that paragraph in the evening papers?" said Felpham without preface. "By George! That's serious news! What a pity that Hyde ever made that statement about his doings on the night of the murder! It would have been far better if he'd held his tongue altogether."

"He insisted on it–in the end," answered Viner. "And in my opinion he was right. But–you think this is very serious?"

"Serious? Yes!" exclaimed Felpham. "He says he spent the night in a shed in the Harrow Road district. Now the things that were taken from Ashton's body are discovered in such a place–nay, the very place; for if you remember, Hyde particularized his whereabouts. What's the obvious conclusion? What can anybody think?"

"I see two or three obvious conclusions, and I think several things," remarked Viner. "I'll tell you what they are when we've seen Drillford. I'm not alarmed about this discovery, Felpham. I think it may lead to finding the real murderer."

"You see further than I do, then," muttered Felpham. "I only see that it's highly dangerous to Hyde's interests. And I want first-handed information about it."

Drillford, discovered alone in his office, smiled as the two men walked in–there was an irritating I-told-you-so air about him.

"Ah!" he said. "I see you gentlemen have been reading the afternoon papers! What do you think about your friend now, Mr. Viner?"

"Precisely what I thought before and shall continue to think," retorted Viner. "I've seen no reason to alter my opinion."

"Oh–but I guess Mr. Felpham doesn't think that way?" replied Drillford with a shrewd glance at the solicitor. "Mr. Felpham knows the value of evidence, I believe!"

"What is it that's been found, exactly?" asked Felpham.

Drillford opened a locked drawer, lifted aside a sheet of cardboard, and revealed a fine gold watch and chain and a diamond ring. These lay on two or three sheets of much crumpled paper of a peculiar quality.

"There you are!" said Drillford. "Those belonged to Mr. Ashton; there's his name on the watch, and a mark of his inside the ring. They were found early this morning, hidden, in the very place in which Hyde confessed that he spent most of the night after Ashton's murder–a shed belonging to one Fisher, a greengrocer, up the Harrow Road.

"Who found them?" demanded Felpham.

"Fisher himself," answered Drillford. "He was pottering about in his shed before going to Covent Garden. He wanted some empty boxes, and in pulling things about he found–these! Couldn't have made a more important find, I think.

"Were these things loose?" asked Viner.

"Wrapped loosely in the paper they're lying on," replied Drillford.

Viner took the paper out of the drawer, examined it and lifted it to his nose.

"I wonder, if Hyde really did put those things there," he said, "how Hyde came to be carrying about with him these sheets of paper which had certainly been used before for the wrappings of chemicals or drugs?"

Felpham pricked his ears.

"Eh?" he said. "What's that?"

"Smell for yourself," answered Viner. "Let the inspector smell too. I draw the attention to both of you to the fact, because we'll raise that point whenever it's necessary. Those papers have at some time been used to wrap some strong-smelling drug."

"No doubt of it!" said Felpham, who was applying the papers to his nose. "Smell them, Drillford! As Mr. Viner says, what would Hyde be doing with this stuff in his pocket?"

"That's a mere detail," remarked Drillford impatiently. "These chaps that mooch about, as Hyde was doing, pick up all sorts of odds and ends. He may have pinched them from a chemist's shop. Anyway, there's the fact–and we'll hang him on it! You'll see!"

"We shall never see anything of the sort!" said Viner. "You're on the wrong tack, Inspector. Let me put two or three things to your intelligence. Where's Ashton's purse? I know for a fact that Ashton had a purse full of money when he went out of his house that night–Mrs. Killenhall and Miss Wickham saw him take it out just before he left to give some cash to the parlourmaid, and they saw him replace it in his trousers pocket; I also know for another fact where he spent money that evening–in short, I know now a good deal about his movements for some hours before his death."

"Then you ought to tell us, Mr. Viner," said Drillford a little sulkily. "You oughtn't to keep any information to yourself."

"You're going on the wrong tack, or I might," retorted Viner. "But you'll know all in good time. Now, I ask you again–where's Ashton's purse? You know as well as I do that when his clothing was examined, almost immediately after his death, all his effects were gone– watch, chain, rings, pocketbook, purse. If Hyde took the whole lot, do you think he would ever have been such a consummate ass as to wait until next morning to pawn that ring in Edgware Road? The idea is preposterous!"

"And why, pray?" demanded Drillford, obviously nettled at the turn which the conversation was taking.

"I wonder your own common sense doesn't tell you," said Viner with intentional directness. "If Hyde took everything from his victim, as you say he did, he would have had a purse full of ready money. He could have gone off to some respectable lodging-house. He could have put a hundred miles between himself and London by breakfast-time. He would have had ready money to last him for months. But—he was starving when he went to the pawnbrokers! Hyde told you the truth—he never had anything but that ring."

"Good!" muttered Felpham. "Good, Viner! That's one in the eye for you, Drillford."

"Another thing that you're forgetting, Inspector," continued Viner: "I suppose you attach some value to probabilities? Do you, as a sensible man, believe for one moment that Hyde, placed in the position he is, would be such a fool, such a suicidal fool, as to tell you about that particular shed if he'd really hidden those things there? The mere idea is absurd—ridiculous!"

"Good again, Viner!" said Felpham. "He wouldn't!"

Drillford, obviously ill-pleased, put the strongly-smelling paper and the valuables which had been wrapped in it, back in the drawer and turned the key.

"All very well talking and theorizing, Mr. Viner," he said sullenly. "We know from his own lips that Hyde did spend the night in that shed. If he didn't put these things there, who did?"

Viner gave him a steady look.

"The man who murdered and robbed Ashton!" he answered. "And that man was not Hyde."

"You'll have that to prove," retorted Drillford, derisively. "I know what a jury'll think with all this evidence before it!"

"We shall prove a good many things that'll surprise you," said Viner quietly. "And you'll see, then, the foolishness of jumping at what seems to be an obvious conclusion."

He motioned Felpham to follow, and going outside, turned in the direction of the Harrow Road.

"I'm going to have a look at the place where these things were found," he said. "Come with me. You see for yourself," he continued as they walked on, "how ridiculous it is to suppose that Hyde planted them. The whole affair is plain enough, to me. The real murderer read–or may have heard–Hyde's statement before the coroner, and in order to strengthen the case against Hyde and divert suspicion from himself, sought out this shed and put the things there. Clumsy! If Hyde had ever had the purse, which more certainly disappeared with the rest of the property, he'd never have gone to that shed at all."

"We'll make the most of all that," said Felpham. "But I gathered, from what you said just now to Drillford, that you know more about this case than you've let out. If it's in Hyde's favour–"

"I can't tell you what I know," answered Viner. "I do know some strange things, which will all come out in good time. If we bring the murder home to the right man, Hyde of course will be cleared. I'll tell everything as soon as I can, Felpham."

They walked quickly forward until they came to the higher part of the Harrow Road; there, at a crowded point of that dismal thoroughfare, where the shops were small and mean, Felpham suddenly lifted a finger towards a sign which hung over an open front with the cheaper sorts of vegetables.

"Here's the place," he said, "a corner shop. The shed, of course, will be somewhere behind."

Viner looked with interest at the refuge which Hyde had chosen after his hurried flight from the scene of the murder. A shabby looking street ran down from the corner of the greengrocer's shop; the first twenty yards of it on that side were filled with palings, more or less broken and dilapidated; behind them lay a yard in which stood a van, two or three barrows, a collection of boxes and baskets and crates, and a lean-to shed, built against the wall of the adjoining house. The door of this yard hung loosely on its rusty hinges; Viner saw at once that nothing could be easier than for a man to slip into this miserable shelter unseen.

"Let's get hold of the tenant," he said. "Better show him your card, and then he'll know we're on professional business."

The greengrocer, a dull-looking fellow who was measuring potatoes, showed no great interest on hearing what his callers wanted. Summoning his wife to mind the shop, he led Viner and Felpham round to the yard and opened the door of the shed. This was as untidy as the yard, and filled with a similar collection of boxes, baskets and crates. In one corner lay a bundle of empty potato sacks–the greengrocer at once pointed to it.

"I reckon that's where the fellow got a bit of a sleep that night," he said. "There was nothing to prevent him getting in here–no locks or bolts on either gate of the yard or that door. He may have been in here many a night, for all I know."

"Where did you find those valuables this morning?" asked Viner.

The greengrocer pointed to a shelf in a corner above the bundle of sacking.

"There!" he answered. "I wanted some small boxes to take down to Covent Garden, and in turning some of these over I came across a little parcel, wrapped in paper–slipped under a box that was turned top downwards on the shelf, you understand? So of course I opened it, and there was the watch and chain and ring."

"Just folded in the papers that you handed to the police?" suggested Viner.

"Well, there was more paper about 'em than what I gave to Inspector Drillford," said the greengrocer. "A well-wrapped-up bit of parcel it was–there's the rest of the paper there, where I threw it down."

He pointed to some loose sheets of paper which lay on the sacking, and Viner went forward, picked them up, looked quickly at them, and put them in his pocket.

"I suppose you never heard anybody about, that night?" he asked turning to the greengrocer.

"Not I!" the man replied. "I sleep too sound to hear aught of that sort. There's nothing in here that's of any value. No–a dozen folk could come into this yard at night and we shouldn't hear 'em–we sleep at the front of the house."

Viner slipped some silver into the greengrocer's hand and led Felpham away. And when they reached a quieter part of the district, he pulled out the papers which he had picked out of the corner in the shed and held them in front of his companion's eyes.

"We did some good in coming up here, after all, Felpham!" he said, with a grim smile. "It wasn't a mere desire to satisfy idle curiosity that made me come. I thought I might, by sheer good luck, hit on something, or some idea that would help. Now then, look at these things. That's a piece of newspaper from out of a copy of the *Melbourne Argus* of September 6th last. Likely thing for Langton Hyde to be carrying in his pocket, eh?"

"Good heavens, that's certainly important!" exclaimed Felpham.

"And so is this, and perhaps much more so," said Viner, making a second exhibit. "That's a sheet of brown wrapping-paper with the name and address of a famous firm of wholesale druggists and chemical manufacturers on one side–printed. It's another likely thing for Hyde to possess, and to carry about, isn't it?"

"And the same bitter, penetrating smell about it!" said Felpham.

"Hyde, of course, if Drillford is correct, had all this paper in his pocket when he went into that shed," said Viner. "But I have a different idea, and a different theory. Here," he went on, folding his discoveries together neatly, "you take charge of these—and take care of them. They may be of more importance than we think."

He went home full of thought, restored the sisters to something like cheerfulness by assuring them that the situation was no worse, and possibly rather better, and spent the rest of the evening in his study, silently working things out. Viner, by the time he went to bed, had evolved an idea, and it was still developing and growing stronger when he set out next morning to accompany Mr. Pawle to Lord Ellingham's solicitors.

17
THE CLAIMANT

Carless and Driver practised their profession of the law in one of the old houses on the south side of Lincoln's Inn Fields–a house so old that it immediately turned Viner's thought to what he had read of the days wherein Inigo Jones exercised his art up the stately frontages, and duels were fought in the gardens which London children now sport in. In one of these houses lived Blackstone; in another Erskine; one ancient roof once sheltered John Milton; another heard the laughter of Nell Gwynn; up the panelled staircase which Mr. Pawle and his companion were presently conducted, the feet of many generations had trod. And the room into which they were duly conducted was so old-world in appearance with its oaken walls and carving and old-fashioned furniture that nothing but the fact that its occupants wore twentieth century garments would have convinced Viner that he had not been suddenly thrown back to the days of Queen Anne.

Lord Ellingham was already there when they arrived–in conference with his solicitor, Mr. Carless, a plump, rosy, active gentleman who wore mutton-chop whiskers and–secretly–prided himself on his likeness to the type of fox-hunting squire. It was very evident to Viner that both solicitor and client were in a state of expectancy bordering on something very like excitement; and Mr. Carless, the preliminary greetings being over, plunged at once into the subject.

"I say, Pawle," he exclaimed, turning at once to his fellow-practitioner, "this appears to be a most extraordinary business! His lordship has just been telling me all about the two calls he had yesterday–first from two men whom he'd never seen before–then from you two, who were also strangers. He has also told me what both lots of his callers had to say, and hang me if I ever heard of two such curious unfoldings coming one on top of the other. Sounds like a first-class mystery!"

"You forget," remarked Mr. Pawle with a glance at Lord Ellingham, "that we don't know–Mr. Viner and myself–what it was that his lordship's first couple of callers told him. He left that until today."

Mr. Carless looked at his client, who nodded his head as if in assent to something in the glance.

"Well, as I'm now in possession of the facts," said he, "I'll tell you, Pawle–His Lordship has given me a clear account of what his first callers said, and what you and Mr. Viner added to it. The two men whom you saw coming away from Ellingham House were Methley and Woodlesford, two solicitors who are in partnership in Edgware Road–I know of them: I think we've had conveyancing business with them once or twice. Quite a respectable firm–in a smallish way, you know, but all right so far as I know anything of them. Now, they came to Lord Ellingham yesterday afternoon with a most extraordinary story. His lordship tells me that he learned from your talk with him yesterday afternoon that you are pretty well acquainted, you and Mr. Viner, with his family history, so I'll go straight to the point. What do you think Methley and Woodlesford came to tell him? You'd never guess!"

"I won't try!" answered Mr. Pawle. "What, then?"

Mr. Carless smiled grimly.

"That the long-lost Lord Marketstoke was alive and in England!" he said. "Here, in fact, in London!"

Mr. Pawle smiled too. But his smile was not grim–it was, rather, the smile of a man who hears what he has been expecting to hear.

"I thought it would be something of that sort!" he exclaimed. "Aye, I fancied that would be the game!"

"You think it a game?" suggested Mr. Carless.

"And a highly dangerous one–as somebody will find out," responded Mr. Pawle. "But–what did these fellows really say!"

"His lordship will correct me if I miss anything pertinent," answered Mr. Carless with a glance at his client. "They said this–that they had been called upon by a gentleman now staying at one of the private residential hotels in Lancaster Gate, who was desirous of legal assistance in an important matter and had been recommended to them by a fellow-boarder at the hotel. He then told them that though he was now passing under the name of Cave–"

"Ah!" exclaimed Mr. Pawle, with a snort which denoted a certain sort of surprised satisfaction. "Ah, to be sure! Cave, of course! But I interrupt you–pray proceed."

"I see your point," remarked Mr. Carless with a smile. "Well–although he was passing under the name of Cave, he was, in strict reality, the Lord Marketstoke who disappeared from England many years ago, who was never heard of again, and whose death had been presumed. He was, therefore, the rightful Earl of Ellingham, and as such entitled to the estates. He proceeded to tell Methley and Woodlesford his adventures.

"He had, he said, never at any time from boyhood been on good terms with his father: there had always been mutual dislike. As he grew to manhood, his father had thwarted him in every conceivable way. He himself as a young man, had developed radical and democratic ideas–this had caused a further widening of the breach. Eventually he had made up his mind to clear out of England altogether. He had a modest amount of money of his own, a few thousands which had been left him by his mother. So he took this and quietly disappeared.

"According to his own account he became a good deal of a rolling stone, going to various out-of-the-way parts of the earth, and taking particular pains, wherever he went, to conceal his identity. He told these people Methley and Woodlesford, that he had at one time or another lived and traded in South Africa, India, China, Japan and the Malay Settlement–finally he had settled down in Australia. He had kept himself familiar with events at home–knew of his father's death, and he saw no end of advertisements for himself. He was aware that legal proceedings were taken as regards the presumption of his death and the administration of the estates; he was also aware of the death of his younger brother and that title and estates were now in possession of his nephew–His Lordship there. In fact, he was very well up in the whole story, according to Methley and Woodlesford," said Mr. Carless, with a smile. "And Lord Ellingham believed that Methley and Woodlesford were genuinely convinced by him."

"Seemed so, anyway, both of 'em," agreed Lord Ellingham.

"However," continued Mr. Carless, "Methley and Woodlesford, like you and I, Pawle, are limbs of the law. They asked two very pertinent questions. First–why had he come forward after this long interval? Second–what evidence had he to support and prove his claim?"

"Good!" muttered Mr. Pawle. "And I'll be bound he had some excellent replies ready for them."

"He had," said Mr. Carless. "He answered as regards the first question that of late things had not gone well with him. He was still comfortably off, but he had lost a lot of money in Australia through speculation. He replied to the second by producing certain papers and documents."

"Ah!" exclaimed Mr. Pawle, nudging Viner. "Now we're warming to it!"

"And according to what Methley and Woodlesford told Lord Ellingham," continued Mr. Carless, "these papers and documents are of a very convincing nature. They said to His Lordship frankly that they were greatly surprised by them. They had thought that this man might possibly be a bogus claimant, who had somehow gained a thorough knowledge of the facts he was narrating, but the papers he produced, which, he alleged, had never been out of his possession since his secret flight from London, were–well, staggering. After inspecting them, Methley and Woodlesford came to the conclusion that their caller really was what he claimed to be–the missing man!"

"What were the papers?" demanded Mr. Pawle.

"Oh!" replied Mr. Carless, looking at his client. "Letters, certificates, and the like,–all, according to Methley and Woodlesford, excellent proofs of identity."

"Did they show them to Your Lordship?" asked Mr. Pawle.

"Oh, no! They only told me of them," answered Lord Ellingham. "They said, of course, that they would be shown to me, or to Mr. Carless."

"Aye!" muttered Mr. Pawle. "Just so! Yes, and they will have to be shown!"

"That follows as a matter of course," observed Mr. Carless. "But now, Pawle, we come to the real point of the case. Methley and Woodlesford, having informed His Lordship of all this when they called on him yesterday afternoon then proceeded to tell him precisely what their client, the claimant, as we will now call him, really wanted, for he had been at some pains, considerable pains, to make himself clear on that point to them, and he desired them to make themselves clear to Lord Ellingham, whom he throughout referred to as his nephew. He had no desire, he told them, to recover his title, nor the estates. He did not care a cent–his own phrase–for the title. He was now sixty years of age. The life he had lived had quite unfitted him for the positions and duties of an English nobleman. He wanted to go back to the country in which he had settled. But as title and estates really were his, he wanted his nephew, the present holder, to make him a proper payment, in consideration of the receipt of which he would engage to preserve the silence which he had already kept so thoroughly and effectively for thirty-five years. Eh?"

"In plain language," said Mr. Pawle, "he wanted to be bought."

"Precisely!" agreed Mr. Carless. "Of course, Methley and Woodlesford didn't quite put it in that light. They put it that their client had no wish to disturb his nephew, but suggested, kindly, that his nephew should make him a proper payment out of his abundance."

Mr. Pawle turned to Lord Ellingham.

"Did they mention a sum to Your Lordship?" he asked.

"Yes," replied Lord Ellingham, with a smile at Carless. "They did—tentatively."

"How much?" asked Mr. Pawle.

"One hundred thousand pounds!"

"On receipt of which, I suppose," observed Mr. Pawle dryly, "nothing would ever be heard again of your lordship's long-lost uncle, the rightful owner of all that Your Lordship possesses?"

Lord Ellingham laughed.

"So I gathered!" he answered.

"I wish I'd been present when Methley and Woodlesford put forward that proposition," exclaimed the old lawyer. "Did they seem serious?"

"Oh, I think they were quite serious," replied Lord Ellingham. "They seemed so; they spoke of it as what they called a domestic arrangement."

"Excellent phrase!" remarked Mr. Pawle. "And what said your lordship to their—or the claimant's proposition?"

"I told them that the matter was so serious that they and I must see my solicitors about it," answered Lord Ellingham, "and I arranged to meet them here at one o'clock today. They quite agreed that that was the proper thing to do, and went away. Then—you and Mr. Viner called."

"With, I understand, another extraordinary story," remarked Mr. Carless. "The particulars of which His

Lordship has also told me. Now, Pawle, what do you really say about all this?"

Mr. Pawle smote his clenched right fist on the palm of his open left hand.

"I will tell you what I say, Carless!" he exclaimed with emphasis. "I say that whatever the papers and documents were which were produced by this man to Methley and Woodlesford, they were stolen from the body of John Ashton, who was foully murdered in Lonsdale Passage only last week. I'll stake all I have on that! Now, then, did this claimant steal them? Did he murder John Ashton for them? No–a thousand times no, for no man would have been such a fool as to come forward with them so soon after his victim's death! This claimant doesn't know how or where or when they were obtained–he doesn't suspect that murder's in it. Now, then–where did he get them? Who's at the back of him? Who–to be plain–who's making a cat's-paw of him? Find that out, and we shall know who murdered John Ashton!"

Viner, glancing at Lord Ellingham and at Mr. Carless, saw that Mr. Pawle's words had impressed them greatly, the solicitor especially. He nodded sympathetically, and Mr. Pawle went on speaking.

"Listen here, Carless!" he continued. "Mr. Viner and I have been investigating this case as far as we could, largely to save a man whom we both believe to be absolutely innocent of murder. I have come to certain conclusions. John Ashton, many years ago, fell in with the missing Lord Marketstoke, then living under the name of Wickham, in Australia, and they became close friends. At some time or other, Wickham told Ashton the real truth about himself, and when he died, left his little daughter–"

Carless looked sharply round.

"Ah!" he exclaimed. "So there's a daughter?"

"There is a daughter, and her name is Avice–a name borne by a good many women of the Cave-Gray family," answered Mr. Pawle with a significant glance at his fellow-practitioner. "But let me go on: Wickham left his daughter, her mother being dead, in Ashton's guardianship. She was then about six years of age. Ashton sent her to school here in England. About twelve or thirteen years later, he came home and settled in Markendale Square. He brought Avice Wickham to live with him. He handed over to her a considerable sum, which, he said, her father had left in his hands for her. And then, secretly, Ashton went down to Marketstoke and evidently made certain inquiries and investigations. Whether he was going to reveal the truth as to what I have just told you, we don't know–probably he was. But he was murdered, and we all know when and where. And I say he was murdered for the sake of these very papers which we now know were produced to Methley and Woodlesford by this claimant. Now, then–"

Mr. Carless suddenly bent forward.

"A moment, Pawle!" he said. "If this man Wickham really was the lost Lord Marketstoke, and he's dead, and he left a daughter, and the daughter's alive–"

"Well?" demanded Mr. Pawle. "Well?"

"Why, then, of course, that daughter," said Mr. Carless slowly, "that daughter is–"

A clerk opened the door and glanced at his employer.

"Mr. Methley and Mr. Woodlesford, sir," he announced. "By appointment."

18
LET HIM APPEAR!

The meeting between the solicitors suggested to Viner and to Lord Ellingham, who looked on curiously while they exchanged formal greetings and explanations, a certain solemnity—each of them seemed to imply in look and manner that this was an unusually grave occasion. And Mr. Carless, assuming the direction of things, became almost judicial in his deportment.

"Well, gentlemen," he said, when they had all gathered about his desk. "Lord Ellingham has informed me of what passed between you and himself at his house yesterday. In plain language, the client whom you represent claims to be the Lord Marketstoke who disappeared so completely many years ago, and therefore the rightful Earl of Ellingham. Now, a first question—do you, as his legal advisers, believe in his claim?"

"Judging by the proofs with which he has furnished us, yes," answered Methley. "There seems to be no doubt of it."

"We'll ask for these proofs presently," remarked Mr. Carless. "But now a further question: Your client—whom we'll now call the claimant—had, I understand, no desire to take up his rightful position, and suggests that the secret shall remain a secret, and that he shall be paid a hundred thousand pounds to hold his tongue?"

"If you put it that way—yes," replied Methley.

"I don't know in what other way it could be put," said Mr. Carless grimly. "It's the plain truth. But now, if Lord Ellingham refuses that offer, does your client intend to commence proceedings?"

"Our instructions are—yes," answered Methley.

"Very good," said Mr. Carless. "Now, then—what are these proofs?"

Methley turned to his partner, who immediately thrust a hand in his breastpocket and produced a long envelope.

"I have them here," said Woodlesford. "Our client intrusted them to us so that we might show them to Lord Ellingham, if necessary. There are not many documents—they all relate to the period of our client's life before he left England. There are one or two important letters from his father, the seventh Earl, two or three from his mother; there is also his mother's will. There is one letter from his younger brother, to whom he had evidently, more than once, announced his determination of leaving home for a considerable time. There are two letters from your own firm, relating to some property which Lord Marketstoke disposed of before he left London. There is a schedule or memorandum of certain personal effects which he left in his rooms at Ellingham Hall: there is also a receipt from his bankers for a quantity of plate and jewellery which he had deposited with them before leaving—these things had been left him by his mother. There are also two documents which he seems to have considered it worthwhile to preserve all these years," concluded Woodlesford with a smile. "One is a letter informing him that he had been elected a member of the M.C.C.; the other is his commission as a justice of the peace for the county of Buckinghamshire."

As he detailed these things, Woodlesford laid each specified paper before Mr. Carless, and then they all gathered round, and examined each exhibit. The various documents were somewhat faded with age, and the edges of some were worn as if from long folding and keeping in a pocketbook. Mr. Carless hastily ran his eye over them.

"Very interesting, gentlemen," he remarked. "But you know, as well as I do, that these things don't prove your client to be the missing Lord Marketstoke. A judge and jury would want a lot more evidence than that. The mere fact that your man is in possession of all these documents proves nothing whatever. He may have stolen them!"

"From what we have seen of our client, Mr. Carless," observed Methley, with some stiffness of manner, "there is no need for such a suggestion."

"I dare say we shall all see a good deal of your client before this matter is settled, Mr. Methley," retorted Mr. Carless. "And even when I have seen a lot of him, I should still say the same–he *may* have stolen them! What else has he to prove that he's what he says he is?"

"He is fully conversant with his family history," said Woodlesford. "He can give a perfectly full and–so far as we can judge–accurate account of his early life and of his subsequent doings. He evidently knows all about Ellingham Hall, Marketstoke and the surroundings. I think if you were to examine him on these points, you would find that his memory is surprisingly fresh."

"I have no doubt that it will come to his being examined on a great many points and in much detail," said Mr. Carless with a dry smile. "Of course, I shall be much interested in seeing him. You see, I remember the missing Lord Marketstoke very well indeed–he was often in here when I, as a lad of nineteen or twenty, was articled to my own father. And now, gentlemen, I'll ask you a question and commend it to your intelligence and common sense: if your client is this man he claims to be, why didn't he come straight to Carless and Driver, whom he would remember well enough, instead of going to Methley and Woodlesford? Come, now?"

Neither visitor answered this question, and Mr. Pawle suddenly turned on them with another.

"Did your client mention to you that he knew Carless and Driver as the family solicitors?" he asked.

"No, I can't say that he did," admitted Methley. "After all, thirty-five years' absence, you know–"

"You said just now that his memory was surprisingly fresh," interrupted Mr. Pawle.

"Surely," replied Woodlesford, "surely you can't expect a man who has been away from England all that time to remember everything!"

"I should have expected Lord Marketstoke to have gone straight to the family solicitors, anyway," retorted Mr. Pawle. "Obvious thing to do–if his story is a true one."

Woodlesford glanced at his partner, and repossessing himself of the documents, began to arrange them in the envelope from which he had drawn them.

"We cannot, of course, say positively who our client is or who he is not," he said. "All we can say is that he came to us with an introduction from an old client of ours whom we knew very well, and that his story seems to us to be quite credible. No doubt he can bring further proof. That he did not come here in the first instance–"

"I'll tell you why I, personally, am very much surprised that he didn't," interrupted Mr. Carless. "You told Lord Ellingham yesterday that your client saw no end of advertisements for him at the time of his father's death. Now, we, Carless and Driver, sent out those advertisements–our name was appended to every one of them, wherever they appeared. Why, then, when this man–if he is the real man–returned home, did he not come to us? For there are three persons in this office who–but wait!"

He touched a bell; the clerk who had announced Methley and Woodlesford put his head in at the door.

"Ask Mr. Portlethwaite to come here," commanded Mr. Carless. "And just find out if Mr. Driver is in his room. Portlethwaite can tell me when he comes."

An elderly, grey-haired man presently appeared and closed the door behind him as if aware of the sacred nature of the proceedings.

"Mr. Driver is out, Mr. Carless," he said. "You wanted me, I think?"

"Our senior clerk," observed Mr. Carless, by way of introduction. "Portlethwaite, you remember the Lord Marketstoke who disappeared some thirty-five years ago?"

Mr. Portlethwaite smiled.

"Quite well, Mr. Carless!" he answered. "As if it were yesterday. He used to come here a good deal, you know."

"Do you think you'd know him again, Portlethwaite, after all these years?" asked Mr. Carless. "Thirty-five years, mind!"

The elderly clerk smiled—more assuredly than before. Then he looked significantly at a corner of the room, and Mr. Carless took the hint, and rising from his chair, went aside with him. Portlethwaite whispered something in his employer's ear, and Carless suddenly laughed and nodded.

"To be sure—to be sure—I remember now!" he said aloud. "Thank you, Portlethwaite: that's all. Well, gentlemen," he continued, returning to his desk when the clerk had gone. "I think the best thing you can do is to bring your client here—if he is the real and genuine article, he will, I am sure, be very glad indeed to meet three persons who knew him quite intimately in the old days—Mr. Driver, Mr. Portlethwaite and myself. And I really don't know that there's any more to do or say."

The two visitors rose, and Methley looked at Mr. Carless in a questioning fashion.

"Am I to go away with the impression that you believe our client to be an impostor?" he said quietly.

"Frankly I do!" answered Mr. Carless.

"So do I!" exclaimed Mr. Pawle. "Emphatically so!"

"In that case," said Methley, "I see no advantage in bringing him here."

"Not even anything to your own advantage?" suggested Mr. Carless, with a keen glance which passed from one partner to the other. "You, as reputable practitioners of our profession, don't want to be mixed up with an impostor?"

"We should be very sorry to be mixed up in any way with an impostor, Mr. Carless!" said Methley.

Mr. Carless pursed his lips for a moment as if he were never going to open them again; then he suddenly relaxed them.

"I tell you what it is, gentlemen!" he said. "I'm only anticipating matters in saying what I'm going to say, and I'm saying it because I feel sure you are quite sincere and genuine in this affair and are being deceived. If you will bring your client here, there are three of us in this office who, as my old clerk has just reminded me, can positively identify him on the instant if he is the man he claims to be. Positively, I say, and at once! There!"

"May one ask how?" said Woodlesford.

"No!" exclaimed Mr. Carless. "Bring him! Telephone an appointment–and we'll settle the matter as soon as he sets foot inside that door."

"May we tell him that?" asked Methley.

"You can do as you like," answered Mr. Carless. "Between ourselves, I shouldn't! But I assure you–we can tell in one glance! That's a fact!"

The two solicitors went away; and Viner, who had closely watched Methley during the interview, followed them out and hailed Methley in the corridor outside Mr. Carless' room.

"May I have a word with you?" he asked, drawing him aside. "I don't know if you remember, but I saw you the other night in the parlour of that old tavern in Notting Hill–you came in while I was there?"

"I had some idea that I remembered your face when we were introduced just now," said Methley. "Yes, I think I do remember–you were sitting in a corner near the hearth?"

"Just so," agreed Viner. "And I heard you ask the landlord a question about a gentleman whom you used to meet there sometimes–you left some specimen cigars with the landlord for him."

"Yes," assented Methley wonderingly.

"You never knew that man's name?" continued Viner. "Nor who he was? Just so–so I gathered. Then I'll tell you. There was a good reason why he had not been to that tavern for some nights. He was John Ashton, the man who was murdered in Lonsdale Passage!"

Viner was watching his man with all the keenness of which he was capable, and he saw that this announcement fell on Methley as an absolute surprise. He started as only a man can start who has astounding news given to him suddenly.

"God bless me!" he exclaimed. "You don't mean it! Of course, I know about that murder–our own district. And I saw Ashton's picture in the paper–but then there are so many elderly men of that type–broad features, trimmed grey beard! Dear me, dear me! A very pleasant, genial fellow. I'm astonished, Mr. Viner."

Viner resolved on a bold step–he would take it without consulting Mr. Pawle or anybody. He drew Methley further aside.

"Mr. Methley," he said. "You're a man of honour, and I trust you with a secret, to be kept until I release you from the obligation of secrecy. I have reasons for getting at the truth about Ashton's murder–so has Mr. Pawle. He and I have been making investigations and inquiries, and we are convinced, we are positive, that these papers which your partner now has in his pocket were stolen from Ashton's dead body–that, in fact, Ashton was murdered for the possession of them. And I tell you, for your own sake–find out who this client of yours is! That he was the actual murderer I don't believe for a second–he is probably a mere cat's-paw. But–who's behind him? If you can do anything to find out the truth, do it!"

That Methley was astonished beyond belief was so evident that Viner was now absolutely convinced of his sincerity. He stood staring open-mouthed for a moment: then he glanced at Woodlesford, who was waiting at some distance along the corridor.

"Mr. Viner!" he said. "You amaze me! Listen: my partner is as sound and honest a fellow as there is in all London. Let me tell him this–I'll engage for his secrecy. If you'll consent to that, I'll see that, without a word from us as to why, this man who claims to be the missing Lord Marketstoke is brought here. If what you say is true, we are not going to be partners to a crime. Let me tell Woodlesford–I'll answer for him."

Viner considered this proposition for a moment.

"Very well!" he said at last. "Tell him–I shall trust you both. Remember–it's between the three of us. I shan't say a word to Pawle, nor to Carless. You know there's a man's life at stake–Hyde's! Hyde is as innocent as I am–he's an old schoolfellow of mine."

"I understand," said Methley. "Very well, trust to me, Mr. Viner."

He went off with a reassuring nod, and Viner returned to Mr. Carless' room. The three men he had left there were deep in conversation, and as he entered, Mr. Carless smote his hand on the desk before him.

"This is certain!" he exclaimed. "We must have this Miss Avice Wickham here–at once!"

19
UNDER EXAMINATION

Mr. Pawle nodded assent to this proposition and rose from his chair. "It's the only thing to do," he said. "We must get to the bottom of this as quickly as possible–whether Miss Wickham can tell us much or little, we must know what she can tell. Let us all meet here again at three o'clock–I will send one of my clerks to fetch her. But let us be clear on one point–are we to tell this young lady what our conclusions are, regarding herself?"

"Your conclusions!" said Mr. Carless, with a sly smile. "We know nothing yet, you know, Pawle."

"My conclusions, then," assented Mr. Pawle. "Are we–"

Lord Ellingham quietly interrupted the old lawyer.

"Pardon me, Mr. Pawle," he said, "but before we go any further, do you mind telling me, briefly, what your conclusions really are!"

"I will tell your lordship in a few words," answered Mr. Pawle, readily. "Wrong or right, my conclusions are these: From certain investigations which Mr. Viner and I have made since this affair began–with the murder of Ashton–and from certain evidence which we have unearthed, I believe that Ashton's friend Wickham, the father of the girl we are going to produce this afternoon, was in reality your lordship's uncle, the missing Lord Marketstoke. I believe that Ashton came to England in order to prove this, and that he was probably about to begin proceedings when he was murdered–for the sake of those papers which we have just seen. And I believe, too, that we have not seen all the papers which were stolen from his dead body. What was produced to us just now by

Methley and Woodlesford was a selection—the probability is that there are other and more important papers in the hands of the murderer, whose cat's-paw or accomplice this claimant, whoever he may be, is. I believe," concluded Mr. Pawle, with emphasis, "that my conclusions will be found to be correct ones, based on indisputable fact."

Lord Ellingham looked from one solicitor to the other.

"Then," he said, with something of a smile, "if Wickham was really my uncle, Lord Marketstoke, and this young lady you tell me of is his daughter—what, definitely, is my position?"

Mr. Pawle looked at Mr. Carless, and Mr. Carless shook his head.

"If Mr. Pawle's theory is correct," he said, "and mind you, Pawle, it will take a lot of proving. If Mr. Pawle's theory is correct, the position, my lord, is this. The young lady we hear of is Countess of Ellingham in her own right! She would not be the first woman to succeed to the title: there was a Countess of Ellingham in the time of George the Third. She would, of course, have to prove her claim before the House of Lords—if made good, she succeeds to titles and estates. That's the plain English of it—and upon my honour," concluded Mr. Carless, "it's one of the most extraordinary things I ever heard of. This other affair is nothing to it!"

Lord Ellingham again inspected the legal countenances.

"I see nothing at all improbable about it," he said. "We may as well face that fact at once. I will be here at three o'clock, Mr. Carless. I confess I should like to meet my cousin—if she really is that!"

"Your Lordship takes it admirably!" exclaimed Mr. Carless. "But really—well, I don't know. However, we shall see. But, 'pon my honour, it's most odd! One claimant disposed of, another, a more formidable one, comes on!"

"But we have not disposed of the first, have we?" suggested Lord Ellingham.

"I don't anticipate any trouble in that quarter," answered Mr. Carless. "As I said to those two who have just gone out–send or bring the man here, and we'll tell in one minute if he's what he claims to be!"

"But–how?" asked Lord Ellingham. "You seem very certain."

"Dead certain!" asserted Mr. Carless. He looked round his callers and laughed. "I may as well tell you," he said. "Portlethwaite drew me aside to remind me of it. The real Lord Marketstoke, if he were alive, could easily be identified. He lost a finger when a mere boy."

"Ah!" exclaimed Mr. Pawle. "Good–excellent! Best bit of evidence I've heard of. Hang this claimant! Now we can tell if Wickham really was Lord Marketstoke. If necessary, we can have his body exhumed and examined."

"It was a shooting accident," continued Mr. Carless. "He was out shooting in the park at Ellingham when a boy of fourteen or fifteen; he was using an old muzzle-loading gun; it burst, and he lost his second finger–the right hand. It was, of course, very noticeable. Now, that small but very important fact is most likely not known to Methley and Woodlesford's client–but it's known to Driver and to Portlethwaite and to me, and now to all of you. If this man comes here–look at his right hand! If he possesses his full complement of fingers, well–"

Mr. Carless ended with a significant grimace, and Mr. Pawle, nodding assent, returned to the question which he was putting when Lord Ellingham interrupted him.

"Now let us settle the point I raised," he said. "Are we to tell Miss Wickham what my conclusions are, or are we to leave her in ignorance until we get proof that they are correct?"

"Or–incorrect!" answered Mr. Carless with an admonitory laugh. "I should say–at present, tell her nothing. Let us find out all we can from her; there are several questions I should like to ask her, myself, arising out of what you have told us. Leave all the rest until a later period. If your theory is correct, Pawle, it can be established, if it isn't, the girl may as well be left in ignorance that you ever raised it."

"Until three o'clock, then," said Mr. Pawle.

Three o'clock found the old lawyer and Viner pacing the pavement of Lincoln's Inn Fields in expectation of Miss Wickham's arrival. She came at last in the taxicab which Mr. Pawle had sent for her, and her first words on stepping out of it were of surprise and inquiry.

"What is it, Mr. Pawle?" she demanded as she shook hands with her two squires. "More questions? What's it all about?"

Mr. Pawle nudged Viner's arm.

"My dear young lady," he answered in grave and fatherly fashion, "you must bear in mind that a man's life is in danger. We are doing all we can to clear that unfortunate young fellow Hyde of the dreadful charge which has been brought against him, and to do that we must get to know all we can about your late guardian, you know."

"I know so little about Mr. Ashton," said Miss Wickham, looking apprehensively at the building towards which she was being conducted. "Where are you taking me?"

"To a solicitor's office–friends of mine," answered Mr. Pawle. "Carless and Driver–excellent people. Mr. Carless wants to ask you a few questions in the hope that your answers will give us a little more light on Ashton's history. You needn't be afraid of Carless," he added as they began to climb the stairs. "Carless is quite a pleasant fellow–and he has with him a very amiable young gentleman, Lord Ellingham, of whom you needn't be afraid, either."

"And why is Lord Ellingham, whoever he may be, there?" inquired Miss Wickham.

"Lord Ellingham is also interested in your late guardian," replied Mr. Pawle. "In fact, we are all interested. So now, rub up your memory–and answer Mr. Carless' questions."

Viner remained in the background, quietly watching, while Mr. Pawle effected the necessary introductions. He was at once struck by what seemed to him an indisputable fact–between Lord Ellingham and Miss Wickham there was an unmistakable family likeness. And he judged from the curious, scrutinizing look which Mr. Carless gave the two young people as they shook hands that the same idea struck him–Mr. Carless wound up that look in a significant glance at Mr. Pawle, to whom he suddenly muttered a few words which Viner caught.

"By Jove!" he whispered. "I shouldn't wonder if you're right."

Then he placed Miss Wickham in an easy-chair on his right hand, and cast a preliminary benevolent glance on her.

"Mr. Pawle," he began, "has told us of your relationship with the late Mr. Ashton–you always regarded him as your guardian?"

"He was my guardian," answered Miss Wickham. "My father left me in his charge."

"Just so. Now, have you any recollection of your father?"

"Only very vague recollections. I was scarcely six, I think, when he died."

"What do you remember about him?"

"I think he was a tall, handsome man–I have some impression that he was. I think, too, that he had a fair complexion and hair. But it's all very vague."

"Do you remember where you lived?"

"Only that it was in a very big town–Melbourne, of course. I have recollections of busy streets–I remember, too, that when I left there it was very, very hot weather."

"Do you remember Mr. Ashton at that time?"

"Oh, yes–I remember Mr. Ashton. I had nobody else, you see; my mother had died when I was quite little; I have no recollection whatever of her. I remember Mr. Ashton's house, and that he used to buy me lots of toys. His house was in a quiet part of the town, and he had a big, shady garden."

"How long, so far as you remember, did you live with Mr. Ashton there?"

"Not very long, I think. He told me that I was to go to England, to school. For a little time before we sailed, I lived with Mrs. Roscombe, with whom I came to England. She was very kind to me; I was very fond of her."

"And who was Mrs. Roscombe?"

"I didn't know at the time, of course—I only knew she was Mrs. Roscombe. But Mr. Ashton told me, not long before his death, who she was. She was the widow of some government official, and she was returning to England in consequence of his death. So she took charge of me and brought me over. She used to visit me regularly at school, every week, and I used to spend my holidays with her until she died."

"Ah!" said Mr. Carless. "She is dead?"

"She died two years ago," answered Miss Wickham.

"I wish she had been living," observed Mr. Carless, with a glance at Mr. Pawle. "I should have liked to see Mrs. Roscombe. Well," he continued, turning to Miss Wickham, "so Mrs. Roscombe brought you to England, to school. What school?"

"Ryedene School."

"Ryedene! That's one of the most expensive schools in England, isn't it?"

"I don't know. I—perhaps it is."

"I happen to know it is," said Mr. Carless dryly. "Two of my clients have daughters there, now. I've seen their bills! Do you know who paid yours?"

"No," she answered, "I don't know. Mr. Ashton, I suppose."

"You had everything you wanted, I dare say! Clothes, pocket-money, and so on?"

"I've always had everything I wanted," replied Miss Wickham.

"And you were at Ryedene twelve years?"

"Except for the holidays–yes."

"You must be a very learned young lady," suggested Mr. Carless.

Miss Wickham looked round the circle of attentive faces.

"I can play tennis and hockey very well," she said, smiling a little. "And I wasn't bad at cricket the last season or two–we played cricket there. But I'm not up to much at anything else, except that I can talk French decently."

"Physical culture, eh?" observed Mr. Carless, smiling. "Very well! Now, then, in the end Mr. Ashton came home to England, and of course came to see you, and in due course you left school, and came to his house in Markendale Square, where he got a Mrs. Killenhall to look after you. All that correct? Yes? Well, then, I think, from what Mr. Pawle tells me, Mr. Ashton handed over a lot of money to you, and told you it had been left to you, or left in his charge for you, by your father? That is correct too? Very well. Now, did Mr. Ashton never tell you anything much about your father?"

"No, he never did. Beyond telling me that my father was an Englishman who had gone out to Australia and settled there, he never told me anything. But," here Miss Wickham paused and hesitated for a while, "I have an idea," she continued in the end, "that he meant to tell me something–what, I, of course, don't know. He once or twice–hinted that he would tell me something, some day."

"You didn't press him?" suggested Mr. Carless.

"I don't think I am naturally inquisitive," replied Miss Wickham. "I certainly did not press him. I knew he'd tell me, whatever it was, in his own way."

"One or two other questions," said Mr. Carless. "Do you know who your mother was?"

"Only that she was someone whom my father met in Australia."

"Do you know what her maiden name was?"

"No, only her Christian name; that was Catherine. She and my father are buried together."

"Ah!" exclaimed Mr. Carless. "That is something else I was going to ask. You know where they are buried?"

"Oh, yes! Because, before we sailed, Mrs. Roscombe took me to the churchyard, or cemetery, to see my father's and mother's grave. I remembered that perfectly. Her own husband was buried there too, close by. I remember how we both cried."

Mr. Carless suddenly pointed to the ornament which Miss Wickham was wearing.

"Will you take that off, and let me look at it?" he asked. "Thank you," he said, as she somewhat surprisedly obeyed. "I believe," he continued, as he quietly passed the ornament to Lord Ellingham, "that Mr. Ashton gave you this and told you it had belonged to your father? Just so! Well," he concluded, handing the ornament back, "I think that's all. Much obliged to you, Miss Wickham. You won't understand all this, but you will, later. Now, one of my clerks will get you a car, and we'll escort you down to it."

"No," said Lord Ellingham, promptly jumping to his feet. "Allow me–I'm youngest. If Miss Wickham will let me–"

The two young people went out of the room together, and the three men left behind looked at each other. There was a brief and significant silence.

"Well, Carless?" said Mr. Pawle at last. "How now?"

"'Pon my honour," answered Mr. Carless, "I shouldn't wonder if you're right!"

20
SURPRISING READINESS

Mr. Pawle made a gesture which seemed to denote a certain amount of triumphant self-satisfaction.

"I'm sure I'm right!" he exclaimed. "You'll find out that I'm right! But there's a tremendous lot to do, Carless. If only that unfortunate man, Ashton, had lived, he could have cleared this matter up at once. I feel convinced that he possessed papers which would have proved this girl's claim beyond dispute. Those papers, of course–"

"Now, what particular papers are you thinking of?" interrupted Mr. Carless.

"Well," replied Mr. Pawle, "such papers as proofs of her father's marriage, and of her own birth. According to what she told us just now, her father was married in Australia, and she herself was born there. There must be documentary proof of that."

"Her father was probably married under his assumed name of Wickham," observed Mr. Carless. "You'll have to prove that Wickham and Lord Marketstoke were identical–were one and the same person. The fact is, Pawle, if this girl's claim is persisted in, there'll have to be a very searching inquiry made in Australia. However much I may feel that your theory may be–probably is– right, I should have to advise my client, Lord Ellingham, to insist on the most complete investigation."

"To be sure, to be sure!" assented Mr. Pawle. "That's absolutely necessary. But my own impression is that as we get into the secret of Ashton's murder, as I make no doubt we shall, there will be more evidence forthcoming.

Now, as regards this man, whoever he is, who claims to be the missing Lord Marketstoke–"

At that moment a clerk entered the room and glanced at Mr. Carless.

"Telephone message from Methley and Woodlesford, sir," he announced. "Mr. Methley's compliments, and if agreeable to you, he can bring his client on to see you this afternoon–at once, if convenient."

Mr. Carless looked at Mr. Pawle, and Mr. Pawle nodded a silent assent.

"Tell Mr. Methley it's quite agreeable and convenient," answered Mr. Carless. "I shall be glad to see them both–at once. Um!" he muttered when the clerk had withdrawn. "Somewhat sudden, eh, Pawle? You might almost call it suspicious alacrity. Evidently the gentleman has no fear of meeting us!"

"You may be quite certain, Carless, if my theory about the whole thing is a sound theory, that the gentleman will have no fear of meeting anybody, not even a judge and jury!" answered Mr. Pawle sardonically. "If I apprehend things rightly, he'll have been very carefully coached and prepared."

"You think there's a secret conspiracy behind all this?" suggested Mr. Carless. "With this claimant as cat's-paw–well tutored to his task?"

"I do!" affirmed Mr. Pawle. "Emphatically, I do!"

"Aye, well!" said Mr. Carless. "Don't forget what I told you about the missing finger–middle finger of the right hand. And I'll have Driver in here, and Portlethwaite, too; we'll see if he knows which is which of the three of us. I'll go and prepare them."

He returned presently with his partner, a quiet, elderly man; a few minutes later Portlethwaite, evidently keenly interested, joined them. They and Mr. Pawle began to discuss certain legal matters connected with the immediate business, and Viner purposely withdrew to a corner of the room, intent on silently watching whatever followed on the arrival of the visitors. A quarter of an hour later Methley was shown into the room, and the five men gathered there turned with one accord to look at his companion, a tall, fresh-coloured, slightly grey-haired man of distinctly high-bred appearance, who, Viner saw at once, was much more self-possessed and assured in manner than any of the men who rose to meet him.

"My client, Mr. Cave, who claims to be Earl of Ellingham," said Methley, by way of introduction. "Mr. Car–"

But the other man smiled quietly and immediately assumed a lead.

"There is no need of introduction, Mr. Methley," he said. "I remember all three gentlemen perfectly! Mr. Carless–Mr. Driver–and–yes, to be sure, Mr. Portlethwaite! I have a good memory for faces." He bowed to each man as he named him, and smiled again. "Whether these gentlemen remember me as well as I remember them," he remarked, "is another question!"

"May I offer you a chair?" said Mr. Carless.

The visitor bowed, sat down, and took off his gloves. And in the silence which followed, Viner saw that the eyes of Driver, Carless, Pawle and Portlethwaite were all steadily directed on the claimant's right hand–he himself turned to it, too, with no small interest. The next instant he was conscious that an atmosphere of astonishment and surprise had been set up in that room. For the middle finger of the man's right hand was missing!

Viner felt, rather than saw, that the three solicitors and the elderly clerk were exchanging glances of amazement. And he fancied that Mr. Carless' voice, which had sounded cold and noncommittal as he offered the visitor a seat, was somewhat uncertain when he turned to address him.

"You claim, sir, to be the Lord Marketstoke who disappeared so many years ago?" he asked, eyeing the claimant over.

"I claim to be exactly what I am, Mr. Carless," answered the visitor with another ready and pleasant smile. "I hope your memory will come to your aid."

"When a man has disappeared—absolutely—for something like thirty-five years," remarked Mr. Carless, "those whom he has left behind may well be excused if their memories don't readily respond to sudden demands. But I should like to ask you some questions? Did you see the advertisements which were issued, broadcast, at the time of the seventh Earl of Ellingham's death?"

"Yes—in several English and Colonial papers," answered the claimant.

"Why did you not reply to them?"

"At that time I still persevered in my intention of never again having anything to do with my old life. I had no desire—at all—to come forward and claim my rights. So I took no notice of your advertisements."

"And since then—of late, to be exact—you have changed your mind?" suggested Mr. Carless dryly.

"To a certain extent only," replied the visitor, whose calm assurance was evidently impressing the legal practitioners around him. "I have already told Mr. Methley and his partner, Mr. Woodlesford, that I have no desire to assume my title nor to require possession of the estates which are certainly mine. I have lived a free life too long to wish for—what I should come in for if I established my claim. But I have a right to a share in the property which I quite willingly resign to my nephew—"

"In plain language," said Mr. Carless, "if you are paid a certain considerable sum of money, you will vanish again into the obscurity from whence you came? Am I right in that supposition?"

"I don't like your terminology, Mr. Carless," answered the visitor with a slight frown. "I have not lived in obscurity, and—"

"If you are what you claim to be, sir, you are Earl of Ellingham," said Mr. Carless firmly, "and I may as well tell you at once that if you prove to us that you are, your nephew, who now holds title and estates, will at once relinquish both. There will be no bargaining. It is all or nothing. Our client, whom we know as Earl of Ellingham, is not going to traffic. If you are what you claim to be, you are head of the family and must take your place."

"We could have told you that once for all, if you had come to us in the first instance," remarked Mr. Driver. "Any other idea is out of the question. It seems to me most remarkable that such a notion as that which you suggest should ever enter your head, sir. If you are Earl of Ellingham, you are!"

"And that reminds me," said Mr. Carless, "that there is another question I should like to ask. Why, knowing that we have been legal advisers to your family for several generations, did you not come straight to us, instead of going–Mr. Methley, I'm sure, will pardon me– to a firm of solicitors which, as far as I know, has never had any connection with it!"

"I thought it best to employ absolutely independent advice," replied the visitor. "And I still think I was right. For example, you evidently do not admit my claim?"

"We certainly admit nothing, at present!" declared Mr. Carless with a laugh. "It would be absurd to expect it. The proofs which your solicitors showed us this morning are no proofs at all. That those papers belonged to the missing Lord Marketstoke there is no doubt, but your possession of them at present does not prove that you are Lord Marketstoke or Lord Ellingham. They may have been stolen!"

The claimant rose from his chair with a good deal of dignity. He glanced at Methley.

"I do not see that any good can come of this interview, Mr. Methley," he remarked in quiet, level tones. "I am evidently to be treated as an impostor. In that case,"–he bowed ceremoniously to the men gathered around Mr. Carless' desk–"I think it best to withdraw."

Therewith he walked out of the room; and Methley, after a quiet word with Carless, followed—to be stopped in the corridor, for a second time that day, by Viner, who had hurried after him.

"I'm not going to express any opinion on what we've just heard," whispered Viner, drawing Methley aside, "but in view of what I told you this morning, there's something I want you to do for me."

"Yes!" said Methley. "What?"

"That unlucky fellow Hyde, who is on remand, is to be brought before the magistrate tomorrow morning," answered Viner. "Get him—this claimant there, to attend the court as a spectator—go with him! Use any argument you like, but get him there! I've a reason—which I'll explain later."

"I'll do my best," promised Methley. "And I've an idea of what's on your mind. You want to find out if Hyde can recognize him as the man whom he met at the Markendale Square end of Lonsdale Passage?"

"Well, that is my idea!" assented Viner. "So get him there."

Methley nodded and turned away; then he turned back and pointed at Carless' room.

"What do they really think in there?" he whispered. "Tell me—between ourselves?"

"That he is an impostor, and that there's a conspiracy," replied Viner.

Methley nodded again, and Viner went back. The men whom he had left were talking excitedly.

"It was the only course to take!" Mr. Carless was declaring. "Uncompromising hostility! We could do no other. You saw—quite well—that he was all for money. I will engage that we could have settled with him for one half of what he asked. But—who is he?"

"The middle finger of his right hand is gone!" said Mr. Pawle, who had been very quiet and thoughtful during the recent proceedings. "Remember that, Carless!"

"A most extraordinary coincidence!" exclaimed Mr. Carless excitedly. "I don't care twopence what anybody says–we all know that the most surprising coincidences do occur. Nothing but a coincidence! I assert–what is it, Portlethwaite?"

The elderly clerk had been manifesting a strong desire to get in a word, and he now rapped his senior employer's elbow.

"Mr. Carless," he said earnestly, "you know that before I came to you, now nearly forty years ago, I was a medical student: you know, too, you and Mr. Driver, why I gave up medicine for the law. But–I haven't forgotten all of that I learned in the medical schools and the hospitals."

"Well, Portlethwaite," demanded Mr. Carless, "what is it? You've some idea?"

"Gentlemen," answered the elderly clerk. "I was always particularly interested in anatomy in my medical student days. I've been looking attentively at what I could see of that man's injured finger since he sat down at that desk. And I'll lay all I have that he lost the two joints of that finger within the last three months! The scar over the stump had not long been healed. That's a fact!"

Mr. Carless looked round with a triumphant smile.

"There!" he exclaimed. "What did I tell you? Coincidence–nothing but coincidence!"

But Portlethwaite shook his head.

"Why not say design, Mr. Carless?" he said meaningly. "Why not say design? If this man, or the people who are behind him, knew that the real Lord Marketstoke had a finger missing, what easier–in view of the stake they're playing for–than to remove one of this man's fingers? Design, sir, design. All part of the scheme!"

The elderly clerk's listeners looked at each other.

"I'll tell you what it is!" exclaimed Mr. Pawle with sudden emphasis. "The more we see and hear of this

affair, the more I'm convinced that it is, as Portlethwaite
says, a conspiracy. You know, that fellow who has just
been here was distinctly taken aback when you, Carless,
informed him that it was going to be a case of all or
nothing. He–or the folk behind him–evidently expected
that they'd be able to effect a money settlement. Now, I
should say that the real reason of his somewhat hasty
retirement was that he wanted to consult his principal or
principals. Did you notice that he was not really affronted
by your remark? Not he! His personal dignity wasn't
ruffled a bit. He was taken aback! He's gone off to
consult. Carless, you ought to have that man carefully
shadowed, to see where and to whom he goes."

"Good idea!" muttered Mr. Driver. "We might see to
that."

"I can put a splendid man on to him, at once, Mr.
Carless," remarked Portlethwaite. "If you could furnish
me with his address–"

"Methley and Woodlesford know it," said Mr. Carless.
"Um–yes, that might be very useful. Ring Methley's up,
Portlethwaite, and ask if they would oblige us with the
name of Mr. Cave's hotel–some residential hotel in
Lancaster Gate, I believe."

Mr. Pawle and Viner went away, ruminating over the
recent events, and walked to the old lawyer's offices in
Bedford Row. Mr. Pawle's own particular clerk met them
as they entered.

"There's Mr. Roland Perkwite, of the Middle Temple,
in your room, sir," he said, addressing his master. "You
may remember him, sir–we've briefed him once or twice
in some small cases. Mr. Perkwite wants to see you about
this Ashton affair–he says he's something to tell you."

Mr. Pawle looked at Viner and beckoned him to
follow.

"Here a little, and there a little!" he whispered. "What
are we going to hear this time?"

21
The Marseilles Meeting

The man who was waiting in Mr. Pawle's room, and who rose from his chair with alacrity as the old lawyer entered with Viner at his heels, was an alert, sharp-eyed person of something under middle-age, whose clean-shaven countenance and general air immediately suggested the Law Courts. And he went straight to business before he had released the hand which Mr. Pawle extended to him.

"Your clerk has no doubt already told you what I came about, Mr. Pawle?" he said. "This Ashton affair."

"Just so," answered Mr. Pawle. "You know something about it? This gentleman is Mr. Richard Viner, who is interested in it—considerably."

"To be sure," said the barrister. "One of the witnesses, of course. I read the whole thing up last night. I have been on the Continent—the French Riviera, Italy, the Austrian Tyrol—for some time, Mr. Pawle, and only returned to town yesterday. I saw something, in an English newspaper, in Paris, the other day, about this Ashton business, and as my clerk keeps the *Times* for me when I am absent, last night I read over the proceedings before the magistrate and before the coroner. And of course I saw your request for information about Ashton and his recent movements."

"And you've some to give?" asked Mr. Pawle.

"I have some to give," assented Mr. Perkwite, as the three men sat down by Mr. Pawle's desk. "Certainly—and I should say it's of considerable importance. The fact is I met Ashton at Marseilles, and spent the better part of the week in his company at the Hotel de Louvre there."

"When was that?" asked Mr. Pawle.

"About three months ago," replied the barrister. "I had gone straight to Marseilles from London; he had come there from Italy by way of Monte Carlo and Nice. We happened to get into conversation on the night of my arrival, and we afterwards spent most of our time together. And finding out that I was a barrister, he confided certain things to me and asked my advice."

"Aye—and on what, now?" enquired the old lawyer.

"It was the last night we were together," replied Mr. Perkwite. "We had by that time become very friendly, and I had promised to renew our acquaintance on my return to London, where, Ashton told me, he intended to settle down for the rest of his life. Now on that last evening at Marseilles I had been telling him, after dinner, of some curious legal cases, and he suddenly remarked that he would like to tell me of a matter which might come within the law, and on which he should be glad of advice. He then asked me if I had ever heard of the strange disappearance of Lord Marketstoke, heir to the seventh Earl of Ellingham. I replied that I had at the time when application was made to the courts for leave to presume Lord Marketstoke's death.

"Thereupon, pledging me to secrecy for the time being, Ashton went on to tell me that Lord Marketstoke was well known to him and that he alone knew all the facts of the matter, though a certain amount of them was known to another man, now living in London. He said that Marketstoke, after a final quarrel with his father, left England in such a fashion that no one could trace him, taking with him the fortune which he had inherited from his mother, and eventually settled in Australia, where he henceforth lived under the name of Wickham. According to Ashton, he and Marketstoke became friends, close friends, at a very early period of Marketstoke's career in Australia, and the friendship deepened and existed until

Marketstoke's death some twelve or thirteen years ago. But Ashton never had the slightest notion of Marketstoke's real identity until his friend's last days. Then Marketstoke told him the plain truth; and the fact who he really was at the same time was confided to another man–who, however, was not told all the details which were given to Ashton.

"Now, Marketstoke had married in Australia. His wife was dead. But he had a daughter who was about six years of age at the time of her father's death. Marketstoke confided her to Ashton, with a wish that she should be sent home to England to be educated. He also handed over to Ashton a considerable sum of money for this child. Further, he gave him a quantity of papers, letters, family documents, and so on. He had a purpose. He left it to Ashton–in whom he evidently had the most absolute confidence–as to whether this girl's claim to the title and estates should be set up. And when Ashton had finished telling me all this, I found that one of his principal reasons in coming to England to settle down, was the wish to find out how things were with the present holder of the title: if, he said, he discovered that he was a worthy sort of young fellow, he, Ashton, should be inclined to let the secret die with him. He told me that the girl already had some twelve thousand pounds of her own, and that it was his intention to leave her the whole of his own fortune, and as she was absolutely ignorant of her real position, he might perhaps leave her so. But in view of the possibility of his setting up her claim, he asked me some questions on legal points, and of course I asked him to let me see the papers of which he had spoken."

"Ah!" exclaimed Mr. Pawle, with a sigh of relieved satisfaction. "Then you saw them?"

"Yes–he showed me the whole lot," replied Mr. Perkwite. "Not so many, after all–those that were really pertinent, at any rate. He carried those in a pocketbook; had so carried them, he told me, ever since Marketstoke had handed them to him; they had never, he added, been out of his possession, day or night, since Marketstoke's death. Now, on examining the papers, I at once discovered two highly important facts. Although Marketstoke went to and lived in Australia under the name of Wickham, he had taken good care to get married in his own proper name, and there, amongst the documents, was the marriage certificate, in which he was correctly described. Further, his daughter had been correctly designated in the register of her birth; there was a copy, properly attested, of the entry."

Mr. Pawle glanced at Viner, and Viner knew what he was thinking of. The two documents just described by Mr. Perkwite had not been among the papers which Methley and Woodlesford had exhibited at Carless & Driver's office.

"A moment," said Mr. Pawle, lifting an arresting finger. "Did you happen to notice where this marriage took place?"

"It was not in Melbourne," replied Mr. Perkwite.

"My recollection is that it was at some place of a curious name. Ashton told me that Marketstoke's wife had been a governess in the family of some well-to-do-sheep-farmer—she was an English girl, and an orphan. The child, however, was certainly born in Melbourne and registered in Melbourne."

"Now, that's odd!" remarked Mr. Pawle. "You'd have thought that when Lord Marketstoke was so extensively advertised for some years ago, on the death of his father, some of these officials—"

"Ah! I put that point to Ashton," interrupted Mr. Perkwite. "He said that Marketstoke, though he had taken good care to be married in his own name and had exercised equal precaution about his daughter, had pledged everybody connected with his marriage and the child's birth to secrecy."

"Aye!" muttered Mr. Pawle. "He would do that, of course. But continue."

"Well," said the barrister, "after seeing these papers, I had no doubt whatever that the case as presented by Ashton was quite clear, and that his ward Miss Avice Wickham is without doubt Countess of Ellingham (the title, I understand, going in the female as well as the male line) and rightful owner of the estates. And I told him that his best plan, on reaching England, was to put the whole matter before the family solicitors. However, he said that before doing that, there were two things he wanted to do. One was to find out for himself how things were–if the young earl was a satisfactory landlord and so on, and likely to be a credit to the family; the other was that he wanted to consult the man who shared with him the bare knowledge that the man who had been known in Melbourne as Wickham was really the missing Lord Marketstoke. And he added that he had already telegraphed to this man to meet him in Paris."

"Ah!" exclaimed Mr. Pawle with a look in Viner's direction. "Now we are indeed coming to something! He was to meet him in Paris! Viner, I'll wager the world against a China orange that that's the man whom Armitstead saw in company with Ashton in the Rue Royale, and–no doubt–the man of Lonsdale Passage! Mr. Perkwite, this is most important. Did Ashton tell you the name of this man?"

The old lawyer was tremulous with excited interest, and Mr. Perkwite was obviously sorry to disappoint him.

"Unfortunately, he did not!" he replied. "He merely told me that he was a man who had lived in Melbourne for some time and had known Marketstoke and himself very intimately–had left Melbourne just after Marketstoke's death, and had settled in London. No, he did not mention his name."

"Disappointing!" muttered Mr. Pawle. "That's the nearest approach to a clue that we've had, Perkwite. If we only knew who that man was! But–what more can you tell us?"

"Nothing more, I'm afraid," answered the barrister. "I promised to call on Ashton when I returned to London, and when he'd started housekeeping, and we parted–I went on next morning to Genoa, and he set off for Paris. He was a pleasant, kindly, sociable fellow," concluded Mr. Perkwite, "and I was much grieved to hear of his sad fate."

"He didn't correspond with you at all after you left him at Marseilles?" asked Mr. Pawle.

"No," replied the barrister. "No–I never heard of or from him until I read of his murder."

Pawle turned to Viner.

"I think we'd better tell Perkwite of all that's happened, within our own ken," he said, and proceeded to give the visitor a brief account of the various important details. "Now," he concluded, "it seems to me there's only one conclusion to be arrived at. The man who shared the secret with Ashton is certainly the man whom Armitstead saw with him in Paris. He is probably the man whom Hyde saw leaving Londsdale Passage, just before Hyde found the body. And he is without doubt the murderer, and is the man to whom this claimant fellow is acting as cat's-paw. And–who is he?"

"There must be some way of finding that out," observed Mr. Perkwite. "If your theory is correct, that this claimant is merely a man who is being put forward, then surely the thing to do is to get at the person or persons behind him, through him!"

"Aye, there's that to be thought of," asserted Mr. Pawle. "But it may be a tougher job than we think for. It would have been a tremendous help if Ashton had only mentioned a name to you."

"Sorry, but he didn't," said Mr. Perkwite. "You feel," he continued after a moment's silence, "you feel that this affair of the Ellingham succession lies at the root of the Ashton mystery–that he was really murdered by somebody who wanted to get possession of those papers?"

"And to remain sole repository of the secret," declared Mr. Pawle. "Isn't it established that beyond yourself and this unknown man nobody but Ashton knew the secret?"

"There is another matter, though," remarked Viner. He turned to the visitor. "You said that you and Ashton became very friendly and confidential during your stay in Marseilles. Pray, did he never show you anything of a valuable nature which he carried in his pocketbook?"

The barrister's keen eyes suddenly lighted up with recollection.

"Yes!" he exclaimed. "Now you come to suggest it, he did! A diamond!"

"Ah!" said Mr. Pawle. "So you saw that!"

"Yes, I saw it," assented Mr. Perkwite. "He showed it to me as a sort of curiosity—a stone which had some romantic history attaching to it. But I was not half as much interested in that as in the other affair."

"All the same," remarked Mr. Pawle, "that diamond is worth some fifty or sixty thousand pounds, Perkwite—and it's missing!"

Mr. Perkwite looked his astonishment.

"You mean—he had it on him when he was murdered?" he asked.

"So it's believed," replied Mr. Pawle.

"In that case it might form a clue," said the barrister.

"When it's heard of," admitted Mr. Pawle, with a grim smile. "Not till then!"

"From what we have heard," remarked Viner, "Ashton carried that diamond in the pocketbook which contained his papers—the papers you have told me of, and some of which have certainly come into possession of this claimant person. Now, whoever stole the papers, of course got the diamond."

Mr. Perkwite seemed to consider matters during a moment's silence; finally he turned to the old lawyer.

"I have been thinking over something that might be done," he said. "I see that the coroner's inquest was adjourned. Now, as that inquest is, of course, being held to inquire into the circumstances of Ashton's death, I suggest that I should come forward as a witness and should prove that Ashton showed certain papers relating to the Ellingham peerage to me at Marseilles; I can tell the story, as a witness. It can then be proved by you, or by Carless, that a man claiming to be the missing Lord Marketstoke showed these stolen papers to you. In the meantime, get the coroner to summon this man as a witness, and take care that he's brought to the court. Once there, let him be asked how he came into possession of these papers? Do you see my idea?"

"Capital!" exclaimed Mr. Pawle. "An excellent notion! Much obliged to you, Perkwite. It shall be done—I'll see to it at once. Yes, to be sure, that will put this fellow in a tight corner."

"Don't be surprised if he hasn't some very clever explanation to give," said the barrister warningly. "The whole thing is evidently a well-concocted conspiracy. But when is the adjourned inquest?"

"Day after tomorrow," replied Mr. Pawle, after glancing at his desk-diary.

"And tomorrow morning," remarked Viner, "Hyde comes up before the magistrate again, on remand."

He was half-minded to tell Mr. Pawle there and then of his secret dealings with Methley that day, but on reflection he decided that he would keep the matter to himself. Viner had an idea which he had not communicated even to Methley. It had struck him that the mysterious *deux ex machina* who was certainly at the back of all this business might not improbably be so anxious about his schemes that he would, unknown and unsuspected, attend the magistrates' court. Would Hyde, his wits sharpened by danger, be able to spot him as the muffled man of Lonsdale Passage?

22
ON REMAND

When Langton Hyde was brought up before the magistrate next morning, the court was crowded to its utmost limits; and Viner, looking round him from his seat near the solicitors' table saw that most of the people interested in the case were present. Mr. Carless was whispering with Mr. Pawle; Lord Ellingham had a seat close by; in the front of the public gallery Miss Penkridge, grim and alert, was in charge of the timid and shrinking sisters of the unfortunate prisoner. There, too, were Mr. Armitstead and Mr. Isidore Rosenbaum, and Mr. Perkwite, all evidently very much alive to certain possibilities. But Viner looked in vain for either Methley or Woodlesford or their mysterious client; they were certainly not present when Hyde was put into the dock, and Viner began to wonder if the events of the previous day had warned Mr. Cave and those behind him to avoid publicity.

Instructed by Viner, who was determined to spare neither effort nor money to clear his old schoolmate, Felpham had engaged the services of one of the most brilliant criminal barristers of the day, Mr. Millington-Bywater, on behalf of his client; and he and Viner had sat up half the night with him, instructing him in the various mysteries and ramifications of the case. A big, heavy-faced, shrewd-eyed man, Mr. Millington-Bywater made no sign, and to all outward appearance showed no very great interest while the counsel who now appeared on behalf of the police, completed his case against the prisoner.

The only new evidence produced by the prosecution was that of the greengrocer on whose premises Hyde had admitted that he passed most of the night of the murder, and in whose shed the missing valuables had been found. The greengrocer's evidence as to his discovery was given in a plain and straightforward fashion–he was evidently a man who would just tell what he actually saw, and brought neither fancy nor imagination to bear on his observation. But when the prosecution had done with him, Mr. Millington-Bywater rose and quietly asked the police to produce the watch, chain and ring which the greengrocer had found, in their original wrappings. He held up the wrapping-papers to the witness and asked him if he could swear that this was what he had found the valuables in and had given to the police. The greengrocer was positive as to this; he was positive, too, that the other wrappings which Felpham had carefully preserved were those which had been on the outside of the parcel and had been thrown aside by himself on its discovery and afterwards picked up by Viner. Mr. Millington-Bywater handed all these papers up to the magistrate, directing his attention to the strong odour of drugs or chemicals which still pervaded them, and to the address of the manufacturing chemists which appeared on the outer wrapping. The magistrate seemed somewhat mystified.

"What is the object of this?" he asked, glancing at the defending counsel. "It is admitted that these are the wrappings in which the watch, and chain and ring were found in the witness's shed, but"–he paused, with another inquiring look–"you propose to–what?" he asked.

"I propose, Your Worship, to prove that these things were never put there by the prisoner at all!" answered Mr. Millington-Bywater, promptly and with an assurance which was not lost on the spectators. "I intend to show that they were purposely placed in that outhouse by the real murderer of John Ashton after the statement made by the prisoner at the inquest became public–placed there, of course, to divert any possible suspicion of himself.

"And now," he continued, after the greengrocer had left the box and the prosecuting counsel had intimated that he had no more evidence to bring forward at present, "now I will outline the defence which I shall set up on behalf of my client. I intend to prove that John Ashton was murdered by some man not yet discovered, who killed him in order to gain possession of certain papers which he carried on him–papers of extreme importance, as will be shown. We know where certain of those papers are, and we hope before very long to know where the rest are, and also where a certain very valuable diamond is, which the murdered man had on him at the time of his death. I shall, indeed, prove that the prisoner–certainly through his own foolishness–is wrongly accused. It will be within your worship's recollection that when the prisoner was first before you, he very unwisely refused to give his name and address or any information–he subsequently repented of that and made a statement, not only to the police but before the coroner. Now, I propose to put him into that box so that he may give evidence, and I shall then call certain witnesses who will offer evidence which will go to prove that what I say as regards the murder of Ashton is more than probable–namely, that he was murdered for the sake of the documents he had on him, and that the spoiling of his money and valuables was a mere piece of bluff, intended to mislead. Let the prisoner go into the box!"

There was a continued deep silence in court while Hyde, under examination, repeated the story which he had told to Viner and Drillford and before the coroner and his jury. It was a plain, consecutive story, in which he set forth the circumstances preceding the evening of the murder and confessed his picking up of the ring which lay on the pavement by Ashton's body. He kept his eyes steadily fixed on Mr. Millington-Bywater under this examination, never removing them from him save when the magistrate interposed with an occasional remark or question. But at one point a slight commotion in court caused him to look among the spectators, and Viner, following the direction of his eyes, saw him start, and at the same instant saw what it was that he started at. Methley, followed by the claimant, was quietly pushing a way through the throng between the door and the solicitor's table.

Viner leaned closer to Mr. Pawle.

"Do you see?" he whispered. "Hyde evidently recognizes one of those two! Now—which?"

Mr. Pawle glanced at the prisoner. Hyde's face, hitherto pale, had flushed a little, and his eyes had grown bright; he looked as if he had suddenly seen a friend's face in a hostile crowd. But Mr. Millington-Bywater, who had been bending over his papers, suddenly looked up with another question, and Hyde again turned his attention to him.

"All that you really know of this matter," asked Mr. Millington-Bywater, "is that you chanced to turn up Lonsdale Passage, saw a man lying on the pavement and a ring close by, and that, being literally starving and desperate, you snatched up that ring and ran away as fast as you could?"

"Yes—that is all," asserted Hyde. "Except that I had met a man, as I have already told you, at the end of the passage by which I entered."

"You did not even know whether this man lying on the pavement was alive or dead?"

"I thought he might be drunk," replied Hyde. "But after I had snatched up the ring I never thought at all until I had run some distance. I was afraid of being followed."

"Now why were you afraid of being followed?"

"I was famishing!" answered Hyde. "I knew I could get something, some money, on that ring, in the morning, and I wanted to stick to it. I was afraid that the man whom I met as I ran out of the passage, whom I now know to have been Mr. Viner, might follow me and make me give up the ring. And the ring meant food."

Mr. Millington-Bywater let this answer sink into the prevalent atmosphere and suddenly turned to another matter. The knife which had been found in Hyde's possession was lying with certain other exhibits on the solicitor's table, and Mr. Millington-Bywater pointed to it.

"Now about that knife," he said. "It is yours? Very well–how long have you had it?"

"Three or four years," replied Hyde, promptly. "I bought it when I was touring in the United States, at a town called Guthrie, in Oklahoma. And," he added suddenly and with a triumphant smile as of a man who is unexpectedly able to clinch an argument, "there is a gentleman there who was with me when I bought it–Mr. Nugent Starr!"

From the magistrate on his bench to the policeman at the door every person in court turned to look at the man to whom the prisoner pointed an out-stretched finger. And Mr. Pawle let out an irrepressible exclamation.

"Good God!" he said. "The claimant fellow!"

But Viner said nothing. He was staring, as everybody else was, at the man who sat by Methley. He, suddenly aware that Hyde had pointed to him, was obviously greatly taken aback and embarrassed–he looked sharply at the prisoner, knitted his brows, shook his head, and turning to Methley muttered something which no one else caught. Mr. Millington-Bywater looked at him and turned to his client.

"You say there is a gentleman here–that gentleman!– who was with you when you bought that knife?" he asked. "A friend of yours, then?"

"Well–we were playing in the same company," asserted Hyde. "Mr. Moreby-Bannister's company. He was heavy lead–I was juvenile. He knows me well enough. He was with me when I bought that knife in a hardware store in Guthrie."

The magistrate's eye was on the man who sat by Methley, and there was a certain amount of irritation in it. And suddenly Methley whispered something to his companion and the man shyly but with a noticeable composure stood up.

"I beg Your Worship's pardon," he said, quietly, with a polite bow to the bench, "but really, the witness is under a mistaken impression! I don't know him, and I have never been in the town he mentions–in fact, I have never been in the United States. I am very sorry, but, really, there is some strange mistake–I–the witness is an absolute stranger to me!"

The attention of all present was transferred to Hyde. And Hyde flushed, leaned forward over the ledge of the witness-box and gave the claimant a long, steady stare.

"No mistake at all!" he suddenly exclaimed in a firm voice. "That's Mr. Nugent Starr! I played with him for over twelve months."

While this had been going on, Felpham on one side, and Carless on the other, had been whispering to Mr. Millington-Bywater, who listened to both with growing interest, and began to nod to each with increasing intelligence–and then, suddenly, the prosecuting counsel played unexpectedly and directly into his hand.

"If Your Worship pleases," said the prosecuting counsel, "I should like to have the prisoner's assertion categorically denied–it may be of importance. Perhaps this gentleman will go into the box and deny it on oath."

Mr. Millington-Bywater sat down as quickly as if a heavy hand had forced him into his seat, and Viner saw a swift look of gratification cross his features. Close by, Mr. Pawle chuckled with joy.

"By the Lord Harry!" he whispered, "the very thing we wanted! No need to wait for the adjourned coroner's inquest, Viner–the thing'll come out now!"

Viner did not understand. He saw Hyde turned out of the box; he saw the claimant, after an exchange of remarks with Methley, step into it; he heard him repeat on oath the denial he had just uttered, after stating that his name was Cave, and that he lived at the Belmead Hotel, Lancaster Gate; and he saw Mr. Millington-Bywater, after exchanging a few questions and answers in whispers with Hyde over the ledge of the dock, turn to the witness as he was about to step down.

"A moment, sir," he said. "I want to ask you a few questions, with the permission of His Worship, who will soon see that they are very pertinent. So," he went on, "you reside at the Belmead Hotel, in Lancaster Gate, and your name is Edward Cave?"

"At present," answered the witness, stiffly.

"Do you mean that your name is Edward Cave–at present?"

"My name is Edward Cave, and at present I live–as I have stated," replied the witness with dignity.

"You have just stated, on oath, that you are not Nugent Starr, have never been so called, don't know the prisoner, never met him in America, have never set foot in America! Now, then–mind, you're on your oath!–is Edward Cave your real or full name?"

"Well, strictly speaking," answered the witness, after some hesitation, "no, it is not. My full name is Cave-Gray–my family name; but for the present–"

"For the present you wish to be called Mr. Cave. Now, sir, are you not the person who claims to be the rightful Earl of Ellingham?"

A murmur of excited interest ran round the court, and everybody recognized that a new stage of the case had been entered upon. Every eye, especially the observant eyes on the bench, were fixed on the witness, who now looked considerably ruffled. He glanced at Methley–but Methley sat with averted look and made no sign; he looked at the magistrate; the magistrate, it was plain, expected the question to be answered. And the answer came, almost sullenly.

"Yes, I am!"

"That is to say, you are really–or you claim to be really–the Lord Marketstoke who disappeared from England some thirty-five years ago, and you have now returned, though you are legally presumed to be dead, to assert your rights to titles and estates? You absolutely claim to be the ninth Earl of Ellingham?"

"Yes!"

"Where have you been during the last thirty-five years?"

"In Australia."

"What part?"

"Chiefly in Melbourne. But I was for four or five years up-country."

"What name did you go under there?"

Mr. Pawle, Mr. Carless and the rest of the spectators who were in these secrets regarded the witness with keen attention when this question was put to him. But his answer came promptly.

"At first, under the name of Wickham. Later under the one I now use–Cave."

"Did you marry out there?"

"Never!"

"And so, of course, you never had a daughter?"

"I have never been married and have never had daughter or son!"

Mr. Millington-Bywater turned to Mr. Carless, at his left elbow, and exchanged two or three whispered remarks with him. At last he looked round again at the witness.

"Yesterday," he said, "in your character of claimant to the Ellingham title and estates you showed to Messrs. Carless & Driver, of Lincoln's Inn Fields, and to the present holder of the title, certain documents, letters, papers, which would go some way toward establishing your claim to be what you profess to be. Now, I will say at once that we believe these papers to have been stolen from the body of John Ashton when he was murdered. And I will ask you a direct question, on your oath! Have those papers always been in your possession since you left England thirty-five years ago?"

The witness drew himself up and looked steadily at his questioner.

"No!" he answered firmly. "They were stolen from me almost as soon as I arrived in Australia. I have only just regained possession of them."

23
IS THIS MAN RIGHT?

A murmur of astonishment ran through the court as the witness made his last reply, and those most closely interested in him turned and looked at each other with obvious amazement. And for a moment Mr. Millington-Bywater seemed to be at a loss; in the next he bent forward toward the witness-box and fixed the man standing there with a piercing look.

"Do you seriously tell us, on your oath, that these papers–your papers, if you are what you claim to be–were stolen from you many years ago, and have only just been restored to you?" he asked. "On your oath, mind!"

"I do tell you so," answered the witness quietly. "I am on oath."

The magistrate glanced at Mr. Millington-Bywater.

"What is the relevancy of this–in relation to the prisoner and the charge against him?" he inquired. "You have some point, of course?"

"The relevancy is this, Your Worship," replied Mr. Millington-Bywater: "Our contention is that the papers referred to were until recently in the custody of John Ashton, the murdered man–I can put a witness in the box who can give absolute proof of that, a highly reputable witness, who is present,–and that John Ashton was certainly murdered by some person or persons who, for purposes of their own, wished to gain possession of them. Now, we know that they are in possession of the present witness, or rather, of his solicitors, to whom he has handed them. I mean to prove that Ashton was murdered in the way, and for the reason I suggest, and that accordingly the prisoner is absolutely innocent of the charge brought against him. I should therefore like to ask this witness to tell us how he regained possession of these papers, for I am convinced that in what he can tell us lies the secret of Ashton's murder. Now," he continued, turning again to the witness as the magistrate nodded assent, "we will assume for the time being that you are what you represent yourself to be–the Lord Marketstoke who disappeared from England thirty-five years ago. You have just heard what I said to His Worship–about these papers, and what I put forward as regards their connection with the murder of John Ashton? Will you tell us how you lost those papers, and more particularly, how you recently regained possession of them? You see the immense, the vital importance of this to the unfortunate young fellow in the dock?"

"Who," answered the witness with a calm smile, "is quite and utterly mistaken in thinking that he knew me in America, for I have certainly never set foot in America, neither North nor South, in my life! I am very much surprised indeed to be forced into publicity as I have been this morning–I came here as a merely curious spectator and had no idea whatever that I should be called into this box. But if any evidence of mine can establish, or help to establish, the prisoner's innocence, I will give it only too gladly."

"Much obliged to you, sir," said Mr. Millington-Bywater, who, in Viner's opinion, was evidently impressed by the witness's straightforward tone and candid demeanour.

"Well, if you will tell us–in your own way–about these papers, now–always remembering that we have absolute proof that until recently they were in the possession of John Ashton? Let me preface whatever you choose to tell us with a question: Do you know that they were in possession of John Ashton?"

"I have no more idea or knowledge of whose hands they were in, and had been in, for many years, until they were restored to me, than the man in the moon has!"

affirmed the witness. "I'll tell you the whole story—willingly: I could have told it yesterday to certain gentlemen, whom I see present, if they had not treated me as an impostor as soon as they saw me. Well,"–here he folded his hands on the ledge of the witness-box, and quietly fixing his eyes on the examining counsel, proceeded to speak in a calm, conversational tone–"the story is this: I left England about five-and-thirty years ago after certain domestic unpleasantnesses which I felt so much that I determined to give up all connection with my family and to start an absolutely new life of my own. I went away to Australia and landed there under the name of Wickham. I had a certain amount of money which had come to me from my mother. I speculated with it on my arrival, somewhat foolishly, no doubt, and I lost it–every penny.

"So then I was obliged to work for my living. I went up country, and for some time worked as a miner in the Bendigo district. I had been working in this way perhaps fourteen months when an accident occurred in the mine at which I was engaged. There was a serious fall of earth and masonry; two or three of my fellow-workers were killed on the spot, and I was taken up for dead. I was removed to a local hospital–there had been some serious injury to my head and spine, but I still had life in me, and I was brought round. But I remained in hospital, in a sort of semiconscious state, for a long time–months. When I went back, after my discharge, to my quarters–nothing but a rough shanty which I had shared with many other men–all my possessions had vanished. Among them, of course, were the papers I had kept, and a packet of letters written to me by my mother when I was a schoolboy at Eton.

"Of course, I knew at once what had happened–someone of my mates, believing me to be dead, had appropriated all my belongings and gone off with them. There was nothing at all to be wondered at in that–it was

the usual thing in such a society. And I knew there was
nothing to do but to accept my loss philosophically."

"Did you make no effort to recover your possessions?"
asked Mr. Millington-Bywater.

"No," answered the witness with a quiet smile. "I
didn't! I knew too much of the habits of men in mining
centers to waste time in that way. A great many men had
left that particular camp during my illness–it would have
been impossible to trace each one. No–after all, I had left
England in order to lose my identity, and now, of course,
it was gone. I went away into quite another part of the
country–into Queensland. I began trading in Brisbane,
and I did very well there, and remained there many
years. Then I went farther south, to Sydney–and I did
very well there too. It was in Sydney, years after that,
that I saw the advertisements in the newspapers, English
and Colonial, setting forth that my father was dead, and
asking for news of myself. I took no notice of them–I had
not the least desire to return to England, no wish for the
title, and I was quite content that my youngest brother
should get that and the estates. So I did nothing; nobody
knew who I really was–"

"One moment!" said Mr. Millington-Bywater. "While
you were at the mining-camp, in the Bendigo district, did
you ever reveal your secret to any of your fellow-miners?"

"Never!" answered the witness. "I never revealed it to
a living soul until I told my solicitor there, Mr. Methley,
after my recent arrival in London."

"But of course, whoever stole your letters and so on,
would discover, or guess at, the truth?" suggested Mr.
Millington-Bywater.

"Oh, of course, of course!" said the witness. "Well as I
was saying, I did nothing–except to keep an eye on the
papers. I saw in due course that leave to presume my
death had been given, and that my younger brother had
assumed the title, and administered the estate, and I was
quite content. The fact was, I was at that time doing
exceedingly well, and I was too much interested in my

doings to care about what was going on in England. All my life," continued the witness, with a slight smile, "I have had a–I had better call it a weakness–for speculating; and when I had got a goodly sum of money together by my trading venture in Brisbane and Sydney, I began speculating again, in Melbourne chiefly. And–to cut my story short–last year I had one of my periodic bad turns of fortune: I lost a lot of money. Now, I am, as you see, getting on in life, over sixty–and it occurred to me that if I came over to England and convinced my nephew, the present holder of the title and estates, that I am really who I am, he would not be averse–we have always been a generous family–to giving me enough to settle down on in Australia for the rest of my days. Perhaps I had better say at once, since we are making matters so very public, that I do not want the title, nor the estate; I will be quite candid and say what I do want–enough to let me live in proper comfort in Australia, whither I shall again repair as soon as I settle my affairs here."

Mr. Millington-Bywater glanced at the magistrate and then at the witness.

"Well, now, these papers?" he said. "You didn't bring them to London with you?"

"Of course not!" answered the witness. "I had not seen or heard of them for thirty-two years! No I relied, on coming to this country, on other things to prove my identity, such as my knowledge of Marketstoke and Ellingham, my thorough acquaintance with the family history, my recollection of people I had known, like Mr. Carless, Mr. Driver, and their clerk, Mr. Portlethwaite, and on the fact that I lost this finger through a shooting accident when I was a boy, at Ellingham. Curiously," he added with another smile, "these things don't seem to have much weight. But no! I had no papers when I landed here."

"How did they come into your possession, then?" asked Mr. Millington-Bywater. "That is what we most earnestly desire to know. Let me impress upon you, sir, that this is the most serious and fateful question I can possibly put to you! How did you get them?"

"And–from whom?" said the magistrate. "From whom?"

The witness shook his head.

"I can tell you exactly how I got them," he answered. "But I can't tell you from whom, for I don't know! What I can tell you is this: When I arrived at Tilbury from Melbourne, I asked a fellow-passenger with whom I came along to London if he could tell me of a quiet, good hotel in the neighbourhood of the parks–he recommended the Belfield, in Lancaster Gate. I went there and put myself up, and from it I went out and about a good deal, looking up old haunts. I also lunched and dined a good many times at some of the new restaurants which had sprung into being since I left London. I mention this to show you that I was where I could be seen and noticed, as I evidently was. One afternoon, while I was sitting in the smoking-room at my hotel, the page-boy came in with a letter on his tray, approached me, and said that it had been brought by a district messenger. It was addressed simply, 'Mr. Cave'–the name by which I had registered at the hotel–and was sealed; the inclosure, on a half-sheet of note-paper, was typewritten. I have it here," continued the witness, producing a pocketbook and taking out an envelope. "I will read its contents, and I shall be glad to let anyone concerned see it. There is no address and no date, and it says this: 'If you wish to recover the papers and letters which were lost by you when you went into hospital at Wirra-Worra, Bendigo, thirty-two years ago, be at the Speke Monument in Kensington Gardens at five o'clock this afternoon.' There was no signature."

Another murmur of intense and excited interest ran round the court as the witness handed the letter up to the magistrate, who, after looking it over, passed it on to the counsel below. They, in their turn, showed it to Mr.

Carless, Mr. Pawle and Lord Ellingham, Mr. Pawle, showing it to Viner, whispered in his ear:

"If this man's telling the truth," he said, "this is the most extraordinary story I ever heard in my life."

"It seems to me that it is the truth!" muttered Viner. "And I'm pretty certain that at last we're on the way-to finding out who killed Ashton. But let's hear the end."

Mr. Millington-Bywater handed the letter back with a polite bow–it was very obvious to more than one observer that he had by this time quite accepted the witness as what he claimed to be.

"You kept the appointment?" he asked.

"I did, indeed!" exclaimed the witness. "As much out of greatly excited curiosity as anything! It seemed to me a most extraordinary thing that papers stolen from me in Australia thirty-two years ago should be returned to me in London! Yes, I walked down to the Speke Monument. I saw no one about there but a heavily veiled woman who walked about on one side of the obelisk while I patrolled the other. Eventually she approached me, and at once asked me if I had kept secret the receipt of the mysterious letter? I assured her that I had. She then told me that she was the ambassadress of the people who had my letters and papers, and who had seen and recognized me in London and tracked me to my hotel. She was empowered to negotiate with me for the handing over of the papers. There were stipulations. I was to give my solemn word of honour that I would not follow her, or cause her to be followed. I was not to ask questions. And I was to give a post-dated check on the bank at which I had opened an account in London, on receipt of the papers. The check was to be post-dated one month; it was to be made out to bearer, and the amount was ten thousand pounds. I agreed!"

"You really agreed!" exclaimed Mr. Millington-Bywater.

"I agreed! I wanted my papers. We parted, with an agreement that we were to meet two days later at the same place. I was there–so was the woman. She handed me a parcel, and I immediately took it to an adjacent seat and examined it. Everything that I could remember was there, with two exceptions. The packet of letters from my mother, to which I referred just now, was missing; so was a certain locket, which had belonged to her, and of which I had taken great care since her death, up to the time of my accident in the mining-camp. I pointed out these omissions to the woman: she answered that the papers which she had handed over were all that had been in her principal's possession. Thereupon I gave her the check which had been agreed upon, and we parted."

"And that is all you know of her?" asked Mr. Millington-Bywater.

"All!"

"Can you describe her?"

"A tallish, rather well-built woman, but so veiled that I could see nothing of her features; it was, moreover, nearly dark on both occasions. From her speech and manner, she was, I should say, a woman of education and refinement."

"Did you try to trace her, or her principals, through the district messenger who brought the letter?"

"Certainly not! I told you, just now, that I gave my word of honour: I couldn't."

Mr. Millington-Bywater turned to the magistrate.

"I can, if Your Worship desires it, put a witness in the box who can prove beyond doubt that the papers of which we have just heard this remarkable story, were recently in the possession of John Ashton," he said. "He is Mr. Cecil Perkwite, of the Middle Temple–a member of my own profession."

But the magistrate, who appeared unusually thoughtful, shook his head.

"After what we have heard," he said, "I think we had better adjourn. The prisoner will be remanded–as before–for another week."

When the magistrate had left the bench, and the court was humming with the murmur of tongues suddenly let free, Mr. Pawle forced his way to the side of the last witness.

"Whoever you are, sir," he said, "there's one thing certain–nobody but you can supply the solution of the mystery about Ashton's death! Come with me and Carless at once."

24
THE BROKEN LETTER

The man whose extraordinary story had excited such intense interest had become the object of universal attention. Hyde, hitherto the centre of attraction, was already forgotten, and instead of people going away from the court to canvass his guilt or his innocence, they surged round the witness whose testimony, strange and unexpected, had so altered the probabilities of the case. It was with difficulty that Methley got his client away into a private room; there they were joined by Mr. Carless, Mr. Pawle, Mr. Perkwite, Lord Ellingham and Viner, and behind a locked door these men looked at each other and at this centre of interest with the air of those to whom something extraordinary has just been told. After a moment of silence Mr. Carless spoke, addressing the man whose story had brought matters to an undeniable crisis.

"I am sure," he said gravely, and with a side glance at Lord Ellingham, "that if your story is true, sir,–and after what we have just heard, I am beginning to think that my first conclusions may have been wrong ones,–no one will welcome your reappearance more warmly than the young gentleman whom you will turn out of title and property! But you must see for yourself that your claims must be thoroughly investigated–and as what you have now just told affects other people, and we must invite you to full discussion, I propose that, for the time being, we address you as Mr. Cave."

The claimant smiled, and nodded genially to the young man whose uncle he alleged himself to be.

"I wish to remain Mr. Cave," he said. "I don't want to turn my nephew out of title and property, so long as he will do something for his old uncle. Call me Mr. Cave, by all means."

"We must talk—and at once," said Mr. Carless. "There are several points arising out of your evidence on which you must give me information. Whoever is at the back of that woman who handed you those papers is probably the murderer of John Ashton—and that is what must be got at. Now, where can we have a conference—immediately?— Your office, Methley, is not far away, I think."

"My house is nearer," said Viner. "Come—we shall be perfectly quiet in my study, and there will be nothing to interrupt us. Let us go now."

A police official let them out by a side-door, and Viner and Mr. Pawle led the way through some side-streets to Markendale Square, the others coming behind, conversing eagerly about the events of the morning. Mr. Pawle, on his part, was full of excitement.

"If we can only trace that woman, Viner!" he exclaimed. "That's the next thing! Get hold of her, whoever she is, and then—ah, we shall be in sight of the finishing-part."

"What about tracing the whole lot through the check he has given?" suggested Viner. "Wouldn't that be a good way?"

"We should have to wait nearly a month," answered Mr. Pawle. "And even then it would be difficult—simple though it seems at first sight. There are folk who deal in post-dated checks, remember! This may have been dealt with already—aye, and that diamond too; and the man who has got the proceeds may already be many a mile away. Deep, cunning folk they are who have been in this, Viner. And now—speed is the thing!"

Viner led his guests into his library, and as he placed chairs for them round a centre table, an idea struck him.

"I have a suggestion to make," he said with a shy smile at the legal men. "My aunt, Miss Penkridge, who lives with me, is an unusually sharp, shrewd woman. She has taken vast interest in this affair, and I have kept her posted up in all its details. She was in court just now and heard Mr. Cave's story. If no one has any objection, I should like her to be present at our deliberations–as a mysterious woman has entered into the case, Miss Penkridge may be able to suggest something."

"Excellent idea!" exclaimed Mr. Carless. "A shrewd woman is worth her weight in gold! By all means bring Miss Penkridge in–she may, as you say, make some suggestion."

Miss Penkridge, fetched into the room and duly introduced, lost no time in making a suggestion of an eminently practical nature–that as all these gentlemen had been cooped up in that stuffy police-court for two or three hours, they would be none the worse for a glass of wine, and she immediately disappeared, jingling a bunch of keys, to reappear a few minutes later in charge of the parlour-maid carrying decanters and glasses.

"A very comfortable suggestion, that, ma'am," observed Mr. Carless, bowing to his hostess over a glass of old sherry. "Your intuition does you credit! But now, gentlemen, and Miss Penkridge, straight to business! Mr. Cave, the first question I want to put to you is this: on what date did you receive the letter which you exhibited in court this morning?"

Mr. Cave produced a small pocket diary and turned over its pages.

"I can tell you that," he answered. "I made a note of it at the time. It was–yes, here we are–on the twenty-first of November."

"And you received these papers, I think you said, two days later?"

"Yes–on the twenty-third. Here is the entry."

Mr. Carless looked round at the assembled faces.

"John Ashton was murdered on the night of the twenty-second of November," he remarked significantly. "Therefore he had not been murdered when the veiled woman first met Mr. Cave for the first time, and he had been murdered when she met Mr. Cave the second time!"

There was a silence as significant as Mr. Carless' tone upon this–broken at last by Mr. Cave.

"If I may say a word or two," he remarked diffidently. "I don't understand matters about this John Ashton. The barrister who asked me questions–Mr. Millington-Bywater, is it–said that he, or somebody, had positive proof that Mr. Ashton had my papers in his possession for some time previous to his death. Is that really so?"

Mr. Carless pointed to Mr. Perkwite.

"This is the gentleman whom Mr. Millington-Bywater could have put in the box this morning to prove that," he replied. "Mr. Perkwite, of the Middle Temple–a barrister-at-law, Mr. Cave. Mr. Perkwite met Mr. Ashton some three months ago at Marseilles, and Mr. Ashton then not only asked his advice about the Ellingham affair, alleging that he knew the missing Lord Marketstoke, but showed him the papers which you have recently deposited with Mr. Methley here–which papers, Ashton alleged, were intrusted to him by Lord Marketstoke on his deathbed. Ashton, according to Mr. Perkwite, took particular care of these papers, and always carried them about with him in a pocketbook."

Mr. Cave appeared to be much exercised in thought on hearing this.

"It is, of course, absurd to say that Lord Marketstoke –myself!–intrusted papers to anyone on his deathbed, since I am very much alive," he said. "But it is, equally of course, quite possible that Ashton had my papers. Who was Ashton?"

"A man who had lived in Australia for some thirty-five or forty years at least," replied Mr. Carless, "and who recently returned to England and settled down in London, in this very square. He lived chiefly in Melbourne, but we have heard that for some four or five years he was somewhere up country. You never heard of him out there? He was evidently well known in Melbourne."

"No, I never heard of him," replied Mr. Cave. "But I don't know Melbourne very well; I know Sydney and Brisbane better. However, an idea strikes me—Ashton may have had something to do with the purloining of my letters and effects at Wirra-Worra, when I met with the accident I told you of."

"So far as we are aware," remarked Mr. Carless, "Ashton was an eminently respectable man!"

"So far as you know!" said Mr. Cave. "There is a good deal in the saving clause, I think. I have known a good many men in Australia who were highly respectable in the last stages of life who had been anything but that in their earlier ones! Of what class was this Ashton?"

"I met him, occasionally," said Methley, "though I never knew who he was until after his death. He was a very pleasant, kindly, good-humoured man—but," he added, "I should say, from his speech and manners, a man who had risen from a somewhat humble position of life. I remember noticing his hands—they were the hands of a man who at some period had done hard manual labour."

Mr. Cave smiled knowingly.

"There you are!" he said. "He had probably been a miner! Taking everything into consideration, I am inclined to believe that he was most likely one of the men, or the man, who stole my papers thirty-two years ago."

"There may be something in this," remarked Mr. Pawle, glancing uneasily at Mr. Carless. "It is a fact that the packet of letters to which Mr. Cave referred this morning as having been written by the Countess of Ellingham to Lord Marketstoke when a boy at school, was found by Mr. Viner and myself in Ashton's house, and that the locket which he also mentioned is in existence—facts which Mr. Cave will doubtless be glad to know of. But," added the old lawyer, shaking his head, "what does all this imply? That Ashton, of whom up to now we have heard nothing but good, was not only a thief, but an impostor who was endeavouring, or meant to endeavour, to palm off a bogus claimant on people, who, but for Mr. Cave's appearance and evidence, would certainly have been deceived! It is most amazing."

"Don't forget," said Viner quietly, "that Mr. Perkwite says that Ashton showed him at Marseilles a certain marriage certificate and a birth certificate."

Mr. Carless started.

"Ah!" he exclaimed. "I had forgotten that. Um! However, don't let us forget, just now, that our main object in meeting was to do something towards tracking these people who gave Mr. Cave these papers. Now, Mr. Cave, you got no information out of the woman?"

"None!" answered Mr. Cave. "I was not to ask questions, you remember."

"You took her for a gentlewoman?"

"Yes—from her speech and manner."

"Did she imply to you that she was an intermediary?"

"Yes—she spoke of someone, indefinitely, you know, for whom she was acting."

"And she told you, I think, that you had been recognized, in London, since your arrival, by someone who had known you in Australia years before?"

"Yes—certainly she told me that."

"Just let me look at that typewritten letter again, will you?" asked Mr. Carless. "It seems impossible, but we might get something out of that."

Mr. Cave handed the letter over, and once more it was passed from hand to hand: finally it fell into the hands of Miss Penkridge, who began to examine it with obvious curiosity.

"Afraid there's nothing to be got out of that!" sighed Mr. Carless. "The rogues were cunning enough to typewrite the message—if there'd been any handwriting, now, we might have had a chance! You say there was nothing on the envelope but your name, Mr. Cave?"

Mr. Cave opened his pocketbook again.

"There is the envelope," he said. "Nothing but *Mr. Cave*, as you see–that is also typewritten."

Miss Penkridge picked up the envelope as Mr. Cave tossed it across the table. She appeared to examine it carefully, but suddenly she turned to Mr. Carless.

"There *is* a clue in these things!" she exclaimed. "A plain clue! One that's plain enough to me, anyway. I could follow it up. I don't know whether you gentlemen can."

Mr. Carless, who had, up to that point, treated Miss Penkridge with good-humoured condescension, turned sharply upon her.

"What do you mean, ma'am?" he asked. "You really see something in–in a typewritten letter?"

"A great deal!" answered Miss Penkridge. "And in the stationery on which it's typed, and in the envelope in which it's inclosed. Now look here: This letter has been typed on a half-sheet of notepaper. Hold the half-sheet up to the light–what do you see? One half of the name and address of the stationer who supplied it, in watermark. What is that one half?"

Mr. Carless held the paper to the light and saw on the top line, ... "*sforth*," on the middle line, ... "*nd Stationer*" and, ... "*n Hill*" on the bottom line.

"My nephew there," went on Miss Penkridge, "knows what that would be, in full, if the other half of the sheet were here. It would be precisely what it is under the flap of this envelope–there you are! '*Bigglesforth, Bookseller and Stationer, Craven Hill.*' Everybody in this district knows Bigglesforth–we get our stationery from him. Now, Bigglesforth has not such a very big business in really expensive notepaper like this–the other half of the sheet, of course, would have a finely engraved address on it–and you can trace the owner of this paper through him, with patience and trouble.

"But here's a still better clue! Look at this typewritten letter. In it, the letter *o* occurs with frequency. Now, notice–the letter is broken, imperfect; the top left-hand curve has been chipped off. Do you mean to tell me that with time and trouble and patience you can't find out to whom that machine belongs? Taking the fact that this half-sheet of notepaper came from Bigglesforth's, of Craven Hill," concluded Miss Penkridge with emphasis, "I should say that this document–so important–came from somebody who doesn't live a million miles from here!"

Mr. Carless had followed Miss Penkridge with admiring attention, and he now rose to his feet.

"Ma'am," he exclaimed, "Mr. Viner's notion of having you to join our council has proved invaluable! I'll have that clue followed up instantly! Gentlemen, we can do no more just now–let us separate. Mr. Cave–you'll continue to be heard of at the Belfield Hotel?"

"I shall be at your service any time, Mr. Carless," responded Mr. Cave. "A telephone message will bring me at once to Lincoln's Inn Fields."

The assembly broke up, and Viner was left alone with Miss Penkridge.

"That was clever of you!" he said, admiringly. "I should never have noticed that. But–there are a lot of typewriting machines in London!"

"Not so many owned by customers of Bigglesforth's!" retorted Miss Penkridge. "I'd work it out, if I were a detective!"

The parlour-maid looked in and attracted Viner's attention.

"Mr. Felpham wants you at the telephone, sir," she said.

25
THROUGH THE TELEPHONE

Events had crowded so thick and fast upon Viner during the last day or two, that he went to the telephone fully expecting to hear of some new development. But he was scarcely prepared for his solicitor's first words.

"Viner!" said Felpham, whose voice betrayed his excitement. "Is that man Cave still with you?"

"No!" answered Viner. "Why?"

"Listen carefully," responded Felpham. "In spite of all he asserts, and his long tale this morning at the police-court, I believe he's a rank impostor! I've just had another talk with Hyde."

"Well?" demanded Viner.

"Hyde," answered Felpham, "persists that he's not mistaken. He swears that the man is Nugent Starr. He says there's no doubt of it! And he's told me of another actor, a man named George Bellingham, who's now somewhere in London, who can positively identify him as Starr. I'm going to find Bellingham this afternoon–there's some deep-laid plot in all this, and that fellow had been cleverly coached in the event of his being unexpectedly tackled.... Viner!"

"Well–I'm listening carefully," replied Viner.

"Where's this man gone?" demanded Felpham.

"To his hotel, I should think," answered Viner. "He left here just before one."

"Listen!" said Felpham. "Do you think it would be wise to post New Scotland Yard on to him–detectives, you know?"

Viner considered swiftly. In the rush of events he had
forgotten that Carless had already given instructions for
the watching of the pseudo Mr. Cave.

"Why not find this man Bellingham first?" he
suggested. "If he can prove, positively, that the fellow is
Nugent Starr, you'd have something definite to work on.
Where can Bellingham be found?"

"Hyde's given me the address of a theatrical agent in
Bedford Street who's likely to know of his whereabouts,"
replied Felpham. "I'm going over there at once. Hyde saw
Bellingham in town three weeks ago."

"Let me know at once," said Viner. "If you find
Bellingham, take him to the Belfield Hotel and contrive
to show him the man. Call me up later."

He went away from his telephone and sought Miss
Penkridge, whom he found in her room, arraying herself
for out of doors.

"Here's a new development!" he exclaimed, shutting
the door on them. "Felpham's just telephoned to say that
Hyde persists that the man who calls himself Cave is
Nugent Starr! In that case, he won't–"

Miss Penkridge interrupted her nephew with a sniff.

"My dear Richard," she said, with a note of
contemptuous impatience, "in a case like this, you don't
know who's who or who isn't who! It wouldn't surprise me
in the slightest if the man turns out to be Nugent Starr."

"How did he come by such a straight tale, then?"
asked Viner doubtfully.

"Carefully prepared–in case of need," declared Miss
Penkridge as she tied her bonnet-strings with a decisive
tug. "The whole thing's a plant!"

"That's what Felpham says," remarked Viner. "But–
where are you going?" he broke off as Miss Penkridge,
seizing an umbrella, started for the door. "Lunch is just
going in."

"My lunch can wait–I've had a biscuit and a glass of
sherry," asserted Miss Penkridge. "I'm going round to
Bigglesforth the stationer's, to follow up that clue I

suggested just now. I dare say I can do a bit of detective work as well as another, and in my opinion, Richard, there's no time to be lost. I have been blessed and endowed," continued Miss Penkridge, as she laid hold of the door-handle, "with exceedingly acute perceptions, and I saw something when I made that suggestion which I'm quite sure none of you men, with all your brains, saw!"

"What?" demanded Viner.

"I saw that my suggestion wasn't at all pleasing to the man who calls himself Cave!" exclaimed Miss Penkridge. "It was only a flash of his eye, a sudden droop at the corners of his lips–but I saw! And I saw something else, too–that he got away as quickly as ever he could after I'd made that suggestion."

Viner looked at his aunt with amused wonder. He thought she was unduly suspicious, and Miss Penkridge guessed his thoughts.

"You'll see," she said as she opened the door.

"There are going to be strange revelations, Richard Viner, my boy! You said at the beginning of this that you'd suddenly got plunged into the middle of things– well, in my opinion, we're now coming to the end of things, and I'm going to do my bit to bring it about."

With that Miss Penkridge sailed away, her step determined and her head high, and Viner, pondering many matters, went downstairs to entertain his visitors, the unlucky Hyde's sisters, with stories of the morning's proceedings and hopes of their brother's speedy acquittal. The poor ladies were of that temperament which makes its possessors clutch eagerly at any straw of hope floating on the sea of trouble, and they listened eagerly to all that their host could tell.

"Langton has an excellent memory!" declared the elder Miss Hyde. "Don't you remember, sister, what a quantity of poetical pieces he knew by heart when he was quite a child?"

"Before he was seven years of age!" said the younger sister. "And at ten he could recite the whole of the trial scene from 'The Merchant of Venice.' Oh, yes, he always had a marvellous memory! If Langton says he remembers this man in America, dear Mr. Viner, I am sure Langton will be right, and that this is the man. But what a very dreadful person to utter such terrible falsehoods!"

"And on oath!" said the elder Miss Hyde, solemnly. "On oath, sister!"

"Sad!" murmured the younger lady. "Most sad! We find London life very disturbing, dear Mr. Viner, after our quiet country existence."

"There are certainly some disturbing elements in it," admitted Viner.

Just then came another interruption; for the second time since his return from the police-court, he was summoned to the telephone. To his great surprise, the voice that hailed him was Mrs. Killenhall's.

"Is that Mr. Viner?" the voice demanded in its usual brisk, clear tones.

"Yes," answered Viner. "Is that Mrs. Killenhall?"

"Yes!" came the prompt reply. "Mr. Viner, can you be so very kind? Miss Wickham and I have come down to the City on some business connected with Mr. Ashton, and we do so want somebody's help. Can you run down at once and join us? So sorry to trouble you, but we really do want a gentleman here."

"Certainly!" responded Viner. "I'll come to you at once. But where are you?"

"Come to 23 Mirrapore Street, off Whitechapel Road," answered Mrs. Killenhall. "There is someone here who knew Mr. Ashton, and I should like you to see him. Can you come at once? And have you the address right?"

"A moment—repeat it, please," replied Viner, pulling out a memorandum book. He noted the address and spoke again: "I'll be there in half an hour, Mrs. Killenhall," he said. "Sooner, if it's possible."

"Thank you so much," responded Mrs. Killenhall's steady voice. "So good of you–good-bye for the present, then."

"Good-bye," said Viner. He hurried away into the hall, snatched up a hat, and letting himself out of the house, ran to the nearest cab-stand and beckoned to a chauffeur who often took him about. "I want to get along to Mirrapore Street, Whitechapel Road," he said, as he sprang into the car. "Do you know whereabouts it is?"

The chauffeur knitted his brows and shook his head.

"There's a sight of small streets running off Whitechapel Road, both sides, sir," he answered. "It'll be one of them–I'll find it. Mirrapore Street? Right, sir."

"Get there as quickly as possible," said Viner. "The quicker the better."

It was not until he had gone a good half of his journey that Viner began to wonder whatever it was that had taken Miss Wickham and her chaperon down to the far boundaries of the City–or, indeed, farther. Mrs. Killenhall had said the City, but Viner knew his London well enough to know that Whitechapel Road lies without the City confines. She had said, too, that a man who knew Mr. Ashton was there with her and Miss Wickham–what man, wondered Viner, and what doing in a district like that toward which he was speeding?

The chauffeur did the run to Whitechapel Road in unusually good time; it was little more than two o'clock when the car passed the parish church. But the man had gone from one end of the road to the other, from the end of High Street to the beginning of Mile End Road, without success, when he stopped and looked in at his passenger.

"Can't see no street of that name on either side, Mr. Viner," he said. "Have you got it right, sir?"

"That's the name given me," answered Viner. He pointed to a policeman slowly patrolling the side walk. "Ask him," he said. "He'll know."

The policeman, duly questioned, seemed surprised at first; then recollection evidently awoke in him.

"Mirrypoor Street?" he said. "Oh, yes! Second to your left, third to the right–nice sort o' street for a car like yours to go into, too!"

Viner overheard this and put his head out of the window.

"Why?" he demanded.

The policeman, quick to recognize a superior person, touched his helmet and stepped off the curb toward his questioner.

"Pretty low quarter down there, sir," he said, with a significant glance in the direction concerned. "If you've business that way, I should advise you to look after yourself–some queer places down those streets, sir."

"Thanks," responded Viner with a grim smile. "Go on, driver, as quick as you can, and stop at the corner of the street."

The car swung out of Whitechapel Road into a long, dismal street, the shabbiness of which increased the further the main thoroughfare was left behind; and Viner, looking right and left, saw that the small streets running off that which he was traversing were still more dismal, still more shabby. Suddenly the car twisted to the right and stopped, and Viner was aware of a long, narrow street, more gloomy than the rest, wherein various doubtful-looking individuals moved about, and groups of poorly clad children played in the gutters.

"All right," he said as he got down from the car, and the chauffeur made a grimace at the unlovely vista. "Look here–I don't want you to wait here. Go back to Whitechapel Road and hang about the end of the street we've just come down. I'll come back there to you."

"Not afraid of going down here alone, then, sir?" asked the chauffeur. "It's a bit as that policeman said."

"I'm all right," repeated Viner. "You go back and wait. I may be some time. I mayn't be long."

He turned away down the street—and in spite of his declaration, he felt that this was certainly the most doubtful place he had ever been in. There were evil and sinister faces on the sidewalks; evil and sinister eyes looking out of dirty windows; here and there a silent-footed figure went by him in the gloom of the December day with the soft step of a wild animal; here and there, men leaning against the wall, glared suspiciously at him or fixed rapacious eyes on his good clothes. There were shops in this street such as Viner had never seen the like of—shops wherein coarse, dreadful looking food was exposed for sale; and there were public-houses from which came the odour of cheap gin and bad beer and rank tobacco; an atmosphere of fried fish and something far worse hung heavily above the dirty pavements, and at every step he took Viner asked himself the same question—what on earth could Miss Wickham and Mrs. Killenhall be doing in this wretched neighbourhood?

Suddenly he came to the house he wanted—Number 23. It was just like all the other houses, of sombre grey brick, except for the fact that it looked somewhat cleaner than the rest, was furnished with blinds and curtains, and in the front downstairs window had a lower wire blind, on which was worked in tarnished gilt letters, the word *Surgery*. On the door was a brass plate, also tarnished, across which ran three lines in black:

"Dr. Martincole.
Attendance: 3 to 6 p. m.
Saturdays. 5 to 9.30 p. m."

Before Viner took the bell in hand, he glanced at the houses which flanked this East-end surgery. One was a poor-looking, meanly equipped chemist's shop; the other a second-hand clothing establishment. And comforting himself with the thought that if need arose the apparently fairly respectable proprietors of these places might reasonably be called upon for assistance, he rang the bell of Number 23 and awaited the opening of the door with considerable curiosity.

The door was opened by Mrs. Killenhall herself, and Viner's quick eye failed to notice anything in her air or manner that denoted uneasiness. She smiled and motioned him to enter, shutting the door after him as he stepped into the narrow entrance hall.

"So very good of you to come, Mr. Viner, and so quickly," she said. "You found your way all right?"

"Yes, but I'm a good deal surprised to find you and Miss Wickham in this neighbourhood," answered Viner. "This is a queer place, Mrs. Killenhall. I hope–"

"Oh, we're all right!" said Mrs. Killenhall, with a reassuring smile. "It is certainly a queer neighbourhood, but Dr. Martincole is an old friend of mine, and we're safe enough under his roof. He'll be here in a few minutes, and then–"

"This man who knew Mr. Ashton?" interrupted Viner. "Where is he?"

"Dr. Martincole will bring him in," said Mrs. Killenhall, "Come upstairs, Mr. Viner."

Viner noticed that the house through which he was led was very quiet, and larger than he should have guessed at from the street frontage. From what he could see, it was well furnished, but dark and gloomy; gloomy, too, was a back room, high up the stairs, into which Mrs. Killenhall presently showed him. There, looking somewhat anxious, sat Miss Wickham, alone.

"Here's Mr. Viner," said Mrs. Killenhall. "I'll tell Dr. Martincole he's come."

She motioned Viner to a chair and went out. But the next instant Viner swung quickly round. As the door closed, he had heard the unmistakable click of a patent lock.

26
THE DISMAL STREET

Unknown to those who had taken part in the conference at Viner's house, unknown even to Carless, who in the multiplicity of his engagements, had forgotten the instructions which he had given on the previous afternoon to Portlethwaite, a strict watch was being kept on the man around whom all the events of that morning had centred. Portlethwaite, after Methley and his client had left Carless and Driver's office, had given certain instructions to one of his fellow-clerks, a man named Millwaters, in whose prowess as a spy he had unlimited belief. Millwaters was a fellow of experience. He possessed all the qualities of a sleuth-hound and was not easily baffled in difficult adventures. In his time he had watched erring husbands and doubtful wives; he had followed more than one high-placed wrong-doer running away from the consequences of forgery or embezzlement; he had conducted secret investigations into the behaviour of persons about whom his employers wanted to know something. In person and appearance he was eminently fitted for his job—a little, inconspicuous, plain-featured man who contrived to look as if he never saw anything. And to him, knowing that he was to be thoroughly depended upon, Portlethwaite had given precise orders.

"You'll go up to Lancaster Gate tonight, Millwaters, and get a good look at that chap," Portlethwaite had told him. "Take plenty of money—I'll speak to the cashier about that—and be prepared for anything, even to following, if he bolts. Once you've seen him, you're not to lose sight of him; make sure of him last thing today and first thing tomorrow. Follow him wherever he goes, make a note of wherever he goes, and particularly of whoever he meets. And if there's need, ring me up here, and let's know what's happening, or if you want assistance."

There was no need for Millwaters to promise faithful compliance; Portlethwaite knew well enough that to put him on a trail was equivalent to putting a hound on the scent of a fox or a terrier to the run of a rat. And that evening, Millwaters, who had clever ways of his own, made himself well acquainted with the so-called Mr. Cave's appearance, and assured himself that his man had gone peacefully to rest at his hotel, and he had seen him again before breakfast next morning and had been in quiet and unobtrusive attendance upon him when, later, he visited Methley's office and subsequently walked away with Methley to the police-court. And Millwaters was in the police-court, meditatively sucking peppermint lozenges in a corner, when Mr. Cave was unexpectedly asked to give evidence; he was there, too, until Mr. Cave left the court.

Cave's remarkable story ran off Millwaters' mentality like raindrops off a steep roof. It mattered nothing to him. He did not care the value of a brass button if Cave was Earl of Ellingham or Duke of Ditchmoor; his job was to keep his eye on him, whoever he was. And so when Viner and his party went round to Markendale Square, Millwaters slunk along in their rear, and at a corner of the Square he remained, lounging about, until his quarry reappeared. Two or three of the other men came out with Cave, but Millwaters noticed that Cave immediately separated from them. He was evidently impressing upon them that he was in a great hurry about something or other, and sped away from them, Millwaters's cold eye upon him. And within a minute Millwaters had observed what seemed to him highly suspicious circumstance– Cave, on leaving the others, had shot off down a side-street in the direction of Lancaster Gate, but as soon as he was out of sight of Markendale Square, had doubled in his tracks, hurried down another turning and sped away as fast as he could walk towards Paddington Station.

Millwaters, shorter in the leg than the tall man in front, had to hurry to keep him in sight, but he was never far behind as Cave hastened along Craven Road and made for the terminus. Once or twice in this chase the quarry lifted a hand to an approaching taxicab, only to find each was engaged; it was not until he and his pursuer were in front of the Great Western Hotel that Cave found an empty cab, hailed it, and sprang in. Millwaters grinned quietly at that; he was used to this sort of chase, and he had memorized car and number before Cave had been driven off. It was a mere detail to charter the next, and to give a quiet word and wink to its chauffeur, who was opening its door for Millwaters when a third person came gently alongside and tapped the clerk's shoulder. Millwaters turned sharply and encountered Mr. Perkwite's shrewd eyes.

"All right, Millwaters!" said the barrister. "I know what you're after! I'm after the same bird. We'll go together."

Millwaters knew Mr. Perkwite very well as a promising young barrister whom Carless and Driver sometimes favoured with briefs. Mr. Perkwite's presence did not disturb him; he moved into the farther corner, and Mr. Perkwite slipped inside. The car moved off in pursuit of the one in front.

"So you're on that game, Mr. Perkwite?" remarked Millwaters. "Ah! And who might have got you on to it, if one may ask?"

"You know that I was at your people's office yesterday?" said Perkwite.

"Saw you there," replied Millwaters.

"It was about this business," said the barrister. "Did you see me in the police-court this morning?"

"I did–listening for all you were worth," answered the clerk.

"And I dare say you saw me go with the rest of them to Mr. Viner's, in Markendale Square?" said Perkwite.

"Right again, sir," assented Millwaters. "I did."

"This fellow in front," observed Perkwite, "made some statements at Viner's, in answer to your principal, Mr. Carless, which incline me to the opinion that he's an impostor in spite of his carefully concocted stories."

"Shouldn't wonder, Mr. Perkwite." said Millwaters. "But that's not my business. My job is to keep him under observation."

"That's what I set out to do when I came out of Viner's," said the barrister. "He's up to something. He assured us as we left the house that he'd a most pressing engagement at his hotel in Lancaster Gate; the next minute, happening to glance down a side-street, I saw him cutting off in the direction of Paddington. And now he's evidently making for the City."

"Well, I'm after him," remarked Millwaters. He leaned out of his window, called the chauffeur, and gave him some further instructions. "Intelligent chap, this, Mr. Perkwite," he said as he sat down again. "He understands–some of 'em are poor hands at this sort of game."

"You're a pretty good hand yourself, I think?" suggested the barrister, with a smile.

"Ought to be," said Millwaters. "Had plenty of experience, anyway."

It seemed to Perkwite that his companion kept no particular observation on the car in front as it sped along to and through the northern edge of the City and beyond. But Millwaters woke to action as their own car progressed up Whitechapel Road, and suddenly he gave a warning word to the barrister and a smart tap on the window behind their driver. The car came to a halt by the curb; and Millwaters, slipping out, pushed some money into the man's hand and drew Perkwite amongst the people who were crowding the sidewalk. The barrister looked in front and around and seemed at a loss.

"Where is he?" he asked. "Hang it, I've lost him!"

"I haven't!" said Millwaters. "He left his car before we left ours. Our man knew what he was after–he slowed up and passed him until I saw where he went." He twisted Perkwite round and pointed to the mouth of a street which they had just passed.

"He's gone down there," he said. "Nice neighbourhood, too! I know something of it. Now, Mr. Perkwite, if you please, we'll separate. You take the right of that street–I'll take the left. Keep a look out for my gentleman's Homburg hat–grey, with a black band–and keep the tail of your eye on me, too."

Cave's headgear was easily followed down the squalid street. Its owner went swiftly ahead, with Millwaters in pursuit on one pavement, and the barrister on the other, until he finally turned into a narrower and shabbier thoroughfare. Then the clerk hurried across the road, attracted Perkwite's attention, winked at him as he passed without checking his pace, and whispered two or three words.

"Wait–by the street-corner!"

Perkwite pulled up, and Millwaters went down the dismal street in pursuit of the Homburg hat. This excellent indication of its owner's presence suddenly vanished from Perkwite's sight, and presently Millwaters came back.

"Ran him to earth–for the time being, anyway," he said. "He's gone into a surgery down there–a Dr. Martincole's. Number 23–brass plate on door–next to a drug-shop. Suspicious sort of spot, altogether."

"Well?" demanded Perkwite. "What next? You know best, Millwaters."

The clerk jerked a thumb down the side of the dismal street on which they were standing.

"There's a public-house down there," he said, "almost opposite this surgery. Fairly decent place for this neighbourhood–bar-parlour looking out on the street.

Better slip in there and look quietly out. But remember, Mr. Perkwite–don't seem to be watching anything. We're just going in for a bottle of ale, and talking business together.

"Whatever you recommend," said Perkwite.

He followed his companion down the street to the tavern, a joyless and shabby place, the bar-parlour of which, a dark and smoke-stained room was just then empty, and looked over its torn half-blind across the way.

"Certainly a queer place for a man who professes to be a peer of the realm to visit!" he muttered. "Well, now, what do you propose to do, Millwaters?"

"Hang about here and watch," whispered the clerk. "Look out!"

A face, heavy and bloated, appeared at a hatch-window at the back of the room, and a gruff voice made itself heard.

"Any orders, gents?"

"Two bottles o' Bass, gov'nor," responded Millwaters promptly, dropping into colloquial Cockney speech. He turned to Perkwite and winked. "Well, an' wot abaht this 'ere bit o' business as I've come rahnd abaht, Mister?" he went on, nudging his companion, in free-and-easy style.

"Yer see, it's this ere wy wiv us–if yer can let us have that there stuff reasonable, d'yer see–" He drew Perkwite over to the window and began to whisper, "That'll satisfy him," he said with a sharp glance at the little room behind the hatch where the landlord was drawing corks. "He'll think we're doing a bit of trade, so we've nothing to do but stand in this window and keep an eye on the street. Out of this I'm not going till I see whether that fellow comes out or stops in!"

Some time had passed, and Millwaters had been obliged to repeat his order for bottled Bass before anything took place in the street outside. Suddenly he touched his companion's elbow.

"Here's a taxicab coming along and slowing up for somewhere about here," he whispered. "And–Lord, if there aren't two ladies in it–in a spot like this! And–whew!" he went on excitedly. "Do you see 'em, Mr. Perkwite? The young un's Miss Wickham, who came to our office about this Ashton affair. I don't know who the old un is–but she evidently knows her way."

The berry-faced landlord had now shut down the hatch, and his two bar-parlour customers were alone and unobserved. Perkwite drew away from the window, pulling Millwaters by the sleeve.

"Careful!" he said. "There's something seriously wrong here, Millwaters! What's Miss Wickham being brought down here for? See, they've gone into that surgery, and the car's going off. Look here–we've got to do something, and at once!"

But Millwaters shook his head.

"Not my job, Mr. Perkwite!" he answered. "My business is with the man–Cave! I've nothing to do with Miss Wickham, sir, nor with the old lady that's taken her in there. Cave's my mark! Queer that the young lady's gone there, no doubt, but–no affair of mine."

"It's going to be an affair of mine, then," said Perkwite. "I'm going off to the police!"

Millwaters put out a detaining hand.

"Don't, Mr. Perkwite!" he said. "To get police into a quarter like this is as bad as putting a light to dry straw. I'll tell you a better plan than that, sir–find the nearest telephone-box and call up our people–call Mr. Carless, tell him what you've seen and get him to come down and bring somebody with him. That'll be far better than calling the police in."

"Give me your telephone-number, then," said Perkwite, "and keep a strict watch while I'm away."

Millwaters repeated some figures and a letter, and Perkwite ran off up the street and toward the Whitechapel Road, anxiously seeking for a telephone booth. It was not until he had got into the main thoroughfare that he found one; he then had some slight delay in getting in communication with Carless and Driver's office; twenty minutes had elapsed by the time he got back to the dismal street. At its corner he encountered Millwaters, lounging about hands in pockets. Millwaters wagged his head.

"Here's another queer go!" he said. "There's been another arrival at Number 23–not five minutes since. Another of our little lot!"

"Who?" demanded Perkwite.

"Viner!" replied Millwaters. "Came peeping and perking along the street, took a glimpse of the premises and the adjacent purlieus, rang at Number 23, and was let in by–the party that came with Miss Wickham! Now, whatever can he be doing there, Mr. Perkwite?"

"Whatever can any of them be doing there!" muttered Perkwite. "Viner! What business can he have in this place? It seems–by George, Millwaters," he suddenly exclaimed, "what if this is some infernal plant–trap– something of that sort? Do you know, in spite of what you say, I really think we ought to get hold of the nearest police and tell them–"

"Wait, Mr. Perkwite!" counselled Millwaters. "Our governor is a pretty cute and smart sort, and he's vastly interested in this Miss Wickham; so Portlethwaite and he'll be on their way down here now, hot foot; and with help, too, if he thinks she's in any danger. Now, *he* can go straight to that door and demand to see her, and–"

"Why can't we?" interrupted Perkwite. "I'd do it! Lord, man, she may be in real peril–"

"Not while Viner's in there," said Millwaters quietly. "I might possibly have gone and rung the bell myself, but for that. But Viner's in there–wait!"

And Perkwite waited, chafing, at the corner of the dismal street, until a quarter of an hour had passed. Then a car came hurrying along and pulled up as Millwaters and his companion were reached, and from it sprang Mr. Carless, Lord Ellingham and two men in plain-clothes, at the sight of whom Perkwite heaved a huge sigh of intense relief.

27

THE BACK WAY

Viner was so sure that the sound which he had heard on Mrs. Killenhall's retirement was that caused by the turning of a key or slipping of a lock in the door by which he had entered, that before speaking to Miss Wickham he instantly stepped back and tried it. To his astonishment it opened readily, but the anteroom outside was empty; Mrs. Killenhall had evidently walked straight through it and disappeared.

"That's odd!" he said, turning to Miss Wickham. "I distinctly thought I heard something like the snap of a lock, or a bolt or something. Didn't you?"

"I certainly heard a sound of that sort," admitted Miss Wickham. "But–the door's open, isn't it?"

"Yes–that is so," answered Viner, who was distinctly puzzled. "Yet–but then, all this seems very odd. When did you come down here?"

"About an hour ago," replied Miss Wickham, "in a hurry."

"Do you know why?" asked Viner.

"To see a Dr. Martincole, who is to tell us something about Mr. Ashton," replied his fellow-sharer in these strange quarters. "Didn't Mrs. Killenhall ask you to come down for the same purpose, Mr. Viner?"

Viner, before he replied, looked round the room. Considering the extreme shabbiness and squalour of the surrounding district, he was greatly surprised to find that the apartment in which he and Miss Wickham waited was extremely well furnished, if in an old-fashioned and rather heavy way. The walls were panelled in dark, age-stained oak, to the height of several feet; above the panelling were arranged good oil pictures, which Viner would have liked to examine at his leisure; here and there, in cabinets, were many promising curiosities; there were old silver and brass things, and a shelf or two of well-bound books—altogether the place and its effects were certainly not what Viner had expected to find in such a quarter.

"Yes," he said at last, turning to his companion, "that's what I was brought here for. Well—have you seen this doctor?"

"No," answered Miss Wickham. "Not yet."

"Know anything about him?" suggested Viner.

"Nothing whatever! I have heard of him," said Miss Wickham with a glance of surprise. "I suppose he—somehow—got into touch with Miss Killenhall."

"Queer!" remarked Viner. "And why doesn't he come in?"

Then, resolved to know more, he walked into the anteroom, and after a look round it, tried the door by which Mrs. Killenhall had admitted him after coming up the stairs from the street; a second later he went back to Miss Wickham and shook his head.

"It's just as I supposed," he remarked quietly. "We're trapped! Anyway, the door of that anteroom is locked—and it's a strong lock. There's something wrong."

The girl started, and paled a little, but Viner saw at once that she was not likely to be seriously frightened, and presently she laughed.

"How very queer!" she said. "But—perhaps Mrs. Killenhall turned the key in the outer lock so that no—patients, or other callers, perhaps—should come in?"

"Sorry, but that doesn't strike me as a good suggestion," replied Viner. "I'm going to have a look at that window!"

The one window of the room, a long, low one, was set high in the wall, above the panelling; Viner had to climb on a bookcase to get at it. And when he had reached it, he found it to be securely fastened, and to have in front of it, at a distance of no more than a yard, a blank whitewashed wall which evidently rose from a passage between that and the next house.

"I don't like the look of this at all!" he said as he got down from the bookcase. "It seems to me that we might be kept here for a long time."

Miss Wickham showed more astonishment than fear.

"But why should anyone want to keep us here for any time?" she asked. "What's it mean?"

"I wish I knew!" exclaimed Viner. He pulled out his watch and made a mental note of the time. "We're being kept much longer than we should be in any ordinary case," he remarked.

"Of course!" admitted Miss Wickham. "Well past three o'clock, isn't it? If we're delayed much longer, Mrs. Killenhall will be too late for the bank."

"What bank?" asked Viner.

"My bank. I always give Mrs. Killenhall a check for the weekly bills every Friday, and as we were coming through the City to get here, she said, just before we left home, that I might as well give her the check and she could call and cash it as we drove back. And," concluded Miss Wickham, "the bank closes at four."

Viner began to be suspicious.

"Look here!" he said suddenly. "Don't think me inquisitive, but what was the amount of the check you gave her?"

"There was no amount stated," replied Miss Wickham. "I always give her a blank check–signed, of course–and she fills in the amount herself. It varies according to what she wants."

Without expressing any opinion on the wisdom of handing checks to other people on this plan, Viner turned to Miss Wickham with a further question.

"Do you know anything about Mrs. Killenhall's movements this morning?" he asked. "Did she go out anywhere?"

"Yes," replied Miss Wickham. "She went to the police-court, to hear the proceedings against Mr. Hyde. She wanted me to go, but I wouldn't–I dislike that sort of thing. She was there all the morning."

"So was I," said Viner. "I didn't see her. But the place was crowded."

"And she was veiled," remarked Miss Wickham. "Naturally, she didn't want people to see her in a place like that."

"Do you know whether she went to the previous sitting? I mean when Hyde was brought up the first time?" inquired Viner. "I remember there were some veiled ladies there–and at the coroner's inquest, too."

"She was at the coroner's inquest, I know," replied Miss Wickham. "I don't know about the other time."

Viner made no remark, and Miss Wickham suddenly lowered her voice and bent nearer to him.

"Why?" she asked. "Are you–suspecting Mrs. Killenhall of anything, Mr. Viner?"

Viner gave her a quick glance.

"Are you?" he said in low tones.

Miss Wickham waved a hand towards the anteroom.

"Well!" she whispered. "What's it look like? She brings me down here in a hurry, on a message which I myself never heard nor saw delivered in any way; after I get here, you are fetched–and here we are! And–where is she?"

"And–possibly a much more pertinent question," said Viner, "where is this Dr. Martincole? Look here: this is a well-furnished room; those pictures are good; there are many valuable things here; yet the man who practises here is only in attendance for an hour or two in an afternoon, and once a week for rather longer in the evening. He can't earn much here; certainly an East End doctor could not afford to buy things like this or that. Do you know what I think? I think this man is some West End man, who for purposes of his own has this place down here–a man who probably lives a double life, and may possibly be mixed up in some nefarious practices. And so I propose, as we've waited long enough, to get out of it, and I'm going to smash that window and yell as loud as I can–somebody will hear it!"

Miss Wickham pointed to a door in the oak panelling, a door set in a corner of the room, across which hung a heavy curtain of red plush, only halfdrawn.

"There's a door there," she remarked, "but I suppose it's only a cupboard."

"Sure to be," said Viner. "However, we'll see." He went across, drew the curtain aside, tried the door, looked within, and uttered an exclamation. "I say!" he called back. "Stairs!"

Miss Wickham came across and looked past his shoulder. There was certainly the head of a staircase before him, and a few stairs to be seen before darkness swallowed up the rest–but the darkness was deep and the atmosphere that came up from below decidedly musty.

"Are you going down there?" she asked. "I don't like it!"

"It seems our only chance," answered Viner. He looked back into the room, and seeing some wax candles standing on a writing-table, seized one and lighted it. "Come along!" he said. "Let's get out of this altogether."

Miss Wickham gathered up her skirts and followed down the stairs, Viner going cautiously in front, with the light held before him in such a fashion that he could see every step. At a turn in the stairway he came across a door, and opening it, saw that it stood at the end of a narrow passage running through the house; at the farther end of the passage he recognized an oak cabinet which he had noticed when Mrs. Killenhall first admitted him.

"I see how these people, whoever they are, manage matters," he remarked over his shoulder as he led his companion forward. "This place has a front and a back entrance. If you don't want to be seen, you know, well, it's convenient. We're approaching the back–and here it is."

The stairs came to an end deep down in the house, terminating in a door which Viner, after leaving his silver-sticked candle, only blown out, on the last step, carefully opened. There before him lay a narrow whitewashed yard, at the end of which they could see a street, evidently pretty much like the rest of the streets in that district. But in the yard a pale-cheeked, sharp-eyed urchin was feeding a couple of rabbits in a wire-faced soap-box, and him Viner immediately hailed.

"You're a smart-looking lad," he said. "Would you like five shillings? Well, have you seen Dr. Martincole this afternoon? You know, the doctor who comes to the house behind us?"

"See him go out abaht an hour ago, guv'nor–wiv anuvver gent," said the lad eagerly, his bright eyes wavering between Viner's face and the hand which he had thrust in his pocket. He pointed to the distant entrance of the yard. "Went aht that way, they did."

"Ah! And what was the other gentleman like?" asked Viner.

"Swell!" answered the informant. "Proper swell, he was!"

"And Dr. Martincole?" Viner continued. "You've seen him many a time, of course. Now what's he like!"

"He's a tall gentleman," said the boy, after some evidently painful thought.

"Yes, but what else–has he got a beard?" asked Viner.

"Couldn't tell you that, guv'nor, d'yer see," said the lad, "'cause he's one o' them gents what allus wears a white silk handkercher abaht his face–up to his eyes. But he's a big man–wears black clothes."

Viner gave the boy his promised reward, and was passing on when Miss Wickham touched his arm.

"Ask if he's seen a lady go out this way," she said. "That's equally important."

The boy, duly questioned nodded his head.

"I see Mrs. Killerby go out not so long since," he answered. "Her what used to live here one time. Know her well enough."

"Come along!" muttered Viner. "We've hit it! Mrs. Killerby–who is Mrs. Killenhall–used to live here at one time! Good–which means very bad, considering that without doubt the doctor who wears a white silk handkerchief about his face is the muffled man of Lonsdale Passage. Miss Wickham, something has alarmed these birds and they've flown."

"But why were we brought here?" asked Miss Wickham.

"I've an idea as to why you were," said Viner, "and I propose to find out at once if I'm right. Let's get away, find a taxicab, and go to your–but, good heavens!" he went on, breaking off as two men came into the yard. "Here's one of Carless' clerks, and Perkwite the barrister.–What are you doing here?" he demanded, as Millwaters and Perkwite hurried up. "Are you after anybody along there–in that house–the one at the end?"

"We're after a good many things and people in Dr. Martincole's place, Mr. Viner," answered Millwaters. "Mr. Perkwite and I traced Mr. Cave here early in the afternoon; he went in, but he's never come out; we saw you enter–here you are. We saw Miss Wickham and Mrs. Killenhall–there's Miss Wickham, but where's the other lady? And where–"

Viner stopped the clerk's questions with a glance, and he laughed a little as he gave him his answer.

"My dear fellow," he said, "you should have posted somebody at the back here. Why, we don't quite know yet, but Miss Wickham and myself were trapped in there. As for Cave, he must be the man who went away with Martincole. As for Mrs. Killenhall, she too has gone. That boy down there saw all three go, some time ago, while we were locked up. But–what made you watch these people?"

"We followed Cave," said Perkwite, "because Millwaters had been ordered to do so, and because I considered his conduct mysterious. Then, when we saw what was going on here,–your arrival following on that of Miss Wickham and Mrs. Killenhall,–we telephoned for Mr. Carless and more help. Carless and Lord Ellingham, and a couple of detectives, are at the front now. Millwaters and I heard from a denizen of these unlovely parts that there was a back entrance. We'd tried in vain for admittance at the front–"

"But they've got in now, Mr. Perkwite!" exclaimed Millwaters suddenly. "See, there's Mr. Carless at a back window, waving to us to come in. I suppose we can get in by the back, Mr. Viner?"

"Yes–if you like to take the risk of entering people's houses without permission!" said Viner sardonically. "I don't think you'll find anybody or anything there. As for Miss Wickham and myself, we've an engagement elsewhere."

He hurried his companion away, through the street on which they emerged from the whitewashed yard, and out into the Whitechapel Road; he hurried her, too, into the first taxicab which came along empty.

"Now," he said, as they stepped in, "tell this man the name of your bank, and let him go there, quick!"

28
THE TRUTH

Four o'clock had struck, and the doors of the bank were closed when Miss Wickham and Viner hurried up to it, but there was a private entrance at the side, and the man who answered their summons made no difficulty about admitting them when Miss Wickham said who she was. And within a few minutes they were closeted with a manager, who, surprised when they entered, was astonished before many words had been exchanged. For during their dash from the Whitechapel streets Viner had coached his companion as to the questions he wished her to put on arrival at the bank, and she went straight to the point.

"I wanted to know if my companion, Mrs. Killenhall, had called here this afternoon?" begun Miss Wickham.

"She has," answered the manager. "I happened to see her, and I attended to her myself."

"Did she present a check from me?" inquired Miss Wickham.

"Certainly—and I cashed it," said the manager. He gave his customer and her companion a look of interrogation which had a good deal of surprise in it.

"Why?" he continued, glancing at Miss Wickham, "wasn't it in order?"

"That," replied Miss Wickham, "depends upon the amount."

"The amount!" he exclaimed. "You know—if the drawer! It was for ten thousand pounds!"

"Then Mrs. Killenhall has done me, or you, out of that," said Miss Wickham. "The check I gave her was to have been filled up for the amount of the usual weekly bills–twenty pounds or so. Ten thousand? Ridiculous!"

"But–it all seemed in order!" exclaimed the concerned manager. "She was as plausible, and all that–and really, you know, Miss Wickham, we know her very well–and, in addition to that, you have a very large balance lying here. Mrs. Killenhall merely mentioned that you wanted this amount, in notes, and that she had called for it–and of course, I cashed the check–your check, remember!–at once."

"I hadn't filled in the amount," remarked Miss Wickham.

"Mrs. Killenhall had often presented checks bearing your signature in which you hadn't filled in the amount," said the manager. "There was nothing unusual, I assure you, in any detail of the affair."

"The most important detail, now," observed Viner dryly, "is to find Mrs. Killenhall."

The manager, who was obviously filled with amazement at Mrs. Killenhall's audacity, looked from one to the other of his visitors, as if he could scarcely credit their suggestion.

"You really mean me to believe that Mrs. Killenhall has got ten thousand pounds out of Miss Wickham by a trick?" he asked, fixing his gaze at last on Viner.

"What I really mean you to believe," said Viner, rising, "is that a rapid series of events this afternoon has proved to me that Mrs. Killenhall is one of a gang who are responsible for the murder of John Ashton, who stole his diamond and certain papers, and who have endeavoured, very cleverly, to foist one of their number, a scoundrelly clever actor, on the public, as a peer of the realm who had been missing. Mrs. Killenhall–who has another name–probably got wind of possible detection about noon today, and took advantage of Miss Wickham's habit of giving her a weekly check, to provide herself with ample funds. That's really about the truth–and I think Miss Wickham and I had better be seeing the police."

"The very best thing you can do!" responded the manager with alacrity. "And take my advice and go straight to headquarters–go to New Scotland Yard. Just think what this woman–and her accomplices–could do! If she or they had one hour's start of you, they can have already put a good distance between themselves and London; they can be halfway to Dover, or Harwich, or Southampton. And therefore–"

"And therefore all the more reason why we should set somebody on their trail," interrupted Viner, and hurried Miss Wickham out of the manager's room and away to the taxicab which he had purposely kept in waiting. "I don't think Mrs. Killenhall, or Killerby, or whatever her name is, will have hurried away as quickly as all that," he remarked as they sped along toward Whitehall. "My own idea is that, having got hold of your money, she'll probably have made for the headquarters of this precious gang, she and they are sure to have one, for I should say the place in Whitechapel was only an outpost,–and they'll be better able to arrange an escape from there than she would to make an immediate flight. She–but what are you thinking?"

"That I seem to be involved, somehow, in a very strange and curious combination of things," answered Miss Wickham.

"Just so!" agreed Viner. "So do I–and I was literally pitchforked into the very midst of it all by sheer accident. If I hadn't happened to go out for a late stroll on the night on which it began, I should never have–but here we are!"

The official of the Criminal Investigation Department with whom they were shortly closeted, listened carefully and silently to Viner's account of all that had happened. He was one of those never-to-be-sufficiently-praised individuals who never interrupt and always understand, and at the close of Viner's story he said exactly what the narrator was thinking. "The real truth of all this, Mr. Viner," he said, "is that this is probably one of the last chapters in the history of the Lonsdale Passage murder. For if you find this woman and the men who are undoubtedly her accomplices, you will most likely have found, in one or other of them, the murderer of John Ashton!"

"Precisely!" agreed Viner. "Precisely!"

The official rose from his seat and turned to the door.

"Drillford, of your nearest police-station, had this case in charge," he remarked. "I'll just call him on the telephone."

He left the room and was away for several minutes; when he returned there was something like a smile on his face.

"If you and Miss Wickham will drive along and see Drillford, Mr. Viner," he said. "I think you'll find he's some news for you."

"Has he told it to you?" demanded Viner.

"Well—just a little," answered the official with another smile. "But I won't rob him of the pleasure of telling you himself. You ought to be disappointed. However, I'll just tell you enough to whet your appetite for more—Drillford is confident that he's just arrested the real man! No—no more!" he added, with a laugh. "You'll run up there in twenty minutes."

Drillford, cool and confident as ever, was alone in his office when Viner and his companion were shown in. He looked at Miss Wickham with considerable curiosity as he handed her a chair, and Viner noticed that the bow he made her was unusually respectful. But he immediately plunged into the pertinent subject, and turned to Viner with a laugh of self-deprecation.

"Well, Mr. Viner!" he said. "You were right, and I was wrong. It wasn't that young fellow Hyde who killed Mr. Ashton. And now that I know who did, I don't mind saying that I'm jolly glad that his innocence will be established."

"But do you know who did?" asked Viner eagerly.

"I do!" answered Drillford.

"Who, then?" exclaimed Viner.

"He's in the cells at the back, now," said Drillford, "and I only hope he's not one of those chaps who are so clever that they can secrete poison to the very last moment and then cheat the gallows, for now that I know as much as I do, I should say he's as pretty a specimen of the accomplished scoundrel as ever put on fine clothes. Dr. Cortelyon, of your square!"

This sudden and surprising revelation, made in ordinary matter-of-fact tones, produced different effects on the two people to whom it was made. Viner, after a start and a smothered exclamation, stared silently at Drillford as if he scarcely comprehended his meaning. But Miss Wickham, with a quick flush which evidently denoted suddenly-awakened recollection, broke into words.

"Dr. Cortelyon!" she exclaimed. "Ah–I remember now. Mr. Ashton once told me, in quite a casual way as we were passing through the square, that he had known Dr. Cortelyon in Australia, years and years ago!"

Drillford glanced at Viner and smiled.

"I wish you'd remembered that little matter before, Miss Wickham!" he said. "It might have saved a lot of trouble. Well–Cortelyon's the man! And it all came about quite suddenly, this afternoon. Through your aunt, Mr. Viner–Miss Penkridge. Smart lady, sir!"

"My aunt!" exclaimed Viner. "Why, how on earth–"

"Some of your gentlemen had a conference with that fellow Cave at your house, after you left court this morning," said Drillford. "Miss Penkridge was present. Cave told more of his cock-and-bull story, and produced a certain letter which he said had been handed to him at the hotel he'd put up at. All that, and all the stuff he told at the police-court, was bluff–carefully concocted by himself and Cortelyon in case Cave was ever put in a tight corner. Now, according to what she tells me, Miss Penkridge immediately spotted something about that letter which none of you gentlemen were clever enough to see–"

"I know!" interrupted Viner. "She saw that the envelope and paper had been supplied by Bigglesforth, of Craven Gardens, and that a certain letter in the typewriter which had been used was defective."

"Just so," laughed Drillford, "and so, being, as I say, a smart woman, she went round to Bigglesforth, got him to herself, and made some inquiries. And–it's very queer, Mr. Viner, how some of these apparently intricate cases are easily solved by one chance discovery!–she hadn't been talking to Bigglesforth ten minutes before she was on the right track. Bigglesforth, when he'd got to know the main features of the case, was willing enough to help, and your aunt immediately brought him round here to see me. And I knew at once that we'd got right there!"

"Yes–but how, exactly?" asked Viner.

"Bigglesforth," answered Drillford, "told me that he'd supplied stationery to Dr. Cortelyon for some time, and he'd no doubt that the paper and envelope described by Miss Penkridge was some which he'd specially secured for the Doctor. But he told something far more important: Six months ago Cortelyon went to Bigglesforth and asked him if he could get him a good second-hand typewriter. Now, Bigglesforth had a very good one for which he'd no use, and he at once sold it to Cortelyon. Bigglesforth didn't mention the matter to his customer, for the machine was perfect in all other respects, but one of the letters was defective–broken. That was the same letter, Mr. Viner, which was defective in the document which Cave showed to you gentlemen and spoke of previously in court!"

"Extraordinary!" muttered Viner. "What a piece of luck!"

"No, sir!" said Drillford, stoutly. "No luck at all–just a bit of good common-sense thinking on the part of a shrewd woman. But you'll want to know what we did. I was so absolutely certain of the truth of Miss Penkridge's theory that I immediately made preparations for a descent on Cortelyon's house. I got a number of our best men–detectives, of course–and we went round to Markendale Square, back and front. Inquiry showed that Cortelyon was out, but we'd scarcely got that fact ascertained when he drove up in a taxicab with Cave himself. They hurriedly entered the house–I myself was watching from a good point of vantage, and I saw that both men were, to say the least, anxious and excited. Then I began to make final preparations. But before I'd finished telling my men exactly what to do, another party drove up–your companion, Miss Wickham, Mrs. Killenhall. She too entered. Then I moved–quick. Some of us went to the front–I with the others went in by the back. We made straight for Cortelyon's surgery, and we were on him and the other two before they'd time to move, literally. The two men certainly tried to draw revolvers, but we were too many for 'em, and as they'd tried that game, I had 'em handcuffed there and then. It was all an affair of a moment–and of course, they saw it was all up. Now, equally of course, Mr. Viner, in all these cases, in my experience, the subordinates immediately try to save their own skins by denouncing the principal, and it was so in this instance. Mrs. Killenhall and Cave at once denounced Cortelyon as the mainspring, and the woman, who's a regular coward, got me aside and offered to turn King's evidence, and whispered that Cortelyon actually killed Ashton himself, unaided, as he let him out of his back door into Lonsdale Passage!"

"So–that's settled!" exclaimed Viner.

"Yes, I think so," agreed Drillford. "Well, we brought 'em all here, and charged 'em, and examined 'em. Nothing much on Cave, who, of course, is precisely what Hyde said he was–a man named Nugent Starr, an old actor–if he was as good a performer on the stage as he is in private life, he ought to have done well. But on Mrs. Killenhall we found ten thousand pounds in Bank of England notes, and one or two letters from Cortelyon, which she was a fool for keeping, for they clearly prove that she was an accessory. And on Cortelyon we'd a big find! That diamond that Ashton used to carry about, the other ring that Ashton was wearing when he was murdered, and—perhaps most important of all–certain papers which he'd no doubt taken from Ashton's body."

"What are they?" demanded Viner.

Drillford glanced at Miss Wickham.

"Well," he said, "I've only just had time to glance at them, but I should say that they affect Miss Wickham in a very surprising fashion, and I shall be glad to hand them over to her solicitors as soon as they come for them. They're birth certificates, burial certificates, marriage certificates, and a complete memorandum of a certain case, evidently written out with great care by Ashton himself. And of course, knowing what I do now, it's very clear to me how Ashton's murder came about. Cortelyon knew that if Ashton was out of the way, and he himself in possession of the papers, he could use some, suppress others, and foist off an accomplice of his own as claimant to a title which, from what I've seen, appears without doubt to belong to–"

Drillford was again glancing at Miss Wickham, but Viner contrived to stop any further revelations and got to his feet.

"Extraordinary!" he said. "But–my aunt? Where is she?"

"She remained here until we'd safely caged the birds," answered Drillford. "Then she said she'd go home. And I suppose you'll find her there."

Viner took his companion away from the police-station in silence. But at the end of the street Miss Wickham looked back.

"Are those three people really locked up–in cells–close by where we were sitting with the inspector?" she asked.

"Just so," answered Viner.

"And will they all be hanged?" she whispered.

"I sincerely hope one will!" exclaimed Viner.

"What," she inquired, "did the inspector mean about the papers found on Dr. Cortelyon? I have some uneasy feeling that–"

"I think you'd better wait," said Viner. "There'll have to be some queer explanations. We must let Mr. Pawle and Mr. Carless know of what's happened–they're the proper people to deal with this affair."

And then, as they turned into Markendale Square, they saw Mr. Pawle and Mr. Carless, who, with Lord Ellingham, were hurrying from Miss Wickham's house in the direction of Viner's. Mr. Carless quickened his pace and came toward them.

"I was so upset when I heard from Perkwite that Miss Wickham has been in that house in Whitechapel," he said, "that, on learning she'd gone off with you, Viner, Lord Ellingham and I drove to Pawle's and brought him on here to learn if she'd got home and what had happened."

"What had happened?" demanded Mr. Pawle. "What is it, Viner?"

Viner gathered them round him with a look.

"This has happened!" he said. "The whole thing's solved. Ashton's murderer is found, and he and his accomplices are under lock and key. Listen, and I'll tell you all that's been done since one o'clock, up here–while we've been at the other end of the town. But I'll only give you an outline. Well, then–"

The three men listened in dead silence until Viner had repeated Drillford's story; then Mr. Pawle glanced round at the window of Viner's house.

"Miss Penkridge, by all that's wonderful!" he said in a deep voice. "Most extraordinary! Where is she?"

"At home, I should imagine," answered Viner with a laugh.

"Then, my dear sir, by all means let us pay our respects to her!" said Mr. Pawle. "A tribute!"

"By all means!" exclaimed Mr. Carless. "A just tribute—richly deserved!"

"I should like to add my small quota," said Lord Ellingham.

Viner led the way into his house and to the drawing-room. Miss Penkridge, in her best cap, was calmly dispensing tea to the two Hyde sisters, who were regarding her with obvious admiration. She looked round on her nephew and the flood of callers as if to ask what most of them were doing there. And Viner, knowing Miss Penkridge's peculiar humour, rose to the occasion.

"My dear aunt," he said in a hushed voice, "these gentlemen, having heard of your extraordinary achievement this afternoon, have come to lay at your feet their united tribute of—"

Miss Penkridge shot a warning glance through her steel-rimmed spectacles.

"Don't talk nonsense, Richard!" she exclaimed sharply. "Ring the bell for more cups and saucers!"

29
WHO IS TO TELL HER?

But Viner, instead of ordering the teacups, whispered a word or two to Miss Penkridge, and then beckoned Lord Ellingham and the two solicitors to follow him out of the room. He silently led them to his study and closed the door.

"Miss Wickham will be all right for a while under my aunt's care," he said, with a smile that had a certain meaning in it which was not lost on Mr. Pawle or on Mr. Carless, "but there are matters connected with her which ought not to wait, even for ten minutes hanging round Miss Penkridge's tea-table. Now, I have been thrown headlong into this case, and like all the rest of you, I am pretty well acquainted with it. And I take it that now that the murder of Ashton has been solved, the real question is—what is the truth about the young lady who was certainly his ward?"

"That is right!" exclaimed Mr. Pawle. "Carless—and Lord Ellingham—I am sure, agree with me."

"Absolutely—as far as I'm concerned," asserted Mr. Carless. "His Lordship will speak for himself."

Lord Ellingham answered Viner's smile with one equally frank.

"I don't know whether I'm Lord Ellingham or not!" he said. "I have had considerable doubt on that point ever since our conference the other day. But I will say this, gentlemen: I had some conversation with Miss Wickham the other day, after we left your office, Mr. Carless, when she was kind enough to allow me to escort her home, and—well, to be frank, gentlemen, whether she is my cousin or not, I—to me an old-fashioned phrase—desire her better acquaintance! And if she is my cousin, why, then—the title is not mine but hers!"

The two lawyers exchanged significant glances.

"Admirably spoken, My Lord!" said Mr. Pawle. "Excellent!"

"It is just what I would have expected of his Lordship," remarked Mr. Carless. "I have known His Lordship since he was first breeched! But I believe Mr. Viner has something to say?"

"Yes—this," answered Viner. "Drillford found on Cortelyon the papers which are missing from those which Ashton had evidently kept together with a view to proving his ward's right to the title and estates. He is a sharp, fellow, Drillford, and he told me just now that he had glanced over those papers since Cortelyon's arrest, and he—well, I only just stopped him from letting out to Miss Wickham who—if the papers and the deduction to be drawn from them are correct—she really is. I am right in supposing," he continued, suddenly interrupting himself, "that the Ellingham title runs in the female as in the male line?"

"Quite right, Mr. Viner," said Mr. Carless. "Quite right. It does! I believe I mentioned the other day that there has already been one Countess of Ellingham in her own right. The male line came to an end at one period—the daughter of the last male holder succeeded, and the man whom she married took the family name of Cave-Gray, and their eldest son, of course, succeeded on the death of his mother. Quite right, sir."

"Then," suggested Viner, "don't you think it would be advisable, rather than that Lord Ellingham should be kept in suspense, that we should go round to the police-station and inspect the documents? I don't know whether Drillford will give them up until his prisoners have been brought before the magistrate, but he said he would give them to the proper persons eventually, and in any case he will show them to you three gentlemen."

"Good!" said Mr. Pawle. "Let us go at once—it is only a few minutes' walk."

"And in the meantime," suggested Mr. Carless, "Miss Wickham might be asked to remain here—under the wing of the excellent Miss Penkridge?"

Viner laughingly remarked that he had no doubt whatever that Miss Penkridge would willingly assume this position of trust, and leading his callers into the hall, left them for a moment while he returned to the drawing-room. He was smiling when he returned.

"I think Miss Wickham will be safe for some time," he said. "Horrified as she is at the conduct of the wicked Mrs. Killenhall, she is sufficiently feminine to be taking a vast interest in my aunt's account of how she brought off her wonderful stroke of genius this afternoon. So—shall we go round?"

Drillford, found alone in his office, showed no surprise when Viner brought in and introduced his companions. He already knew the two lawyers, and exchanged comprehending words with them, but he looked at Lord Ellingham with the same interest which Viner had seen in him when Miss Wickham was present.

"Of course, you may see the whole lot, gentlemen," he said as he unlocked the drawer. "I don't want you to take these things away now, though, because we'd like to produce them when these people are brought up tomorrow morning. But after they've been shown, I'll hand them over—and in the meantime you can rely on it that they'll be taken care of—rather! Well, now, here's the missing ring! Hyde, you know, admitted to picking up one—this is the other, without doubt. And—there's the fifty-thousand-pound diamond. Of course, Cortelyon robbed Ashton after he'd killed him as a piece of bluff—what he wanted was these papers. He evidently gave Cave, or Starr, his accomplice, certain of the papers, to play the game with, but the really important ones he kept in his own pocket, where I found 'em. There you are, gentlemen."

He handed over a stout linen-lined foolscap envelope to Mr. Carless, and that gentleman, whose fingers trembled a little in spite of his determined attempt to preserve his professional coolness, drew certain papers from it, and laying them on a desk close by, beckoned the other men to his elbows, and began to examine them. For several minutes the four pairs of eyes ran over the various documents, Mr. Carless' finger pointing to one particular passage or another during their hasty perusal, and he and Mr. Pawle nodding assent as they exchanged glances and muttered remarks.

"Not a doubt of it!" exclaimed Mr. Carless suddenly. "Not one doubt! Observe the extraordinary care which the missing Lord Marketstoke took to safeguard his own interests and those of his daughter, in case he ever wished to revive his claims. Here, for instance is his marriage certificate. You see, he took good care to be married in his own real, proper, legal name! Here, again, is the birth certificate of his daughter. You see how she is described—Avice Wickham Cave-Gray, daughter of, et cetera, et cetera. And here is his death certificate—that too is all in order. You see, all these are duly attested copies—we could, of course, insist on having them verified over there, but I've no doubt about their genuineness—what do you say, Pawle?"

"I should say there's no doubt whatever," answered Mr. Pawle readily. "But now, this memorandum, evidently written by Ashton himself, in London, soon after he got here?"

Mr. Carless ran his eye over the document which Mr. Pawle indicated.

"Aye!" he said. "A most important, most valuable piece of evidence. You see that Cortelyon's name is mentioned in it. What's he say—'*The only man besides myself who is in full possession of the facts*,' Gad—that'll hang this scoundrel! Yes, here it is—the full history of the case, very lucidly summarized; he must have been a very good business man, this unfortunate Ashton, poor fellow! But what's this he's put at the end, as a sort of note?"

"'Since arriving in England and making inquiries in London and about Marketstoke and Ellingham as to the character and abilities of the young man who is the present holder of the title and estates which are by right my ward's I have had considerable doubt as to whether or not I should exercise the discretion extended to me by her father. Having nobody of my own, I have left her all my fortune, which is a handsome one, and she will be a rich woman. The young man seems to be an estimable and promising young fellow, and I am much exercised in mind as to whether it might not be best if Cortelyon and I kept the secret to ourselves until our deaths.'"

Mr. Carless read this passage aloud, and then smote the desk heavily with his hand.

"There's the secret of the murder!" he exclaimed. "You see, gentlemen, Ashton, one holder of the secret, was honest; the other, Cortelyon, was a rogue. Ashton wanted nothing for himself; Cortelyon wanted to profit. Cortelyon saw that by killing Ashton he alone would have the secret; he evidently got two accomplices who were necessary to him, and he meant, by suppressing certain facts and enlarging on others, to palm off an impostor who–mark this!–could be squared by one hundred thousand pounds! Oh, a bad fellow! Keep him tight, Mr. Inspector, keep him tight!"

"You needn't bother yourself, Mr. Carless," answered Drillford laconically. "We'll see to that!"

Mr. Carless again cast an eye on the passage he had just read, and then, touching Lord Ellingham's arm, drew his attention to it again, whispering something in his ear at which the young man's cheek reddened. Then he gathered up the papers, carefully replaced them in their linen-lined envelope, and handed them to Drillford.

"Much obliged to you," he said. "Now, at what time are these miscreants to be put in the dock tomorrow? Ten sharp? Then," he declared, with a shrewd glance, "I shall be there—and in all my experience I shall never have set eyes on a worse scoundrel than the chief one of 'em! Now, gentlemen, shall we go?"

Outside, Mr. Carless took Lord Ellingham's arm.

"You know what this really means—to you?" he said.

Lord Ellingham laughed.

"Of course!" he answered.

"Remember," continued Mr. Carless, with a knowing glance at Mr. Pawle, "you needn't give in without a struggle! You can make a big fight. You're in possession; it would take a long time to turn you out. You can have litigation—as much as ever you wish. But—I don't think there's the least doubt that the young woman we're going back to is your cousin, and therefore Countess of Ellingham."

"Neither do I!" said his client with a smile. "Nor, I think, does Mr. Pawle?"

"Not a doubt of it!" affirmed Mr. Pawle.

"Very well," said Mr. Carless, and pulled his companions to a halt. "Then—the question now is—who is to tell her?"

The two lawyers and Viner looked from one another to Lord Ellingham—but Lord Ellingham was already eager and responsive.

"Gentlemen," he said quickly, "I claim that right! If I am to abdicate in favour of another, let me have at any rate the privilege of first greeting the new sovereign! Besides, as I have already said to you—"

Mr. Carless interrupted him by pointing toward Viner's house, of which they were now in sight.

"I dare say our friend Viner, who has, as he says, been strangely mixed up in this strange affair, can manage matters," he said dryly. "And as things are, nothing could be better!"

Viner took his companions back into his library, and opening a door, showed Lord Ellingham a small study which lay beyond.

"I'll bring Miss Wickham to you at once," he said. Then, with a glance at the two lawyers, which went round again to Lord Ellingham, he added quietly, "When you have told her, you'll let us know what she says?"

"Aye, aye!" muttered Mr. Pawle. "Good–we must know that!"

Viner went away to the drawing-room and presently brought Miss Wickham back with him. She looked from one solicitor to the other with something of a smile.

"More mystery?" she asked.

Mr. Carless, with a courtly bow, took the girl's hand.

"My dear young lady," he said, "There is, this time, a mystery to be explained. And–allow me to hand you into this room–there is a young gentleman in here who will explain it, all of it, a thousand times better than we old fogies possibly could!"

He closed the door on her, and turned to Mr. Pawle.

"I'll trouble you for a pinch of that old snuff of yours, Pawle!" he said. "Um–dear me! What extraordinary moments we do pass through! Viner, my dear fellow, you're a book-collector, I know. To–er–pass the time, show me some of your treasures."

Ten minutes, twenty minutes, thirty minutes, went by, while Viner showed some of his most treasured possessions in the way of print and binding to the two old lawyers. They were both past masters in the art of make-believe, and they contrived to show great interest in what was exhibited to them, but Viner knew very well that when Mr. Pawle was expatiating on the merits of an Elzevir or Mr. Carless on the beauties of a Grolier, they were really wondering what the two young people in the next room, so strangely thrown together, were saying to each other. And then, as he was about to unlock a cabinet, and bring out a collection of autograph letters, the door of the inner room was opened, and the two appeared on the threshold, one looking extremely confident, and the other full of blushes and surprise. And–they were holding each other's hands.

"Gentlemen–our very good friends," said Lord Ellingham, "it is only right that we should take you into our confidence at once. There will be no litigation, Mr. Carless–no difficulties, Mr. Pawle. I absolutely insist on resigning–what is not mine–to my cousin, the Countess of Ellingham. And–not in any return, gentlemen!–she has promised to give me something which I shall prize far more than any title or any estate–you understand? And now, if Mr. Viner will excuse me, there are just a few more things we have to say to each other, and then–"

He drew the girl back into the room and closed the door, and the three men, once more left to themselves, solemnly shook hands with each other, heaving sighs of infinite delight and gratification.

THE END

Resurrected Press Mysteries by J. S. Fletcher

The Orange-Yellow Diamond
When an elderly pawnbroker is murdered in the London parish of Paddington, a young, down on his luck writer is accused of the crime. But then it's found the pawnbroker had had in his possession an extraordinary South African diamond worth over eighty-thousand pounds — a diamond that's now missing. It falls to Melky Rubenstein to unravel the mystery and prove the young man's innocence.

The Middle Temple Murder
When an elderly man's body is found on the steps of chambers in the Midde Temple, one of the Inns of Court, it falls to newspaperman Frank Spargo and Detective-Sergeant Rathbury to solve the crime. The murdered man, for indeed it was murder, was found with no money or identification on his person except for a piece of paper with the name and address of a young barrister. Who is the victim? Why was he killed? Who is the murderer?

Scarhaven Keep
Bassett Oliver, the famed actor, has gone missing. When Oliver fails to show for a rehearsal, aspiring playwright Richard Copplestone finds himself sent to the small village of Scarhaven on the northern coast of England to track down the actors movements. What he finds is mystery. Find the answers as Copplestone unravels the mystery of Scarhaven Keep.

Visit www.resurrectedpress.com

Resurrected Press Mysteries by Fergus Hume

The Green Mummy

Professor Braddock hoped to compare the burial practices of the Egyptians with those of the ancient Peruvians with his latest acquisition, the mummy of the last Inca, Caxas. But on arrival, the packing case proved to hold not the mummy, but the body of his assistant Sidney Bolton. It falls to Archie Hope to discover the murderer if he is to marry the professors step-daughter, Lucy Kendal. Who killed Bolton and where is the mummy? Was it the sea captain Hervey? The mysterious Don Pedro? Cockatoo the Polynesian servant? The professor, himself? And what has become of the emeralds? These are the questions that Hope must answer amongst the secrets of the past in The Green Mummy.

The Mystery of a Hansom Cab

"Truth is said to be stranger than fiction, and certainly the extraordinary murder which took place in Melbourne Friday morning goes a long way towards verifying that saying." Thus opens The Mystery of a Hansom Cab, the best selling mystery of the nineteenth century. When a man is found dead in a hansom cab one of Melbourne's leading citizens is accused of the murder. He pleads his innocence, yet refuses to give an alibi. It falls to a determined lawyer and an intrepid detective to find the truth, revealing long kept secrets along the way. Fergus Hume's first and perhaps most famous mystery... The Mystery Of A Hansom Cab.

Visit www.resurrectedpress.com

Resurrected Press Mysteries from the Dr. John Thorndyke Series

Dr. John Thorndyke - Lecturer on Medical Jurisprudence and Forensic Medicine. Before Bones, before CSI, before Quincy, M.E – there was Dr. John Thorndyke solving the most baffling cases of Edwardian London using the latest tools of medical science. Read about his cases in:

The Eye of Osiris
John Bellingham, noted Egyptologist has vanished not once but twice in the same day. Now Dr, Thorndyke must unravel the tangled claims on his estate, solve the riddle of the missing man and find the "Eye of Osiris".

The Mystery of 31 New Inn
When Dr. Jervis is whisked away in a coach with no windows to an unknown location to treat a man in a coma from undivulged causes it is Dr. Thorndyke who must come up with the solution.

The Red Thumb Mark
The first of Dr. Thorndyke's cases finds him trying to prove the innocence of a young man accused of being a diamond thief despite the fact that his finger print was found at the scene of the crime.

John Thorndyke's Cases
More cases of medical mysteries as told by his trusted assistant Jervis, M.D. Eight stories of crime and deduction in Edwardian London.

Visit www.resurrectedpress.com

Resurrected Press Mysteries by John R. Watson & Arthur J. Rees

The Hampstead Mystery

High Court Justice Sir Horace Fewbanks found shot dead in his Hampstead home, a butler with a criminal past, a scorned lover and a hint of scandal. These are the elements of the Hampstead Mystery that Detective Inspector Chippenfield of Scotland Yard must unravel with the assistance of the ambitious Detective Rolfe. But will he be able to sort out the tangled threads of this case and arrest the culprit before he is upstaged by the celebrated gentleman detective Crewe. Follow the details of this amazing case at it plays out across Hampstead, London and Scotland until it reaches a stunning conclusion in the courts of the Old Bailey.

The Mystery of the Downs

When Harry Marsland was caught in a sudden down pour he sought shelter at Cliff Farm. Met at the door by a young woman clearly expecting someone else he is only too glad to get inside to wait out the storm. When they hear a noise upstairs in the deserted house they investigate only to discover the body of the farm's owner, Frank Lumsden, dead of a gunshot wound. Who then, killed Lumsden, and why? Who was the woman expecting and did she have any roll in the murder? These are the questions that private detective Crewe must answer in The Mystery of the Downs.

Visit www.resurrectedpress.com

Other Resurrected Press Mysteries

Mysteries on a Train

Before the Orient Express there was:

The Rome Express by Arthur Griffiths
A man is found dead in his first class sleeping compartment on the express from Rome to Paris. Who was his murderer? The Countess? The English General? His brother the clergy man? The maid who has disappeared? Is the French justice system up to solving the crime? Read about it in The Rome Express.

The Passenger from Calais by Arthur Griffiths
Colonel Basil Annesley finds he is the only passenger on the train from Calais to Lucerne. That is until a mysterious woman shows up at the last minute to book a compartment. Who is after her? What is her secret? Is she a criminal or a victim? Read about it in The Passenger from Calais

Visit us at www.resurrectedpress.com

About Resurrected Press

A division of Intrepid Ink, LLC, Resurrected Press is dedicated to bringing high quality, vintage books back into publication. See our entire catalogue and find out more at www.ResurrectedPress.com.

About Intrepid Ink, LLC

Intrepid Ink, LLC provides full publishing services to authors of fiction and non-fiction books, eBooks and websites. From editing to formatting, from publishing to marketing, Intrepid Ink gets your creative works into the hands of the people who want to read them. Find out more at www.IntrepidInk.com.